# when

# whɛn

## VICTORIA LAURIE

**HYPERION**

Los Angeles   New York

First Edition, January 2015
10 9 8 7 6 5 4 3 2 1
G475-5664-5-14288

Printed in the United States of America

Library of Congress Cataloging-in-Publication Data
Laurie, Victoria.
    When/Victoria Laurie.—First edition.
        pages cm
    Summary: Sixteen-year-old Maddie Flynn cannot help but see the death date of everyone she meets or sees in a photograph or on-screen, and her alcoholic mother exploits this by having her do readings for money, but when Maddie predicts the death of a young boy, she becomes the center of an FBI investigation.
        ISBN 978-1-4847-0008-2—ISBN 1-4847-0008-2
    [1. Psychic ability—Fiction.   2. Death—Fiction.   3. Mothers and daughters—Fiction.   4. Criminal investigation—Fiction.   5. Alcoholism—Fiction.   6. Mystery and detective stories.]   I. Title.
        PZ7.L372792De 2015
        [Fic]—dc23                                        2014008428

Reinforced binding

Visit www.hyperionteens.com

For Brian
May my own date come many years from now,
exactly one day before yours.
<3

# Prologue

I'M NOT EXACTLY SURE WHEN I FIRST STARTED SEE-ing the numbers. My earliest memories are filled with snatches of familiar and unfamiliar faces, each with a set of small black digits floating like shadows just above their fore-heads. The clearest first memory I have of seeing them comes from a muggy summer morning when Dad was sitting across the table from me, already dressed for his mid-morning shift. I remember the blue of his shirt perfectly matching the color of his eyes. That morning the city traffic was loud, streaming in through windows fully open to allow for even the faintest breeze. I was probably three or four—four, I think—and he was showing me on a piece of paper how to draw numbers and what to call them.

I already knew my shapes—circle, square, triangle—so I picked up on the lesson really fast, and I thought Dad was finally revealing the secret. The secret of why those odd little figures kept hovering right above everyone's foreheads.

He taught me one, two, and three; I was so excited. But the elusive number was nine. We went through so many others to get to it, and finally it had a name. I remember repeating it out loud—the last piece of the puzzle in place—and I pointed to him triumphantly and shouted, "Nine-two-three-two-circle-circle-four!"

Then I laughed and laughed, and I remember thinking he'd be so proud of me for saying his numbers back to him. But when I'd settled down, I saw that he had the most puzzled look on his face. He was smiling with me, but also confused.

The memory is bittersweet. I can still see his face so clearly in my mind, the blue of his eyes, the black of his hair, the crook to his nose, and those numbers permanently etched onto his forehead. Small black gravestones against a pale white landscape.

It took us a couple of years to figure out what they meant. Actually, it took two years and one day too many.

Ma was the first one to put it together. I remember it was a Tuesday, because in my first-grade class we had show-and-tell on Tuesdays. Jenny Beaumont (10-14-2074) had brought her collection of Beanie Babies for us to pass around the circle, and I'd fallen in love with a little chipmunk. I'd been holding it greedily when Mrs. Lucas (2-12-2041) had to leave the circle to answer the classroom phone and, almost before she'd turned to stare back at me with wide eyes, I'd known something bad was happening at home.

She rushed me into my coat and told me to go with my Uncle Donny (9-30-2062), who was waiting for me in the principal's office. I hurried down the hall to him, and the moment he saw me he scooped me up into his arms and ran to his car.

He'd driven so fast down the streets, and I could feel the whole car vibrating with fear. We came through the door of the apartment to find Ma, pale and trembling as she sat on the edge of the couch and dialed Dad's cell over and over and over. On the coffee table in front of her was a crayon sketch I'd made in kindergarten the year before of Ma, Dad, and me. I'd drawn in all of our numbers, and Ma had proudly tacked it up on the fridge, where it'd gotten buried under other artwork, coupons, and love notes from Dad.

But that day, Ma had pulled the drawing down, circled the figure of my dad with a pencil, and while the TV broadcasted images of a standoff between a gang of drug dealers and the Brooklyn PD, she'd kept dialing and dialing and dialing.

Donny sat down on the couch and pulled me into his arms, but all of his attention had been on that broadcast. I remember so vividly the images from a helicopter circling above a huge warehouse, the chopper sending shaky images of men that looked like ants crawling over the rooftop while small sparks of gunfire flashed repetitively from the muzzles of their weapons The news reporter kept saying there were multiple officers down, and even at six years old, I knew that scene meant terrible things for us.

We learned later that Dad had left his cell in his patrol car. He'd gone into that warehouse to back up his buddies in blue, and he'd never come out. I've since been haunted by the feeling that Ma wasn't the only one who'd put it together as she dialed and dialed and dialed. What if it'd finally clicked for Dad when he'd entered the building and that hail of gunfire had erupted all around him? And more important... why hadn't it clicked for me in time to save him?

That's another question I can't seem to answer.

How come I can see the exact date that someone will die, but nothing else about the how, where, or even why? What good does it do to know the when, if you can't know at least one of the other three?

Also, why am I seemingly the only person on earth who can see these numbers? Why did fate choose me for such a cruel gift?

It's a question I've asked myself a million times, and I'm still looking for the answer. I think there may not be one, because knowing when someone will die has never changed anything. I've never saved anybody or given them more time. I'm just the messenger.

That's what Ma says to me all the time when one of my clients doesn't take the news so well. Knowing that there's nothing I can do to help them get more time still doesn't take the sting out of it, though.

I started reading for strangers a few years ago after Ma lost her part-time job. I knew she was really worried about money, so I didn't argue with her when she proposed charging people for telling them their deathdates. After a slow start, we now get about a dozen new customers a month.

There's a little room at the back of the house, where Ma likes to seat them. The room is dim and gloomy. I never go in there unless I've got a client.

When I do a reading I have to focus on the forehead of the subject in question, and the numbers themselves are always the same: kinda small, less than a half an inch in size. They're black and thin but perfectly etched, like you'd see printed in an obituary. They hover over the foreheads of everyone I see—even in a photograph or video, they're visible to me. It's why I don't like going to the movies or watching a lot of TV. I know when every star in Hollywood will fall.

Because the numbers themselves are small and thin, I need to be within four or five feet of a person to clearly see their numbers, but if someone wears a hat, or has bangs or very dark skin, I need to be even closer. Beyond five feet, the dates get fuzzy and start to look like wispy dots—unsightly smudges on otherwise unmarred faces. When I walk the halls of my high school those smudges are a constant reminder that death is a mere squint away.

I try not to think about the people who don't have a lot of years left. But it's really hard. I'll pass them in the halls at school, or see them around town, and I want to wince when they go by; their numbers flashing over and over again in my mind like strobe lights at a traffic accident, daring me to walk past them and forget what I've seen.

It can be pretty hard to deal with, so, a few years ago I started a notebook where I'd write down all the death-dates for everyone I know or meet. I add about ten to fifteen names a month—all my clients get listed, and it helps me cope.

When I first started seeing the numbers—these deathdates—they ran together as one long stream, but now my mind puts in the dashes.

6-28-2021. That's Ma's. I grew up knowing I'd be

twenty-three when she died. Twenty-three is too young to be an orphan.

Still, it's not like Ma takes care of herself. She smokes, she drinks, but mostly she doesn't care. Not since Dad died.

A year after we lost him and moved from Brooklyn an hour and forty minutes north to Poplar Hollow, I began telling everybody I met what their deathdate was. I was a little seven-year-old on a mission to save anybody I could. Not surprisingly, I didn't save a soul. Instead, I got sent home with a note from my new second-grade teacher, Mrs. Gilbert (7-18-2006). She had cancer and died the following summer, but she didn't care to know that it was coming, and a few of the kids' parents had complained. After that, Ma told me never to tell anybody their numbers unless she said it was okay.

My neighbor, Mrs. Duncan—her number's coming up really soon. 2-28-2015. She doesn't know it yet, either, but I'm tempted to tell her. She's a sweet old lady who likes to redecorate her house every other month just for something to do and someone to talk to. I think she'd like to know that her time is almost up. I wouldn't even charge her, which might not make Ma happy if she found out, but business has been pretty good lately, and Ma said she's thinking of upping the price for a reading from fifty bucks to seventy-five.

With Ma and me on our own with only the money from my dad's wrongful-death settlement to pay the bills, most of what I bring in goes to cover extras like repairs to the house or food or booze for Ma.

She's been drinking a lot lately, which is why I'm hoping that business slows down. But that's not likely. There are plenty of people out there who're curious or desperate or they simply want to prepare. Lots of my clients come to me with a list and a stack of photos, and they'll ask about everyone in their family except themselves.

Others ask only about themselves. Most people want to know if they can change the date, if they can get more time. I tell them I don't know. And that's what kills me. It'd be easier if I knew that the dates couldn't be changed, that they're set in stone as solid as the gravestone they'll be printed on. If I knew for sure that a deathdate couldn't be changed, I think I'd feel less guilty about my dad.

Then I look at my mom, and I see her leaving me in only six years, and a weight settles onto my chest that makes it hard to breathe.

So I wait and hope for a day when a client sits down in front of me, and I tell them their date, and then a miracle happens: I'll see the date change. Simply by the act of revealing their deathdate I'll get to witness them getting more time. Then I'll have solid proof that there's hope for anyone whose date is too soon. And I'll finally be more than just the messenger.

# 10-19-2014

FROM MY BEDROOM WINDOW, I SAW THE MERCEDES pull up next to our house and realized we were about to have company. Not many Mercedes found their way to our side of town.

"Maddie?" Ma called from downstairs. "I think we have a client."

I closed my Algebra II textbook with a sigh and lay back on the bed where I'd been plodding through equations for the past hour. Mr. Chavez (8-9-2039) had given us a ton of homework and, ironically, I really struggle with math.

"Maddie?" Ma called again. "Honey, are you up there?"

"Coming!"

I rolled off the bed and took a minute to pull my hair back and shrug out of my sweatshirt, trading it for a sweater.

When I got to the landing, Ma was at the bottom of the stairs waiting on me. "She's in the back," she said after I'd made my way down. Smoothing her hand over my ponytail she added, "She seems like a nice lady. She said she only needs one date, so I think this one will be easy. Also, I'm keeping your dinner warm in the oven."

I could smell the pizza from the kitchen. I am so sick of pizza I could scream. Ma rarely cooks anymore, so all we ever seem to have are Hot Pockets, microwave pizza, chicken nuggets, or something else right out of the box. "I have to go to the store for some milk," Ma said as I made my way toward the back of the house. "But I'll wait until you're through."

Ma never left me alone in the house with a client, which was good, but I knew she was itching to go to the store. *Milk* was Ma's code word for *vodka*.

Ma's drinking had stopped burning a hole in my stomach a couple of years ago when I realized I was powerless to stop her. Deep down it still really bothered me, but I tried not to let it show.

When I walked into the back room, the first thing I noticed about the client was that she was really pretty, regal even, dressed in chocolate suede slacks and a cream silk blouse. A thick, luxurious fur coat was draped over the back of her chair. I knew right away that she was from Parkwick. They've got big bucks in Parkwick.

I moved to the chair opposite her and sat down. "Hello, Maddie," she said with a warm smile.

"Hi," I replied, pulling at my sweater. I felt a little self-conscious in her elegant presence.

"How are you this evening?"

I blinked. No one ever bothered to ask how I am. "Uh...fine."

The lady smiled again. "I'm Patricia Tibbolt," she told me, offering me her hand. I shook it, surprised by her easy, relaxed manner. "I'm so sorry to call on you during your dinner hour," Mrs. Tibbolt continued, "but it was the only time I could get away from the hospital, and I barely managed to work up the courage to come see you tonight."

I focused on her for a second. 7-21-2068. That made me relax. If she asked about herself, she'd probably like the answer. "It's okay," I told her, referring to the dinner hour. "We're only having pizza again."

Mrs. Tibbolt sat back and beamed her pretty smile at me. "I used to love pizza when I was your age. You must be fifteen or sixteen, right?"

"Sixteen," I told her.

She continued to study me curiously. I noticed she had a whopper of a diamond on her left ring finger. I wondered if it was heavy. "You're still so young to have such a gift and be able to share it with people."

I smirked. "Yeah, I'm a regular Santa Claus."

Mrs. Tibbolt's eyebrows shot up, and I opened my mouth to apologize—it'd come out a little snarky—but she laughed and winked at me. It was like we'd just shared a secret. "Well, I don't want to keep you too long," she said next. "Your mother tells me that you need a picture to look at?"

I nodded and she took out her wallet. It was tan leather and looked soft as butter. Mrs. Tibbolt opened it and flipped to a row of pictures. She had three kids. After a slight hesitation, she tapped the top picture and said, "This is my CeeCee. Please tell me how long she has."

I squinted at the photo. The little girl in the picture

was maybe five or six, and she was bald. Her face was all puffy, but she wore a band with a little pink bow on her head and she had the hugest smile. The numbers floated up from right below her headband. "June seventeenth, twenty eighty-nine," I said.

For a moment, Mrs. Tibbolt didn't move or speak, but her eyes filled with tears. I was used to people getting emotional. I usually ignored it, but I liked this lady and I could feel a small lump forming in my own throat. I moved a box of Kleenex toward her that Ma had set on the table. She took a tissue and dabbed at her eyes. "My baby will really live that long?" she asked me in a choked whisper.

I nodded. "Yes, ma'am. Her deathday isn't until June seventeenth, twenty eighty-nine."

Mrs. Tibbolt swallowed hard and wiped demurely at her cheeks. "Thank you, Maddie," she said. "You've helped me more than you could possibly know. CeeCee has leukemia, and she's not doing so well right now. Her doctor wants her to participate in this experimental drug trial, but the side effects are awful, and I don't want my little girl to go through that if there's no hope." Mrs. Tibbolt paused to stare down at the photo, smoothing her finger over the image of her daughter. It was a moment before she could speak again. "As a parent, you never want your children to suffer even though you can't bear the thought of life without them. If there wasn't a chance my baby would survive longer than the next six months, I was going to say no to the drug trial. You've given me hope, and I can't thank you enough."

I smiled at her but suddenly felt shy, and I dropped my eyes to the table. My gaze landed on the billfold just as Mrs.

Tibbolt was closing it up, and that's when I saw something that made my breath catch. I reached out to put a hand on her arm. "Wait," I said, squinting at the pictures. There were two other kids there. One was a boy a bit older than me, maybe eighteen or nineteen, with black hair, bright green eyes, and really good looking. The other was a kid a little younger than me—maybe thirteen or fourteen with lighter hair but the same eyes and the same beautiful face. The older kid's numbers were similar to his sister's, 11-19-2075, but the middle son was a completely different story.

"Is he sick, too?" I asked, pointing to his picture.

Mrs. Tibbolt looked quizzically at me and swiveled the billfold around. "Tevon?" she asked. "No, honey. He's perfectly well."

My heart started to pound. I'd never seen numbers that soon on someone so young and healthy before. For a minute I didn't know what to do. She hadn't asked about her youngest son, but how could I *not* tell her, when the kid's deathdate was so close? I decided to tell her—maybe this time it would change things. Pointing to the picture again, I said, "Mrs. Tibbolt, his deathday isn't like your other kids'. It's much sooner."

Mrs. Tibbolt's eyes widened, but she kept her tone level. "Oh? How much sooner?"

"It's next week."

She gasped. Then she shook her head. "No," she said to me. "No. That's not possible. Tevon is fine. He's perfectly healthy."

I stared at the picture to make sure. Biting my lip, I looked up at her again. "I'm not wrong."

She paled and leaned in. "How?"

And there it was. That question I can't answer. I shook my head, feeling the weight of my dad's death settle onto my shoulders. At the same time, Mrs. Tibbolt's eyes narrowed.

I glanced again at Tevon's picture. His numbers remained stubbornly fixed. I knew I had to try to convince her. "I don't know how. An accident maybe? I'm not sure. But something bad is going to happen to him, and if you don't do something, he'll die next week." It was my uncertainty and the vagueness of my answer that she keyed in on. She misread me for a liar. I saw it in her expression as she began to shake her head, and her gaze fell away from me as she closed up her wallet.

Desperate to have her believe me I said, "I can tell you the date—"

"Stop!" she commanded, cutting me off. With her mouth pressed into a thin line, she stood, picked up her designer purse, and pushed her billfold into it. "You and your mom must think you're pretty clever," she said, staring at me like she expected a full confession. When I didn't say anything she added, "Oh, I *knew* this was a hoax!"

I felt my stomach burn. "It's no hoax."

"Really? Weren't you about to tell me that my son has come under some sort of deadly curse and for an additional fee you'd be happy to remove it?"

I stared at her. She glared back at me with contempt. Then, I watched her eyes drift up to a spot above my right shoulder. Ma had put a sign there with big bold letters. ABSOLUTELY *NO* REFUNDS!

Mrs. Tibbolt made a dismissive, puffing sound. "Enjoy

your pizza, Maddie." Then she yanked her coat off the chair, causing it to fall over. She didn't pick it up. Instead, she stalked out of the room without a backward glance.

I sat there for a good ten minutes staring at the tabletop. It felt like I'd been punched in the stomach. Finally, Ma poked her head in. "Your dinner's on the table." Then she looked at the overturned chair. "She didn't take it so well, huh?"

I shook my head.

"Oh, sweetie," Ma said, coming over to squeeze my shoulder. "You have to remember that you're just the messenger. You're not responsible for the date or the way your clients take the news. And how that woman reacted in here is only her first reaction. Give her some time to get over her shock, and she'll come to terms with it."

I swallowed hard. I didn't want to tell Ma what'd happened, because it might lead to an argument. So I simply muttered an "I know, Ma," and followed her out of the room to dinner, but I did little more than pick at my pizza.

After dinner I headed out to meet Stubby, my best friend. Stubby's real name is Arnold Schroder (8-16-2094), but he's gone by the nickname he was given by some bullies on the playground in elementary school for as long as I can remember. It's not flattering, but he says it's better than Arnold.

Stubs and I have been hanging out together ever since third grade when, after Mrs. Gilbert died, none of the other kids wanted anything to do with me. Back then Stubby was a chubby little eight-year-old with bright white-blond hair and a permanent goofy smile. He wore a red cape to school and told everybody that he wanted to grow up to be

Superman. He never lost the chubbiness, but the cape is long retired. Socially, he's super awkward, but inside that pudgy chest beats the heart of a superhero for sure.

He'd texted earlier to meet him at the diner midway between our two houses. Stubs and I live about a half mile apart in a suburb filled with majestic poplar, maple, and oak trees. They line the streets so that some days you can barely see the sun. As I rode my bike to the diner, the wind picked up, sending the leaves above me clapping. It sounded like riding under a canopy of applause. Orange, yellow, and red leaves rained onto my hair and shoulders as I pedaled. They coated the street and caught in my spokes, where they clapped some more.

The diner where Stubby and I meet isn't big—not much more than a couple of booths and a short counter—but it's cheap and we like to hang out there on Sunday nights because Rita (3-20-2022), the older waitress who works that shift, doesn't glare at us when we take up a back booth and don't tip her more than a buck fifty for a couple of Cokes and chocolate cream pies.

As I entered the diner, I noticed Cathy Hutchinson (1-19-2082). She's a sophomore who moved in across the street from me the year before. She was there with her boyfriend, Mike Mendez (8-24-2078), who's a junior. They were making out pretty hot and heavy in a booth diagonal from where Stubs was sitting.

He looked uncomfortable, and I could tell he was trying to avert his eyes while Mike groped Cathy. Stubs is a sweetie, raised by a single mom—and he's sort of old-fashioned about how to treat a girl.

I nodded to him and rolled my eyes as I passed Mike and Cathy. He hid a smile with his hand. "Hey," he said when I approached. "I already ordered for us."

I sat down and glanced over my shoulder at the lovebirds. I turned back to Stubs and shook my head. "How long have they been here?"

"Long enough to annoy Rita," Stubs said, motioning with his chin to the older woman across the diner currently taking another customer's order.

I could only imagine the hard time Mike and Cathy had given the waitress. Mike's got a mean streak in him, and Cathy's not much better. I glanced behind me again, and this time I saw that Cathy had pushed Mike off her and was scowling in our direction.

Cathy's not my biggest fan. In the summer of 2013, she, Stubby, and I had hung out together after she first moved in across the street from me, but the minute school started and she found out from the other kids what I could do, she turned on me quick. In the span of an afternoon she went from being my sweet friend to a backstabbing bitch, and I never could figure out what I'd done personally to her to get her to hate me so much.

I turned away from her back to Stubs, and as I did so I overheard Cathy sing, "Ding dong! The witch is dead."

Cathy likes to tell everybody I'm a witch. I've overheard her say that my mom and I are part of a coven, and that we cast spells on the people who come to see me. Stubby once confessed that he heard Cathy tell all the people at her lunch table that she'd seen a guy come out of my house bleeding from the ears. It was ridiculous.

"Ding dong! The witch is dead," Cathy sang again, and she and Mike both laughed.

I bristled, but Stubby gave me a subtle shake of his head. "They're leaving," he whispered.

I shifted my gaze to the large window behind Stubs, which gave a good reflection of the room behind me, and we both waited in silence until Mike and Cathy left the diner.

A minute later Rita appeared at our table with our pies and drinks. After she left, Stubs said, "So, you had a rough time with a client?"

I'd already texted him the basics, but I was eager to fill him in on the rest.

Stubs sat mouth agape through most of my story. "Her kid's really gonna die next week, Mads?"

I nodded, picking at the pie with my fork. "I tried to get her to listen to me, but she thinks I'm a fake."

Stubby shook his head. "If people don't think you can do what you do, then why do they go to see you?"

"I have no clue," I said moodily.

"So, what're you gonna do?" Stubs asked next.

His question stumped me. "Do? What do you mean?"

"Well, if this kid isn't sick or anything, then shouldn't we do something to try to save him?"

I sighed. I hated knowing how close people were to losing a loved one, especially a young loved one. But I'd told Mrs. Tibbolt about her son's deathdate, and it hadn't changed anything. Those numbers had remained stubbornly fixed. "Stubs, there's nothing I can do. I tried everything to get her to listen to me, and I checked the photo a couple of times. Her kid's date didn't change."

Stubby was quiet for a moment and then he said, "*Can the numbers change, Maddie?*"

"I don't know. I only know that I've never seen them change. Not even once."

"So you think they're fixed," Stubs said.

I pressed my lips together and stared hard at the table. "Maybe. I honestly can't be sure. Sometimes I'll Google a client whose date has passed, and I'll find an obit with the exact date I predicted. Warning people has never bought them more time."

Stubby sighed, and rolled his skateboard back and forth under the table like he always did when he was deep in thought. I knew he was trying to think up a solution. He was one of the best problem solvers I'd ever met. Stubby truly believed there wasn't anything in life or in the classroom that couldn't be solved with a little thought, effort, and time.

At last he said, "If there's even a small chance that the date can change, Mads, don't you think we should try to save that kid?"

"How?" I asked.

Stubby pulled out his smartphone and began to tap at it. After a minute his face lit up, and he showed me the screen. It was a directory listing for a Patricia Tibbolt. I noticed she did live in Parkwick. "Call her," Stubs said, and when I hesitated he added, "You gotta try, Mads. It's her *kid*."

Before I could even agree, Stubby had gone back to tapping at the screen, and then he was shoving the phone at me, urging me to take it. I saw that he'd dialed the Tibbolt's, and then I heard her voice echoing out from the phone. "Hello?" she said. "Hello?"

Reluctantly, I took the phone. "Mrs. Tibbolt?" I asked, my voice shaking.

"Who's this?"

I took a deep breath. "It's Maddie Fynn." When she didn't respond I added, "You came to see me today."

"I know who you are," she said, her voice like ice.

I looked at Stubby as if to beg him to let me hang up, but he nodded and waved his hand to encourage me. "Listen," I said. "I . . . it's . . . I want you to know I'm not a fake. Your son—"

"Stop!" she hissed, cutting me off. "Just stop it. If you call here again, I will notify the police. Leave me and my son alone! Do you hear me? Do you?"

Her rising anger tumbled out of the phone, and by the way that Stubby was now looking at me, I knew he'd heard what she'd said. Beginning to panic, I tapped the END button and cut off the call.

By mentioning the police, Mrs. Tibbolt had awakened my greatest fear. Three years before, Ma was arrested for her second DUI. I'd been thirteen at the time, and I freaked out when Ma didn't come home and I couldn't get ahold of Uncle Donny. I'd called 911, and before I knew it, Child Protective Services was on our front porch. If it hadn't been for Uncle Donny, Ma would've ended up in jail and I would've ended up in foster care.

Since then, Ma's become super anxious about anybody getting too curious about what goes on at our house. She doesn't go outside if she can avoid it, and she never waves to the neighbors. Ma won't even answer the door for sweet Mrs. Duncan, who used to bring over cookies and baked goods all the time.

Stubs eyed me with such sympathy that it was hard not to look away. He knew exactly what I was thinking. At last he reached out and nudged my arm. "Hey," he said. "You did what you could, Mads. And who knows, maybe Mrs. Tibbolt will think about what you said and, just to be on the safe side, next week she'll keep her kid home from school, or take him to the doctor and get him checked out, and his date will change."

"You think?" I asked hopefully.

Stubby nodded. "It's what my mom would do."

I felt the tension in my shoulders ease a bit, even though I doubted Mrs. Tibbolt could prevent Tevon's death. Still, I clung to the small ray of hope that Stubs had given me. "Thanks," I told him.

He nodded, but I noticed as I began to nibble at my pie that his gaze became distant and that skateboard started rolling under the table again.

Later, after I got back home, I found three new bottles of cheap vodka on the counter, and another one half empty. Ma was on the couch, droopy-eyed and slurring. She'd also been crying. When I helped her to her feet, something dropped from her lap and fluttered to the floor.

I knew what it was the second I saw the flash of green construction paper. It was the drawing I'd made in kindergarten—the one of me, Ma, and Dad with our numbers drawn over our foreheads. I bit my lip; the sting of seeing Ma with it opened up old wounds. It was well worn and tearstained, but all these years later Ma refused to throw it away. She'd traced her fingers over Dad's numbers so many times that she'd nearly worn a hole in the paper.

After she'd snatched the paper off the floor, Ma tried to tuck it into her shirt. "I can make it up to bed myself, Maddie," she slurred, her face turned away from me.

I swallowed hard. "Okay," I said finally, letting go.

I watched her wobble up the stairs without saying a word. I couldn't move against the guilt or the shame of the moment.

Before he died, my grandpa Fynn had asked me to look after Ma. Her drinking had become noticeable by then. He'd told me she was trying to cope with the loss of my dad. "Even though it wasn't her fault, she still blames herself," he'd said.

I understood fully what Gramps was trying to tell me, but I knew different. I'd seen the truth in her eyes every time I caught her with that stick-figure drawing.

Ma didn't blame herself for Dad's death. She blamed me. She drank, not because she felt guilty about surviving or being unable to prevent Dad's murder, but because she didn't want to be the kind of mother who blamed her kid for it.

And, truthfully, how could she *not* blame me? It's my "gift." Shouldn't I have known all along what the numbers meant? Shouldn't I have warned my dad?

I think that's the real reason she wanted me to read for clients. It's my penance. So I never say no to a reading. I look those strangers in the eye—because I have no choice but to look them in the eye—and deliver them their mortality. And after every reading, Ma hits the bottle hard because I know she understands how difficult it is for me. And yet she's never told me I could stop. She simply continues to pretend that I'm doing a good thing, and I continue to pretend that it doesn't bother me. The truth is, it's killing us both.

It was a while before I headed upstairs and into my room. After closing the door, I went to my desk and pulled out my notebook of dates and opened it. I couldn't explain why writing them down had always comforted me, but it did. Maybe it was simply the act of getting them out of my head and onto paper that helped me deal, or maybe it was the sense of structure and order it lent to the otherwise random quality of death. Whatever it was, it allowed me to cope.

Turning to a fresh page, I reached for a pen and wrote out Mrs. Tibbolt's name, recorded her deathdate, and added her three kids. It wasn't hard to remember them—all I had to do was close my eyes and recall her face and the photos. The numbers always came up in my mind's eye as easily as recalling their hair color or Tevon's lopsided grin.

Once I'd recorded the names, I stared hard at Tevon's deathdate and thought about Mrs. Tibbolt's harsh words to me on the phone and felt a shudder of foreboding travel up my spine. I hoped she didn't call the police on me and Ma, and I hoped even more that she watched out for her son a week from now

Still, it all felt so futile. I couldn't save Tevon any more than I could bring back my dad. I couldn't save anyone.

To take myself out of the melancholy, I flipped to a

well-worn page in the middle of the notebook. Midway down was the name *Aiden*. No last name—I didn't know it—but seeing his name written there with such care made me feel closer to him.

Aiden was a boy I'd first glimpsed my freshmen year as I was sitting in the stands at a football game. There'd been no good seats on our team's side, so Stubby and I had gone over to the rival team's bleachers and found a good spot in the front row. Aiden had walked right past me on his way to the concession stand, and I'd felt all the breath leave my body. I couldn't believe someone so beautiful had been near enough to touch.

I'd never spoken to him, and I'd only see him a handful of times each year when his high school played against mine, but each time I felt inexplicably drawn to him. It was as if I knew him. As if I'd always known him.

I went to his page in my notebook often. It made me feel better. I liked to tell myself that someday I'd work up the courage to talk to him. "Maybe this year," I whispered.

With a sigh I shut the notebook, tucking it away in the drawer of my nightstand before getting ready for bed. As I drifted off to sleep I made peace with myself about Mrs. Tibbolt and her son, telling myself that I'd tried my best with her. There was nothing more I could do.

# 10-30-2014

A WEEK AND A HALF LATER, I WAS IN SIXTH PERIOD American Lit when someone knocked on the classroom door. We all looked up just as our principal came in.

Principal Harris (4-21-2042) is a short man who walks around like he owns the place. He also has a penchant for using big words so nobody can ever figure out what he's trying to say. "Sarah?" he said when my teacher Mrs. Wilson (6-30-2056) looked up.

"Yes, Principal Harris?"

"I will need to see Madelyn Fynn in my office posthaste." His voice sounded grave.

Twenty-three pairs of eyes swiveled around to look at me, and my heartbeat ticked up. Stubby looked as alarmed as I felt.

From the seat in front of me, Eric Anderson (7-25-2017) said, "Yo, Murdering Maddie, what'd you *do*?"

I felt my mouth go dry. What *had* I done?

"*Mr.* Anderson. Another word from you, and you'll join us," warned Harris.

Eric turned away and snickered along with his best friend, Mario Rossi (7-25-2017).

Feeling my face flush, I gathered up my books and my backpack as fast as I could and followed the principal out of the room.

Harris led me through the empty hallways, his shoes making loud clacks against the terrazzo floors. I practically walked on tiptoe.

We reached his offices and passed through the doors into a large open space. All the school secretaries working there looked up in unison as we arrived. Knowing I'd never be called to the principal's office if I wasn't in trouble, I felt my cheeks sear with heat. "This way, Madelyn," said Principal Harris, waving me forward through the maze of desks to his inner office at the back. The door was closed and all the blinds on the glass windows facing out were drawn. He opened the door and again waved me along inside.

Seated in the chairs in front of his large metal desk were two men about the same age as my mom: one short and heavy with a face like a bulldog; the other tall and broad-shouldered with a handsome face you could've seen in Hollywood. They were both dressed formally in suits and ties, and they each turned to look at me, their gazes steely and suspicious. I tugged at the zipper on my hoodie, jumping as the door closed behind me.

Principal Harris moved to his desk and took his seat, then pointed to a chair to his left. "Sit," he said. It wasn't a request.

I tried to swallow, but my mouth had gone dry. I moved

to the chair and shrugged out of my backpack, holding it in front of me like a shield before I sat down. As I took the chair I noticed a large Word of the Day calendar on Principal Harris's desk next to me. Today's word was DONNYBROOK— A PUBLIC ARGUMENT.

"Madelyn," Harris said, and I jerked, my attention back to him. "This is Special Agent Faraday of the FBI and his partner, Agent Wallace." At the mention of their names, the two men reached into their blazer pockets and pulled out their respective badges, which they held aloft. The shiny shields reminded me of my dad's badge. Ma still kept it in her dresser drawer.

"They're here to discuss a most grievous and pressing situation, Madelyn," Principal Harris said. "Please give them your full attention while they recount the details."

The tall, broad-shouldered guy, Agent Faraday (10-2-2052), subtly rolled his eyes when Principal Harris wasn't looking. Apparently, kids weren't the only ones who found it hard to like our principal.

"Madelyn," Agent Faraday started.

I hugged my backpack, feeling my heart pound against my rib cage. This was about Ma. Something had happened to her or she was in trouble.

"Is it Madelyn?" Faraday asked. "Or Maddie?"

"Maddie," I told him, hating that my voice cracked. I was so nervous about Ma that I didn't know if I could handle what might come next.

Agent Faraday smiled, but it held no warmth. "I thought so," he said. "We have something very important we want to ask you, Maddie."

My brow furrowed. What could he want to ask me about Ma? "Uh...okay."

Agent Faraday nudged Agent Wallace (8-7-2051), and he took out a five-by-seven photograph of a kid dressed in a baseball uniform. "Have you seen this young man recently?" Wallace asked.

The appearance of the photo threw me. This didn't seem to be about Ma at all, but what could the photo of a kid in a baseball outfit possibly have to do with me? I leaned forward to look, and at first all my attention was focused on the kid's numbers, which were hard to read given the cap. I finally made them out, though: 10-29-2014. Yesterday. And then I looked again at the kid's face because that date was familiar, and I realized this was Tevon Tibbolt. I could feel the blood drain from my face, and I could also see that the agents had noticed my reaction. I'd watched enough TV to know that the FBI doesn't come around asking questions about dead kids unless they believe you had something to do with it.

I tried to think about what I should say to them. I didn't know if it was better to tell them about the reading with Mrs. Tibbolt or play dumb. I decided to aim for something in the middle. "I haven't seen him," I said, which was the truth. I'd never met Tevon before.

"He went missing yesterday on his way home from school, around three P.M. Are you *sure* you haven't seen him, Maddie?" Agent Faraday pressed.

I looked right at Faraday. "Yes, I'm sure."

He and Wallace leaned back in their chairs and exchanged a look. I didn't like it—they thought I was lying. Wallace shifted in close to me again, still holding the picture at eye level. "See, the thing is, Maddie, this boy is missing. And his mother seems to think you might know where he is."

My brow furrowed. What? Oh God, I thought. Tevon was missing and these guys didn't know he was dead. Worse yet, the way they were looking at me clearly suggested they thought I might've had something to do with it. I felt on the verge of panic, so I stuck to the truth—or a version of it. I shook my head again and said, "I don't know the kid." This time I even managed to raise my voice a little.

"Then why would his mother say you know him?" Agent Wallace asked casually, as if he was simply asking for a little clarification. "Why would she say that you might know where he is?"

I had no idea what Mrs. Tibbolt had said to the feds, and I felt like a rat caught in a maze with no way out. I tried to hold Wallace's gaze. I failed. "I don't know why she'd say something like that. I didn't know him."

Faraday sat up. Something I'd said alerted him. "You *didn't* know him?" he repeated. "Why use the past tense, Maddie?"

I gulped. I'd just said something really stupid. In the background, I heard the bell ring to signal the end of sixth period.

"Is there something you've done that you're feeling bad about, Maddie?" Faraday asked gently. "We're here to help you, you know. But we can't help you if you won't talk to us."

I didn't trust him for a second. I shook my head again, staring hard at the floor. I was determined not to say another word. Anything I said was bound to get twisted around and be used against me.

Agent Wallace lifted the photo toward me again. "He's only a kid, Maddie. If he's hurt or needs help, you have to tell us."

I glanced again at the photo and quickly away. Tevon's numbers kept floating there above his cap. 10-29-2014. The day before. Faraday said he'd disappeared around three P.M., and I knew I had to think about my alibi. I'd gone to school, then home to find Ma drunk on the couch, so I'd headed to Stubby's and hung out with him until around dinner. Then I'd gone home again, gotten Ma to bed, and studied for a chem test. I went to bed around eleven, and I knew that Stubby could vouch for my time after school at least. Guiltily, I realized I hadn't thought about Tevon since putting his name in my notebook.

Taking a deep breath, I worked up some courage. If I didn't explain myself, then this thing could get way out of control really quick.

"Listen," I began, trying to choose my words carefully. "Mrs. Tibbolt came to see me, okay? I didn't go to her house; she came to mine."

Wallace nodded like he totally understood. "She told us you claim to be some sort of psychic."

I took another deep breath and tried to calm myself. They were twisting everything, and they didn't understand. "I'm not a psychic," I said. "I just see dates."

Faraday cocked an eyebrow. "Dates? What kind of dates?"

"Deathdates."

Next to me I heard Mr. Harris suck in a breath while Wallace and Faraday exchanged another look. I decided to push on with my explanation. "Since I was little I've been able to see the exact date when somebody's going to die. I don't know why I can see it, but I can. So when my mom lost her job and we needed some extra money, we started charging people to have me tell them their deathdate."

Wallace made a noise that sounded like a stifled laugh. Faraday cut him a look, and Wallace regained his composure quick. "So you told Mrs. Tibbolt the date you think she's going to die?" he asked.

"No. She came to me about her daughter, who has cancer. Mrs. Tibbolt wanted me to tell her if it was okay to go ahead with the drug trial."

"I thought you weren't psychic?" Faraday said.

I sighed. This was so frustrating. "I'm not. I told her that her daughter was going to live for, like, another eighty years, so Mrs. Tibbolt knew that she should go ahead and put her daughter in the drug trial."

"How did Tevon figure into this?" Faraday asked.

"I saw his picture."

"You saw his picture?" Wallace repeated.

I nodded. "I don't need to see someone in person to see a deathdate. I can read them off photos just as good."

"So you saw his photo, and then what?" Faraday asked.

"When I saw Tevon's date I asked Mrs. Tibbolt if he was sick, too, and she said no. So then I told her that his death-date was this week, and she didn't believe me. She called me a fraud and left." And then I thought about the phone call at the diner and decided I might as well tell them all of it.

"Later on that same night, I called her to try and convince her that I'm not a fake, but she got really mad at me, so I hung up and left her alone."

"She tells it a little differently, Maddie," Wallace said after a slight pause. "She says you threatened her son. She claims you told her that, if she didn't listen to you, something bad was going to happen to Tevon."

I looked at the photo still in Wallace's hands. "Something bad *has* happened to him," I whispered.

Principal Harris sucked in another breath, and the tension in the room went up another notch. "Where is he, Maddie?" Faraday asked me softly. "Tell us what you did to him and where he is."

My eyes widened. He didn't believe me, and he still thought I did something to Tevon. I knew then that I wasn't going to talk my way out of this, but I also knew who could help me. "I think I should call my uncle," I said, as the warning bell for seventh period sounded.

"Your uncle?" Wallace asked.

I nodded, feeling a little better for thinking of calling Donny. "He's a lawyer, and I think he'd want me to call him right now."

Principal Harris cleared his throat, held up his hand. "Agents Faraday and Wallace, I'm afraid I'm rather uncomfortable with this interview taking place in my office. If you want to question Madelyn further, then I'll need to contact Mrs. Fynn and allow Maddie to call her uncle, as she has a right to have her attorney present. Otherwise, gentlemen, that will be all."

Faraday stood, but Wallace ignored him. He leaned

forward, his gaze intent on me. "Are you sure you want to get attorneys involved here, Maddie? I mean, if you tell us where Tevon is right now, we may be able to cut you a deal. But if you lawyer up on us, it's gonna be worse for you down the road. Let us help you, Maddie. Tell us where Tevon is, and stop torturing his parents, for God's sake."

I hugged my backpack even tighter as the agents looked expectantly at me.

I kept thinking of the stories Donny told me about his clients and how dumb a lot of them were to talk to the police first before they called him. "I don't think I should say anything more to you without my uncle," I said. Faraday nudged Wallace, and the two got up and moved to the door, but after opening it, Agent Faraday turned back to look at me. "We'll be in touch, Maddie. Soon. You can count on it."

His promise left me cold to the bone.

After being released from Principal Harris's office, I didn't go to my seventh period ceramics class. Instead, I headed straight to the girls' restroom and hid in a stall. While I waited on the final bell I called my uncle, but it went straight to voice mail. I left him a message, but I didn't hear from him before the bell. After it rang, I stayed put until most of the students had cleared out of the building, and then I hurried through the nearly empty halls to my locker. After gathering up my books, I made my way to the back entrance next to the pool. My bike was locked up in the bike rack, but there were three smashed eggs on the seat. A smudged piece of paper had the words: *Three little chickies died here, 10-30-2014.*

I recognized Eric Anderson's handwriting. Crumpling up the paper I looked around for something to wipe off the seat. "Hey!" I heard while I searched the ground.

Glancing up I saw Stubby walking toward me, carrying a wad of paper towels and his skateboard. "It was Eric and Mario," he said, handing me the towels.

My hands were shaking while I mopped up the mess. "Thanks, Stubs."

"What the heck did Harris call you to his office for?"

I wanted to tell Stubby all about the encounter in the principal's office, but even more I wanted to get home to tell Ma and maybe have her call Uncle Donny. It wasn't unusual for Donny to wait to call me back, but Ma's calls he always returned.

I didn't know how Ma was gonna react, and that worried me. But then I had another thought. I looked up at Stubs and said, "You remember hanging out with me yesterday, right?"

Stubby's brow furrowed. "Yesterday?"

"Yeah. We hung out and studied for the chem test, remember?"

He nodded. "I remember."

I tossed the paper towels in the trash and unlocked my bike. "If anybody comes to your house and asks about it, you'll vouch for me, right?"

Stubby cocked his head. "Mads, what's going on?"

I hopped onto the bike and shoved off. "I'll call you later; just remember what I said!"

I got home fast, but not fast enough. There was a black sedan parked in front of our house--and I didn't think it was a client's.

I left my bike by the garage, then crept to the back door, which was ajar, but the storm door was shut. Putting my ear to the thin pane of glass, I heard voices—Ma's and someone else's. I recognized Faraday's deep baritone right away.

"It's up to you, Mrs. Fynn. If you'd like to have your brother-in-law present while we question your daughter, that's your right as her guardian. But he's going to tell you not to talk to us, and if something has happened to Tevon Tibbolt, and your daughter knew about it or played a role in it, then I'm afraid it could go bad for her pretty fast."

"Maddie had nothing to do with that boy's disappearance!" Ma snapped.

I strained to hear her, listening for the telltale signs that she'd hit the bottle too hard today, but her speech was only a little thick. Maybe they wouldn't notice.

"But you admit that she threatened the boy's mother," Faraday said.

"Of course she didn't! Maddie wouldn't hurt a fly."

"Can you account for her whereabouts yesterday?" another voice asked. Wallace's, I thought.

"She was right here with me."

I shut my eyes and swore under my breath.

"The whole day?" Faraday asked.

"Well, of course not the whole day! She came straight home from school and we were right here until after dinner watching TV. Then she did her homework and went to bed a little after ten." I realized that Ma was recounting what I did most days, but not yesterday. I knew that her memory was often fuzzy, so I didn't think she was trying to outright lie to the agents.

"What time did she arrive home from school?" Wallace continued.

"The usual time," Ma said. "Two forty-five, I think."

There was a pause, then Faraday said, "The usual time? It's three-ten and she's not home yet."

"That clock is ten minutes fast," Ma said quickly. I knew they were both referring to the antique wooden clock above the mantel. It was Dad's clock. He bought it for Ma on their first anniversary, and he used to set it ten minutes ahead so he'd always be early for his shift. We'd never corrected the time.

"Even accounting for the difference," Faraday continued, "she's still fifteen minutes late."

I took a deep, steadying breath and opened the storm door. It squeaked loudly. "Hey, Ma! I'm home!" I decided to play it like I had no idea what was happening in the living room.

"Maddie?" Ma called back nervously. "Where've you been, honey? You're late."

"Sorry," I said, dropping my backpack on the kitchen table so it'd make some noise. "Someone smeared something slimy on my bike seat, and I had a hard time getting it off."

I then walked into the living room and pretended to come up short. "Oh," I said. "You guys are here."

Faraday cocked an eyebrow. I was pretty sure he could tell a faker a mile away. "You have a bike, Maddie?" he asked in that same casual tone that I didn't trust for a second.

I nodded. "It's in the garage."

Faraday then looked to Wallace. "How many miles between here and Parkwick?"

"Four or five," Wallace said.

"How long would that take on a bike?"

"Ten minutes, maybe."

Faraday turned back to Ma. "You're *sure* your daughter was here with you yesterday between the hours of three and six P.M.?"

Ma looked at me and nodded firmly. "I'm positive. Remember, honey? We watched that show . . . What was it?"

And there it was. I either had to agree with Ma, who looked so earnest in her effort to create an alibi for me, or correct her and make the agents suspect her for a liar. I decided to try and protect us both. "Uh, Ma, I think you're thinking of Tuesday. I was at Stubby's yesterday studying for that chem test. Remember?"

Ma's brow furrowed, and all that confidence that she'd mustered up in front of the agents fell away, and she looked lost. Casting her gaze down to her lap she said, "Oh. I thought that was yesterday." Then she reached for the big plastic glass on the table filled with clear liquid that I knew wasn't water.

"Who's Stubby?" Faraday asked.

"Arnold Schroder. He's my best friend. He can vouch for me."

Faraday made a note in his notebook and asked for Stubby's address. As he was jotting that down, Wallace said, "Do you think your friend Arnold might know the whereabouts of Tevon Tibbolt?"

He'd asked that so casually, like he was asking if I knew where to get the best cheeseburger in town. I sighed and looked at Ma, who was back to frowning at the agents. "My daughter and her best friend had nothing to do with that boy's disappearance. If you want to keep pressing the issue, then I will insist on calling my brother-in-law."

Wallace pursed his lips and considered Ma with a cool, steady glare. "Little early in the day to be drinking, don't you think, Mrs. Faraday?"

I felt my chest tighten and I stopped breathing. This was exactly what I feared.

Ma paled and set the plastic cup down. "I don't know what you mean," she said meekly, then she reached for her cigarette pack and fished one out. Her hands were shaking, and I knew the agents noticed.

Wallace smiled tightly. "No. I'm sure you don't."

Ma glared at him while she lit up, and I saw her spine straighten a little. "Maddie," she said. "Can you bring me the phone? I think it's time we called Donny." I was rooted to the spot for a second. The phone was sitting on a table right between the two agents. I was afraid to retrieve it.

While I hesitated, Faraday tucked his notebook into his pocket, motioned to Wallace, and stood up. Before heading to the door, Faraday pulled out a business card from his inside coat pocket and said, "If you want to call and talk, Madelyn, this is my number. Maybe you didn't have anything to do with Tevon's disappearance, but if you know anything . . . anything at all about what might've happened to him or where he is, you can call me and I'll listen."

After placing it next to the phone, he and Wallace walked to the front door, which sticks. They had to tug on it a couple of times to get it to open, but then they were gone. The minute they pulled the door closed, Ma turned to me. "The phone, honey. I need to call Donny."

My uncle Donny is my dad's younger brother. He's an attorney in Manhattan, and he'd handled the lawsuit against the city Ma filed after Dad died. He also managed the settlement we'd gotten as a result, sending us a check every month to cover most of the bills.

Donny still lives in Brooklyn, and he used to come around to check on us every couple of weeks. Now, though, he hardly visits at all. Ever since Ma's drinking got worse, he and Ma stopped getting along. Still, he's always gotten me a great Christmas gift, and this past summer, he'd taken Stubby and me to Florida. I knew that, if anybody could help explain things to the feds, it was Donny.

After bringing Ma the phone, I headed upstairs to lock myself in my room. The first thing I did was hop on my computer and FaceTime Stubs. He answered on the sixth or seventh ring, and simply seeing his baby-faced smile brought a measure of comfort. "I thought you'd never call," he said, scratching at the light-blond stubble on his chin. "You looked totally freaked out at school. What happened with Harris?"

I explained everything to him, about the feds waiting for me in Harris's office and then again here at home. "Whoa," he said, after I was done. "Maddie, that's bad!"

"I know," I said, feeling like the weight of the world had firmly settled onto my shoulders. And then I remembered that I'd given Stubby as my alibi. "They should be calling you," I told him. "To confirm where I was when Tevon went missing."

"When did he go missing?"

"Yesterday after school. The feds said he never made it home."

Stubby's eyes grew wide. "What do you think happened to him?"

I shook my head. "I have no idea, but when they showed me his picture, his date confirms that he's dead."

"Oh, man," Stubby said. "Maddie, maybe we shoulda done something more to try and save him."

I bit my lip. That's what I'd been thinking, too. I felt terribly ashamed of myself because, even though I'd known it was coming and I'd found it really sad, I hadn't expected Tevon's death to be so mysterious. What if he'd fallen into a ravine and his death had been slow and painful? Or what if he'd been hit by a car on a dirt road and the driver hadn't stopped to report it, and he was simply out there somewhere where nobody would find him for weeks? I couldn't imagine what his mother was going through. No wonder she thought I had something to do with it.

"I feel really bad," Stubby said quietly. "I know she got mad when you called, but maybe I should've gone over to her house and explained to her that I knew you, and that you're not a fake. You're a good person. I bet I could've convinced her."

"You couldn't have known it was going to be like this," I said. It was exactly like Stubs to feel guilty over something he had no control over. For a guy, he was incredibly softhearted.

And then I saw Stubs jerk and look over his shoulder. Turning back to me he said, "Somebody's at the door."

I had a suspicion about who it was. "Is your mom home yet?"

"No," he said. "Hold on a sec and let me see who it is." Stubby darted off, and I was left to wait anxiously for him to return. It took about fifteen minutes, but he finally came back and tried to smile at me encouragingly. "That was them," he said, referring to Wallace and Faraday. "I told them you were here the whole time yesterday after school, studying with me for the chem test."

I relaxed a fraction. "Thanks, buddy. What else did they ask you?"

"They wanted to know if I believed you were really psychic. I told them I didn't know about being psychic, but I knew you could read deathdates. And then they asked me how I knew that, and I told them that you'd told me about my grampa dying right after Christmas last year, and he died the exact day you said."

"Did they believe you?"

Stubby frowned. "I don't think so, but they left after that."

I swallowed hard and looked down at my lap. This whole thing was so bad, I didn't know what to do. When I looked up again I saw that Stubby was studying me. "You gonna be okay?"

I shrugged. "Yeah. I hope they find him soon, Stubbs. I hate to think that Tevon is out there somewhere where no one can find him."

Stubby was quiet for a minute, then he said, "You don't think somebody . . . ?"

"What?"

He grimaced. "Murdered him."

My eyes widened. "In Parkwick? No way." Parkwick was known for its big houses, big money, big parks, and its nearly nonexistent crime rate. It had its own police force, which had a reputation for stopping anybody who looked like they didn't belong in the neighborhood.

But Stubby seemed unconvinced. "Then what happened to him, Mads? And why doesn't anybody know where he is?"

I shrugged, feeling incredibly sad. "I don't know, Stubs. It could be that he simply wandered off into the woods and fell and hit his head or something. Or maybe he got hit by a car and no one's found his body yet. Anything like that might explain it."

Stubs sighed. "Yeah, okay. Listen, I gotta go start dinner for Mom. FaceTime me later if you wanna talk."

After I got off the computer with Stubs, I headed downstairs and found Ma pacing back and forth in the kitchen, her plastic cup nearly empty. She jumped when I entered the room. I could tell she was having a tough time dealing with the visit from the FBI. "I spoke to Donny," she said. "He's had court all day and he had to go back to the office to work late on a case, but he told me that if those agents come back to call him right away."

With a pang I noted that Ma was starting to slur her words. "Want some dinner?" I asked, trying to distract her.

Ma moved over to the pantry where she kept her booze. "No, honey. I'm not hungry. There's some turkey in the fridge, though. I got some from the deli today."

I made myself a sandwich and avoided looking at Ma

while she poured a refill. I made a half of a sandwich for her, too, just in case, and set it down in front of her in the TV room.

I then took my sandwich upstairs to eat it while I did my homework, but it was nearly impossible to concentrate, and I barely got through it. I finally called it quits around eight and went back down to check on Ma. She hadn't touched her sandwich, but she'd nodded off, plastic cup in hand.

It took me a little while to get her up to her bedroom, but at last she was settled for the night. I went back downstairs, where I tried to watch some TV, but I was too wound up and anxious.

For a long time I sat in the dark, listening to the light rhythm of Dad's clock. Now that he was gone, its constant ticktock was the closest thing we had to his heartbeat. I loved listening to it—and to the chimes, soft and sweet, like the first notes of a lullaby.

Dad's photo was on the mantel right under the clock. As the minutes ticked by, I found myself staring at his image and missing him like crazy. In my heart I knew that if he were here, he'd get Faraday and Wallace to believe me. It was yet another example of how little Ma and I mattered to a world without Dad. He'd been our center, the glue that held us together and gave us purpose. His absence was greater than the sum of our parts, and I didn't think we'd ever feel quite whole again.

With a sigh I turned away from the photo and went to the window. Peering out into the night, I saw a sedan come down the street and park a bit up from our house. I could

see that the motor was still running, because the t
was giving off vapor, which sparkled in the light from
streetlamp. Squinting, I could just make out the figures
two people in the car. My heartbeat ticked up. It was Wallace and Faraday. I waited for them to get out of the car and
come to the door, but as the minutes passed they remained
where they were. Finally, after about fifteen minutes, the
agents slowly pulled away from the curb and drove off.

I knew then that no matter what alibi I'd offered them,
this wasn't over.

The next day passed in a fog. I was jumpy and on edge the
whole time, and even Stubby couldn't make me feel better.
"They can't prove you had anything to do with it, Maddie,"
he said as we rode home together.

But I didn't have a good feeling.

Stubby and I parted ways at the midway point between
our houses, and I pedaled hard toward home. It was Halloween, and I had to make sure we had enough money in the
grocery envelope for candy for the few kids brave enough to
ring our doorbell. There're lots of kids in the neighborhood,
but our house never sees much traffic. Too many people have
heard the rumors that Ma and I are witches.

As I sped down the street, my thoughts were occupied by
the need for a backup plan if there was no cash in the envelope. As I turned the corner onto my block, I had to lean to
the side to avoid the large truck parked between our house
and Mrs. Duncan's. Taking a quick glance over my shoulder
to make sure there were no cars behind me, I was ready to

making the turn into our drive when I turned back the road, and all of a sudden, two men, hoisting a plastic-wrapped sofa between them, stepped out from the back of a delivery truck and right into my path.

Tensing, I squeezed the hand brakes with all my strength. It caused the bike to skid, then wobble, then crash right into the front of the sofa.

I went down hard and felt the pavement burn the side of my leg all the way to my thigh. My hip took the brunt of the fall, and it hurt so badly I cried out, squeezing my lids shut as hot tears stung my eyes.

A moment later I heard my neighbor, Mrs. Duncan, exclaim, "Oh, my goodness! Maddie, darling!" followed by a quick shuffle of feet. I focused on the pavement and the cluster of shoes hurrying toward me, while I tried to get my bearings. Then there were hands pulling at the bike and at my arms. It all muddled with the pain searing my leg and thigh.

Belatedly, I realized that the bike was still on top of me, and I was gritting my teeth hard against the pain. "Let go of the bike, sweetie," a male voice said. "Come on...that's it. Let it go."

I unclasped my hands and the bike was lifted off of me. I was crying too hard to do much else. "Oh, dear! I should get your mother!" Mrs. Duncan said, hurrying away.

Meanwhile, the two delivery guys helped me up. One was talking low and gentle, but I couldn't focus on anything but the shock of the crash and the pain that radiated up and down my leg. I couldn't seem to stop sobbing. Deep down I knew it wasn't all about the fall.

"Wes," one of the men said, "get the first aid kit from the truck."

I was handed off, and the guy named Wes disappeared into the cab. "Here, honey," the first guy said. "Let's sit you down on this, okay?" I saw him motion toward Mrs. Duncan's new sofa, which had ended up in the middle of the street.

I took a few shuddering breaths and limped over to the couch, where the guy helping me eased me carefully onto the plastic covering before he bent down to inspect my leg. "Can I roll this up?" he asked, pointing to the cuff of my jeans.

I swallowed a sob and nodded. He rolled up the pant leg, and I hissed as it brushed against my raw skin. He whistled and shook his head, his body partially hiding the wound from my sight.

"Is it...is it bad?" I blubbered.

He lifted his chin. "Yeah," he said gravely, and then the corners of his mouth quirked and with a wink he added, "But I don't think it's fatal." All of the sudden, even though I was having a total meltdown, I laughed. Then I was half-laughing and half-crying, and I couldn't seem to settle on one over the other.

Mrs. Duncan returned, wringing her gnarled hands. "Your mother's not feeling so well, herself," she said, her eyes avoiding mine. Her meaning was clear. All the laughter died in my throat.

The other delivery guy came back then with a small white box, and he was sifting through it with a frown on his face. "I don't think any of these bandages are big enough."

Mrs. Duncan hooked one of her fingers onto the box

to pull it toward her. "Oh, that won't do!" she said. "Come along inside, Wesley. I've got everything we need to patch her up, but you'll have to move those chairs out of the way so I can get to the powder room."

After they'd headed inside Mrs. Duncan's house, the guy who was helping me got up and went to the back of his truck. He took out a couple of orange cones and put them in the street behind and in front of the truck so that anyone who drove by wouldn't get too close. Then he came back to me and pulled out a bandanna from his back pocket. He used it to dab at my bleeding leg. "What else hurts?" he asked me.

Everything hurt—I jumped every time he touched my skin with the cloth. Still, I held up my elbow. I couldn't really see it, but I knew it'd gotten scraped up, too.

"Yikes," he said. "When you go down, you really go down, girl."

I wiped at my cheeks. He seemed really nice. But after glancing up to look at him, I took note of his deathdate, and my chest tightened. Dropping my gaze I said, "I'm okay. Thanks."

"Do any bones hurt?" he asked.

I shook my head.

"Really sorry about that, Maddie," he said kindly. "If your bike's wrecked, we'll pay to have it fixed."

I glanced at my ride. It looked a little scratched up, but otherwise it seemed fine. "I think it's okay."

The delivery guy put the bandanna in my hand. "Here," he said. "You can probably do a better job of that than me."

"Thanks." I continued to avoid his gaze.

"You don't remember me, do you?"

Puzzled, I looked up again. He had a big, square head, with short-cropped gray hair and deep-set eyes. Now that he mentioned it, he did look kind of familiar. I squinted at him but couldn't place how I knew him.

He stuck out his hand, and I put my good palm in his. He shook it gently and said, "Rick Kane. I came to see you about a year ago."

Vaguely, I remembered someone who looked a little like him coming to see me the previous September. It'd been right around the anniversary of my dad's death, which is always a tough time at my house—so I couldn't quite remember the exact details—but his deathdate stood out for me now, which was why I was trying to avoid his gaze.

"It's okay," he said, as if reading my mind. "It's still the same, right? I've only got about five weeks left."

I nodded. "I'm really sorry."

He smiled in a way that seemed sad but still genuine. "Don't be, kiddo. We all gotta go sometime."

I looked back at my lap, wishing Mrs. Duncan and the other guy would come back out.

"You know," he said, "you've really helped me."

I squeezed the bandanna. The heel of my palm was scraped up, too.

"I mean, at first I was a wreck. You tell a guy he's only got about a year left to live, and it'll pretty much tear him up inside. But then I got over it, and I realized I had a whole year to get ready. Most people, they have no idea when they wake up in the morning that it'll be their last day, but I know the exact date, and because of that, I've been taking care of things."

I lifted my chin. "Yeah?"

He nodded and he seemed so at peace about it. "I've taken out extra life insurance," he said. "To get the insurance they had to put me through a physical, and it turns out I've got a few issues. I think that's how it'll happen. My heart will give out or it'll be a stroke or something like that."

"Can't you go to a doctor?" I asked. I wanted so badly for that date on his forehead to change.

"I did, Maddie. My own doc ran a bunch of tests, but nothing obvious jumped off the page at him. My cholesterol is a little elevated, and my blood pressure's not great, but it's not bad enough yet to go on the meds. I even got a second head-to-toe physical, and nothing shows up that could be the culprit. Whatever's going to happen to me, I think it'll be a surprise, and it'll be quick. Which, when I think about it, isn't a bad way to go, you know?"

I nodded, shocked by how well he seemed to be taking it. But then, I'd seen this reaction from some of my clients with terminal diseases. They simply accepted it and got busy getting their affairs in order.

"Anyway," he continued, "with all the added life insurance, my family will never have to worry about money again, and both my kids are gonna get to go to college. I also make sure to tell my sons and my wife how much I love them every day. We've never been closer. And I've been checking things off my bucket list, too. You know, the stuff you always say you want to do but never get to because there's always tomorrow? My whole life I put off doing what I really wanted to do because I was worried about providing for my family and keeping my job. These days if I want to take a day off to do something fun, I do. I don't sweat the small stuff. Not anymore. You freed me, Maddie. I feel more alive right now than I ever have. You gave me that."

I was so moved that I didn't know what to say.

"Here we are!" I heard Mrs. Duncan call from her walkway. She and the other guy were loaded down with gauze, ointments, bandages, and medical tape. My kindly neighbor got right to work, and in no time I was patched up and feeling a little better.

Then Rick got me to my feet, and while his partner put my bike into the garage, he helped me up the drive. "Thanks," I told him once we'd reached the storm door. "For everything."

He offered me a big grin. "You gonna be okay?"

I nodded. "Yeah. It just stings a little right now."

"Take some Advil," he advised. "And no more speed racer on that bike of yours, you hear?" He chuckled and I smiled. Then he and the other guy got back to Mrs. Duncan's delivery, and I limped my way inside.

I found Ma passed out on the couch. I checked the time. It was early for her to be so out of it. I could feel a knot beginning to form in my stomach. She was reacting to the visit from the feds. I didn't like it.

I hobbled over to her and tugged the afghan off the back of the couch, spreading it out over her the best I could. I felt stiff and sore all over, and the scrapes on my leg, elbow, and palm were starting to throb, so I limped up the stairs, and once in my room, eased out of the tight jeans and sweater I was wearing and into the lightest pair of sweats I owned. As I got redressed, I thought again about what Rick had said—that I'd helped him. Telling him his deathdate hadn't changed his numbers, but at least I'd helped him and his family by giving him the news. His wife and kids were going to be sad to lose their dad—I knew that pain well—but his family would also be provided for. A bit like Ma and me had been provided for by the settlement from the lawsuit.

I would've rather had my dad, but at least most of our bills were covered for the time being. That meant a whole lot, when I thought about it.

Moving to my desk I pulled out my deathdates notebook and began to thumb through the pages. I found Rick's entry and the deathdate next to his name: 12-6-2014. I sighed sadly, then looked at all the other names and dates I'd written on the many pages of the notebook.

I always put a capitol C next to my clients, and as I scrolled through the names of the people I'd read for, I wondered if maybe some of them might be doing the same thing as Rick. Maybe some of them were also taking out extra life insurance, and telling their kids and their spouses every day that they loved them. Maybe reading for these people was a good thing after all?

And then I went to Aiden's page and ran my forefinger across his name. I could picture his face, those deep blue eyes, the curve of his jaw, the fullness of his lips.

I'd have a chance to see him in only a week, and I felt my pulse quicken. I hadn't seen him since the previous spring. I wondered if he'd gotten any taller, if his shoulders had gotten broader, if seeing him would still take my breath away.

My smile widened. Of course it would. With a sigh I closed the notebook and tucked it away. Then I limped down the stairs and realized that I still had to go to the store to get some candy for the trick-or-treaters, but how I was going to manage that, I had no idea. In desperation, I texted Stubby— he called me immediately. "What happened?" he asked. I'd only told him in the text that I'd crashed on my bike.

I gave him the quick version of what'd happened, and he offered to come over right away with a bunch of Hershey's minis from his mom's stash. "We always have extra," he said.

While I waited for Stubs, I fixed two grilled cheese sandwiches and some tomato soup. As I was ladling the soup into bowls, Stubby walked in.

"Your timing is perfect," I told him.

He shrugged out of his coat, and I saw that he was only wearing a white T-shirt and jeans underneath. Then I realized he also had his hair slicked back. "James Dean?" I guessed. Stubs loves old movies.

My best friend grinned and nodded at me. "Can I borrow a pack of your mom's cigarettes?" he asked, his gaze traveling to the carton on the counter.

"Why?" I asked sharply. I lived with a smoker, and it was a disgusting habit. I didn't want Stubs to start up.

He rolled his eyes, then he took up one of Ma's half-empty packs, got out a cigarette, dangled it at the corner of his mouth, then rolled the pack up into his shirtsleeve. "Dean used to roll the pack up like this," he explained. "Makes me look cool, right?"

I offered him a skeptical frown. "Don't you think meeting kids at the door with a cigarette hanging out of your mouth might tick off some parents?"

Stubs smiled sheepishly and removed the cigarette

dangling from his lips. "Good point." Then he reached for his backpack and pulled out the candy he'd promised me, like a hunter bringing home a trophy. "Where do you want it?"

"Can you dump it in this and put it on the front porch?" I asked him, handing him our big salad bowl.

Stubs eyed the bowl doubtfully. "You sure, Mads? Usually the first kids at the door take all the candy and run for it."

I bent over to lift up the cuff of my sweats to demonstrate exactly why I wouldn't be getting up and down to answer the door every five minutes. "Yikes," Stubs said, dumping the candy in the bowl. "Got it covered." When he came back to the table, he sat down with me and said, "I can't stay long. Mom wants me to hand out candy while she takes Sam and Grace trick-or-treating."

"Okay." I felt a little disappointed that Stubs couldn't stay longer and keep me company. I hadn't been able to shake my melancholy.

While we sipped at our soup he asked, "Anything new about Tevon?"

"No," I told him. "At least there wasn't a car parked in front of my house today when I got home from school. Not that I noticed much after I crashed."

Stubs offered me a sympathetic frown before brightening. "You gotta heal quick, Mads. Next Friday is the Jupiter game."

I felt a smile tug at the corners of my mouth. "Oh, I'll be there," I said. "No way am I missing it."

Stubby nodded. I could tell he was looking forward to going to the game, too. "Cheerleaders," he said with a loopy grin, and that got me to laugh.

A lot of the kids at school assume Stubs and I are a couple, but the truth is, we're more like brother and sister than anything else.

"You gonna say hi to Aiden this year?" he asked me slyly. "Or are you gonna sit there and pretend you're not seriously crushing on him?"

I pushed him on the shoulder. "Don't rush me," I said. "I'm working up to it."

It was Stubby's turn to laugh. "Working up to it? It's been two years, Mads. At this rate you'll graduate before you even smile at the guy."

I rolled my eyes before reaching over to dunk the rest of his sandwich in his soup. He shook his head, but he was chuckling. "Women!" he said.

We hung out for a while more before Dad's clock chimed six times and Stubs got up, taking his bowl and his plate to the sink. "Gotta go!" he said. "Thanks for dinner. Hope your leg feels better!" With that he banged out the back door with barely a wave good-bye.

After finishing my own meal, I got up and limped over to the sink to rinse out my dishes. The TV was still on in the living room, but I couldn't make out much more than white noise. As I turned off the faucet, however, I thought I heard a familiar name. Moving to the doorway between the kitchen and the living room, I saw that the news was on, and there was a reporter standing in front of a large stately home that had to be in Parkwick. I could tell right away she was talking about Tevon Tibbolt. "...the body of the thirteen-year-old was discovered on the banks of the Waliki River, about six miles from his residence here in Parkwick, where

Tevon was last seen walking home from the bus stop on Wednesday afternoon. Tevon is the son of prominent hedge fund manager Ryan Tibbolt and his wife, socialite Patricia Tibbolt. We have few details other than the boy's body has been positively identified, and police and the FBI have ruled the death a homicide...."

I leaned against the door frame; my knees were threatening to give out from underneath me. I stood there breathing hard as a mounting sense of panic began to overwhelm me. The news reporter rattled off that the FBI was now leading the investigation in the disturbing murder, stating that Tevon's body had been found riddled with wounds, and there were preliminary signs that the boy had been tortured.

When the news cut to commercial I reached a trembling hand toward the phone, but Uncle Donny's line went straight to voice mail again. "Donny? It's Maddie. Did you hear the news? It's Tevon Tibbolt. They found him, and he's been murdered. Please call me, okay? Right away. Please?"

Still gripping the phone, I hobbled over to Dad's old leather chair and collapsed into it. I stared at the TV, but the newscaster had already moved on to a house fire in neighboring Willow Mill.

The doorbell rang twice and shouts of "Trick or Treat!" echoed through the door, but I didn't move out of Dad's chair. Instead I sat there and wept for a long time, feeling so guilty I could barely keep my dinner down. If only I'd insisted that Mrs. Tibbolt listen to me. If only I'd run after her before she left our house and said, "Please don't let him out of the house next Wednesday!" or if I hadn't hung up on her later that night but had tried harder to get her to listen to me, Tevon might still be alive.

At eight o'clock I wiped my eyes with the sleeve of my sweatshirt and stood gingerly. It'd gotten dark in the room, and in spite of Ma sleeping on the couch, I turned on a light, then I hobbled over to the door to check on the candy.

After struggling to get the door open, I saw the plastic bowl smashed and broken at the bottom of the front walk, and a roll of toilet paper hanging from the branches of the small maple tree in our front yard.

I'd been sitting inside and hadn't heard a thing.

My shoulders slumped, and I was about to pick up what remained of the bowl when I saw a dark sedan snake down the street to park a few houses away. The nearby streetlight gave off enough light for me to see two figures inside. I felt cold all over. I knew with certainty that they were looking my way, waiting and watching. It was now official. I was in serious trouble.

# 11-01-2014

UNCLE DONNY DROVE UP TO POPLAR HOLLOW THE
next day, right after the FBI called him to say that they
wanted to talk to me again. He arrived in his shiny BMW,
wearing a black suit and gold tie. Donny always looks good,
but today I could tell he'd put a little bit extra into his
appearance. The sight of him looking so sharp and confident
made me feel better. He walked me to the car after taking
one look at Ma, who'd hit the bottle kind of hard the day
before; even though it was nearly noon, she was still pretty
groggy. Uncle Donny told her she'd better stay home.

Once we were in the car, Donny turned to me and said,
"How you doin', kiddo?"

I shrugged. "Okay, I guess."

"No, really," he pressed, his brow all furrowed and concerned. "How *are* you?"

I almost laughed. It was ridiculous. "I'm fine, Donny.
Can we please go?"

But Donny didn't start the car. Instead he glanced toward the house, then back at me. "You can always come live with me, you know," he said in a serious tone.

I swallowed hard. I loved Donny, but ever since my dad died, I'd had trouble with the city. In fact, it'd been one of the reasons Ma had moved us all the way out here. I'd started having panic attacks and couldn't seem to concentrate at school. Some days in class I would shake so hard I couldn't hold a pencil. Other times I couldn't seem to catch my breath, and I'd nearly pass out.

The minute we moved out of Brooklyn, leaving behind all the noise and people, I'd settled down. But it was hard for me to go into the city to visit Donny for even a day without the shakes and shortness of breath coming back. I couldn't imagine going there to live again.

Then there was Ma to consider. We were an hour and forty minutes by car outside of New York City, two and a half hours by train. I couldn't leave Ma, because who'd get to her quickly if something bad happened?

"Thanks, Donny," I said, "but I'm okay."

Donny sighed and started the car, heading west.

Poplar Hollow, Jupiter, Willow Mill, and Parkwick are all villages technically within the city of Grand Haven, New York. Mostly, the villages circle Grand Haven like planets in a solar system, and the distinctions between the villages are measured more by the sizes of the houses than anything else. Willow Mill is a step down from Poplar Hollow, and Jupiter is a step up, but you'd need a ladder to get into Parkwick. The rest of Grand Haven isn't so grand, though, and most of us kinda thumb our noses at it. We all have our own school system with about a thousand kids in each high school, except that Grand Haven itself has two high schools—North and South—and they have at least two thousand kids in each. Both of their football teams clobber our team every year, but we usually stand a fighting chance against the other schools. Still, it seems we're always duking it out with Jupiter for second-to-last place.

Downtown Grand Haven is on the small side when you compare it to any other major city, especially New York, but every year it gets another few tall office buildings added to it. Now it even has two malls.

The bureau offices are downtown, about a block away from the police station in a building that's new and trendy. Not the kind of place you'd expect to find the FBI.

Donny took up two slots in the parking garage so no one could park too close to his BMW, and then led the way to the stairs—he always takes the stairs—and we finally came out on the third floor. Donny's footfalls were steady and sure as we wound our way through the maze of hallways. I was back on tiptoe.

At last we came out to a central catwalk that encircled the lobby below and wound around to a large staircase with a gleaming brass railing. Donny followed the railing up to a set of double glass doors with a stenciled sign that read, OFFICES OF THE FBI—GRAND HAVEN BRANCH. Before pulling the doors open Donny paused with his palm on the handle and said, "Remember, Maddie, don't answer any question without looking to me to see if I approve; and if I do, *just* answer the question, okay? Nothing else. Don't elaborate beyond the simplest answer."

My mouth had gone dry as we'd stepped onto the third floor, and I wanted a glass of water badly. My legs were trembling, and I found it hard to concentrate on what Donny was saying. Still, I managed to nod when he looked at me and opened the door.

We walked in to find the place pretty busy for a Saturday. "They mostly monitor drug and weapons traffic coming in and out of New York City from here," Donny whispered. That made sense when I thought about it, as Grand Haven sits right next to I-87, which heads straight to Canada.

Donny pointed to a leather chair in the lobby and I sat while he checked in with the receptionist. After letting the feds know we were there, she came over to us. Her death-date read 2-12-2061. "Agents Faraday and Wallace will be with you shortly. Can I get you something to drink while you wait?"

"Coffee," Donny said, flashing a smile. Donny's a big flirt.

"I'll take water please," I told her.

After she came back with our drinks, Agent Faraday appeared and motioned for us to follow him.

He led us to a glass-enclosed office with an open ceiling where he pointed to the two chairs that faced his desk, and as we took our seats Wallace entered the office, pushing a chair in front of him.

Faraday shut the door behind Wallace before taking his seat, and I moved my gaze to his desk. It was cluttered with papers and files, but one corner was fairly neat. Several picture frames were arranged there with their backs to us. I assumed they were of his family, and I felt oddly curious about what his wife and kids looked like. Then I glanced at the wall behind Faraday and saw three rows of mug shots of dangerous-looking felons. All of them had the word CAPTURED in bright red stamped across the top of their mug shots. I couldn't help noticing that a few were already dead.

Belatedly, I realized that Wallace and Faraday were both staring silently at me as if they were waiting for a full confession. I shifted in my seat and looked at Donny, who seemed impatient to get things going.

"Do you guys have questions for us, or should we come back on a day without all this excitement?" Donny said.

Both Faraday and Wallace didn't seem to like his attitude. Wallace glared, and Faraday asked, "You in a hurry, counselor?"

"Yeah, Agent Faraday. I am," Donny replied, pulling at his shirt cuffs and tugging at his tie. He was playing up the hotshot lawyer.

Faraday rolled his eyes a little but turned his attention back to me. "You claimed when we spoke to you a few days ago that you never met Tevon Tibbolt. Is that right, Madelyn?"

I looked at Donny, and he nodded.

"I never met him," I said. I thought I should make it perfectly clear to Faraday, so I added, "I've never met Tevon or talked to him or texted him or e-mailed him. I've never met him in any way at all."

Faraday looked confused. "See, this is what I don't get: if you never met, or talked or texted or e-mailed Tevon, then how exactly could you know that he'd been murdered when we didn't even know that until yesterday?"

I glanced at Donny, a little exasperated. If this was the way it was going to go, then we were going to be here a really long time. Donny put a hand on my arm and said, "My niece and my sister-in-law have both told you that Maddie has a special and unique talent. She has psychic abilities that allow her to accurately predict the deathdate of any individual. She didn't know that Tevon would be murdered, only that he would die, and this information she attempted to share with his mother when she came to see my niece for a professional reading."

Wallace squinted at Donny. I could tell he didn't believe him any more than he had me. "Yeah," he said, drawing out the word. "She's psychic."

I opened my mouth but looked at Donny first. He was glaring at Wallace, so I took a chance and said, "I told you before, I'm not psychic. I see dates. That's all. I don't have visions, and I can't predict the future, and I don't see dead people. All I see is a date, and that's what I tell people. I tell them the day they're going to die."

Wallace shook his head a little. He clearly didn't buy it. "Really?" he asked. "What day am I going to die?"

He said it so flippantly that I opened my mouth to tell him if only to shock him, but Donny put his hand on my arm and gave it a firm squeeze. "We're not playing that game, Agent Wallace," he said.

"Is this a game?" Faraday asked.

"Only to you guys," Donny replied. I totally agreed. Clearly, these two were playing their own game of mean cop/meaner cop.

Faraday snorted and looked back at the file. "I'm curious about the alibi Madelyn has given us for the day Tevon went missing."

"She was with her best friend, Arnold Schroder, studying for a chemistry test," Donny said, his hand still on my arm. "Both she and her best friend have told you that already."

"About Arnold," Faraday said, turning a page in his file. "What's the deal, Madelyn? Are you two an item?"

I didn't know what he was getting at so I looked at Donny, and after a moment he nodded at me to answer. "No," I said. "We're just friends."

"Best friends," Faraday corrected. "Right?"

My palms were sweating. I was so afraid of giving them an answer that might make them suspect me more that I didn't want to confirm or deny anything. But Donny was nodding at me again, so I said, "Yes. We're best friends."

"Would Arnold lie for you if you asked him to?" Faraday asked next.

I knew exactly what he was getting at, and Donny did, too. "He's not lying about her alibi, Agent Faraday. Move on."

"What'd you get on the chemistry test?" Faraday asked almost too casually.

I breathed a tiny bit easier. "A ninety-eight," I said. They could check that if they wanted, and I had no doubt they would.

Donny sat back with a smug grin. He liked my answer, too. "Hardly the score of a young lady who's gone and murdered a thirteen year-old the day before," he said, his tone as mocking as Wallace's had been.

"Did you text or call anyone during that time?" Wallace asked me. He was still fishing.

"No, sir. I was too busy studying for my chem test."

Wallace and Faraday exchanged another look. I saw that they knew they weren't going to poke any more holes in my alibi, which was good. For a minute I had hopes that they'd lay off, but then Wallace leaned over toward the file on Faraday's desk and pulled something out from the back. He slapped it down in front of me. I stared at it, and it took my brain a few seconds to catch up to what my eyes were seeing, and by the time I understood that I was staring at a picture of Tevon Tibbolt, lying dead and bloody in pile of leaves and mud, it was too late to shut my eyes against it. Donny reacted by leaping to his feet and snatching the photo off the desk. I could feel my eyes water, the shock of what I'd seen had caught me totally off guard. *"What the hell?"* Donny roared, throwing the photo back at Agent Wallace.

I bit my lip and dropped my gaze to the ground. I'd heard the news reporter say that Tevon had many wounds and that he'd been tortured. But *seeing* it in the photograph was so, so much worse than anything I could've imagined. The kid's face, torso, and arms were a mass of cuts, burns, and open wounds, and his throat had been slashed wide open. It was the most gruesome thing I'd ever seen, and it was playing over and over in my head, blocking out everything else, even the room I was in and the men who were in it.

I tried to hold it back, but a wave of emotion overcame me, and I bent at the waist and let out a gut-wrenching sob. Tears fell down my cheeks and I shut my eyes, fighting to forget what I'd seen. But the image kept on playing in my head. Tevon's lifeless eyes staring fixedly up, his mouth curled down in a death mask of pain, his fists balled up over his head, and his hair matted with blood. And most of all, I couldn't forget the dark black numbers hovering above his ghostly pale skin. 10-29-2014.

I got to my feet and swayed, feeling my stomach lurch while Donny yelled. Then I bolted out of the office, running along the corridor, trying to keep down the urge to retch before I could find a restroom. I spotted a ladies' room on my right and I pushed my way inside, barely making it into the stall before losing my breakfast.

I hacked and heaved and clutched the bowl for several minutes, sobbing the whole time. "I didn't know!" I whispered over and over. "I didn't know!"

If I had known that *that* was going to happen to Tevon, I never, *ever* would've let his mother leave my house without convincing her that I was for real.

Finally, I sat back and grabbed some toilet paper, wiping my mouth and cheeks. It was that cheap, scratchy kind, but it was a relief to feel something other than nausea and regret.

Suddenly, there was a knock on the stall door and I jerked, knocking my water bottle on its side, where it rolled out under the stall door. I sat still for a couple of seconds. I hadn't heard anyone come in. I then saw a shadow on the floor, and peeking out from under the stall door, I spotted a hand grabbing the water bottle. I managed to get up and open the door. There was a lady (8-14-2058) standing there, wearing a gold badge clipped to her waistband. "You okay?" she asked me.

I took a shuddering breath. "Yeah."

She stared back doubtfully.

I moved to the sink, washed my hands, and splashed cool water onto my face. The whole time I was there, she watched me with a mixture of suspicion and sympathy. Still, something about her presence there felt off.

I wiped my face and hands with a paper towel and then turned back to her. She handed me a fresh bottle of water. "I brought you a new one," she said. But there was something about the exchange that again felt off. "No thanks," I muttered, hurrying out of the restroom. She followed me, and as I got back into the corridor, I saw Donny standing with his arms crossed and a furious look on his face. Next to him were Faraday and Wallace; only Faraday looked like he had an ounce of compassion for me.

Donny put his arm across my shoulders. "You all right?" he asked. I managed to nod, and he turned to the agents. "We're done here."

I was never more grateful in my life, and I leaned against him as we walked away. He didn't let me go until we were next to his car, and he opened the door for me and shut it once I'd gotten seated.

"They pulled that stunt to gauge your reaction," Donny said when he got in. He seemed to be beating himself up pretty good over it. "I'm sorry, Maddie. I should've expected they'd do something like that.'

"It's okay," I told him, wiping my cheeks because the tears wouldn't stop.

Donny glanced out his window toward the building. "Those bastards," he muttered. "If they ever try anything like that again I'll file a complaint with the bureau director."

I didn't say anything. I simply wanted Donny to start the

car and take me home. But he sat there a few more minutes, staring hard at the building. "Hey," he said at last.

"Yeah?"

"Great job on that chem test."

That got me to smile. "Thanks," I said. If Donny was joking with me, then the interview with the feds couldn't have been as bad as it felt.

He laid a hand on my head. "Do me a favor, though, okay?"

"What?"

"No more readings." I gulped and dropped my gaze to my hands. "I mean it, Maddie. Even if the president of the United States calls and says it's a matter of national security, you don't give *anybody* their date."

All I could think was, what was Ma was going to say? Donny was asking us to give up a lot of extra cash, and no matter how many times he'd offered, Ma had never once accepted money from Donny. I didn't know how we were going to make it without the readings.

When I hesitated, Donny added, "Listen, kiddo, if you happen to read someone new who's about to die, and the feds get wind of it . . . Sweetheart, I don't even want to think about how bad that's gonna make you look. You *can't* do any more readings or tell anybody their date. Not a soul. Do you hear?"

I finally nodded reluctantly. "Okay."

"Good girl."

And then I couldn't help adding, "The president doesn't need to worry though. His deathdate isn't for, like, forty more years."

Donny ruffled my hair. "Smartass." He chuckled. But

then he nudged me in the shoulder, and when I looked up, he pointed to the cup holder between us. "Where's your water bottle?"

I blinked. "The FBI lady who came into the restroom took it."

Donny let his head fall forward to the steering wheel. "Well, I guess giving them your fingerprints and a DNA sample was inevitable."

"Wait . . . what?"

"They found cigarette butts at the crime scene. They'll test your saliva from the bottle against the cigarette butts and keep searching the scene for anything that might give them a usable print to compare to yours." Donny shook his head as if he was ticked off at himself. "I didn't think to tell you to bring the bottle with you, but it's not a bad thing. When the DNA comes back as not a match, I can use it in court if they decide charge you."

Donny started the car, and I felt a cold shiver snake up my spine. His words, *if they decide to charge you,* replayed over and over in my mind.

Before we reached home I checked my phone. There were a dozen texts from Stubby. He'd heard about Tevon and he seemed really freaked out. I didn't want to call him from the car, so I waited until we got home when Donny was busy answering all of Ma's questions and telling her that I wasn't allowed to do readings anymore.

Slipping away upstairs I called Stubs. "Ohmigod!" he said the minute he answered the phone. "He's been murdered, Mads! *Murdered!*"

"I know," I told him.

"Oh, man, oh, man, oh, man!" Stubs said, and I could imagine him pacing back and forth, running a nervous hand through his hair. "It's all our fault, Maddie. We should've done something."

I dropped my head and felt my shoulders slump. Stubs had said aloud exactly what I'd felt since hearing they'd discovered Tevon's body. "It gets worse," I whispered.

I heard Stubby's sharp intake of breath, then, "What? What else?"

I filled him in on all that'd happened that morning. Stubby reacted by freaking out a whole lot more. "But you had nothing to do with it!" he practically shouted. "Mads, you have to tell them! You were trying to *help* Mrs. Tibbolt keep Tevon alive!"

"I don't think they believe me, Stubs."

Stubby was silent for a long time. "I should've talked to her at the diner," he said. "Or you and I should've gone over to her house that night. We should've tried harder to get her to listen."

"I know," I agreed, sick with regret about not having done more to prevent Tevon's death. "I didn't know it would end like this. I didn't know he'd be tortured and murdered. I thought he'd die from some freak medical thing that nobody could've detected."

Again Stubby was silent for a long time. Then he said, "I'm sorry, Mads. I didn't mean it when I said it was our fault. You tried to warn Mrs. Tibbolt, but she wouldn't listen. None of this is your fault. I should've been the one to vouch for you."

I sighed. "It's not your fault, either, Stubs. If you'd gotten on the phone, or gone over there, she might've called the cops on both of us."

"Or she might've listened," Stubby countered, his voice heavy with regret. We were both quiet for a minute and then Stubs said, "What'd Donny say?"

I curled my knees up onto the chair and hugged them tight. "He says they don't have a case, but..."

"But what?"

"I can tell he's worried," I whispered, more afraid of sensing that from Donny than anything else that'd happened to me that day. "He doesn't even want me to do readings anymore. He told me flat out that I'm not allowed to tell *anybody* their deathdate until this thing blows over. If it blows over."

I heard Stubby sigh. "Well, if he says there's no case, then I'd believe him. And don't worry, they'll find out who really did this. And then those agents will owe you a big apology."

I squeezed the phone and closed my eyes. It was so typical of Stubby to think positively. I thought it must be in his DNA or something, because he always found the good in everybody and in every situation. But he hadn't seen the photograph of Tevon's body. He hadn't seen the hard, accusing eyes of Agent Wallace.

I could feel myself starting to get really upset again, so I tried to end the call. "Yeah, okay. Listen, I think Donny's calling me. I gotta go."

Stubby seemed to know I was rushing him off the phone. "You gonna be okay?"

"Sure."

"Meet you at the diner tomorrow night?"

"Yeah. Listen, I really gotta go."

"Okay," he said. "Text me later."

I nodded, but my throat had filled with emotion and I couldn't get any more words out. After I hung up, I cried in my room for the rest of the day.

# 11-04-2014

BY THE FOLLOWING TUESDAY AFTERNOON I KNEW IT
wasn't my imagination. It started with Mrs. LeBaron (11-
18-2060), my homeroom teacher. She kept glancing in my
direction during the twenty minutes before classes started.
And it wasn't a nice look. It said, *I know what you did, and I
think you're terrible.*

I tried to shrug it off. Tevon's murder was all over the
news and it was all anybody could talk about at school, but I
didn't think anyone knew that I'd been called in by the FBI.
Well, except for Stubs, and he'd never tell anyone.

But then my chemistry teacher, Mr. Pierce (3-12-2029),
called me over as class was letting out and he said, "Hang in
there, Maddie. In this country you're innocent until *proven*
guilty." And I understood then that all the teachers knew.

Worse yet, Mr. Pierce seemed to be the only teacher who
was on my side. In French class Mrs. Johanson (2-2-2031)
snapped at me for using the wrong preposition while Mike

Dougherty (5-6-2067) had done the very same thing right before and she hadn't even blinked. Stubs leaned forward from behind me and whispered, "Why're they all acting so weird around you?"

I didn't answer him, because out in the hallway I heard Harris call to a student caught out of class after the bell. It suddenly dawned on me that maybe nobody knew I'd been called into the FBI offices over the weekend, but they could know about the meeting in Principal Harris's office. The faculty's reaction was too intense for them to have just learned that I'd met with the agents. They seemed to know the details of the conversation in Harris's office, which meant it could only have come from Harris himself.

I didn't know if he was allowed to tell the other teachers about what was said, but it was pretty obvious that he had, and it really upset me. I started to wonder who else he'd told. The news reporters covering the story were saying what a monster Tevon's murderer was, and after seeing the photo of his dead body, I knew that firsthand. It was bad enough to think that Agents Wallace and Faraday thought me capable of doing something like that to a young kid, but it was a whole different kind of nightmare to think that all my teachers believed I was capable of that, too.

As if to have my worst fears confirmed, a little later as I was leaving Precalc, Mr. Chavez said, "Did you really kill that kid, Fynn?"

He'd spoken so low I almost hadn't heard him, but when I glanced up he was looking at me the way Wallace had, like he simply knew I was guilty. Immediately, I dropped my gaze and bolted out of there. Stubs had to run to catch up.

"Hey!" he called, following me to a barely used stairwell. "Mads! What's going on?"

"It's nothing," I said, trying to hide my face from him. I didn't want to make a bigger deal out of it than it already was, and I was terrified everyone else at school was going to find out.

Stubby frowned and caught my arm to stop me from walking away. "Will you talk to me, please? Seriously, what's up?"

I took a deep breath. "I'm pretty sure Mr. Harris told the other teachers about the meeting with the feds in his office."

"Whoa," he whispered. "Can he *do* that?"

I shrugged. "I don't know, but it doesn't matter now because obviously the word's out, and pretty soon, the whole school will know and everybody's gonna think I'm a murderer."

Stubs eyed me with a bit of humor. He always knew when I was being melodramatic, but this time I wasn't playing. I was actually crazy scared. "Hey," he said. "Don't think like that, okay? None of the kids know yet, right? And maybe the teachers will keep it on the down low until the feds actually catch the guy who did this."

A sudden and terrible thought occurred to me. "But what if they don't, Stubs? What if they never catch the killer and this hangs over me forever?"

Stubby turned me forward to walk with him and nudged me with his shoulder. "You can't let yourself go there. You have to believe that the feds just need a little time to do their thing and figure it out, and then everybody's gonna look totally stupid for thinking it could've been you."

The warning bell rang, and Stubby quickened his steps, hooking his arm through mine. "Come on," he said. "Try not to think about it, okay?"

I let him pull me along to our next class, but for the rest of the day I avoided looking at anything besides the textbook in front of me.

After school I hurried to meet Stubs out by the bike rack. I found him standing next to my bike with a wad of paper towels again. There were even more eggs this time. "I hate those two," I spat as he and I worked to get the gunk off. From nearby we could see Eric and Mario laughing and poking each other.

To add insult to injury, at that moment Cathy and a group of her friends walked by. *"Ewwww,"* they said collectively as we sopped up the mess. I felt my cheeks sear with heat.

"Ignore 'em," Stubby advised.

I knew he was right, but I couldn't help looking up to glare at them as they passed. And it was then that I noticed Principal Harris standing near the door watching Stubs and me. He then looked over at Mario and Eric, who were still laughing it up, and then Harris simply turned and headed back inside.

I felt something bitter twist inside of me.

"There!" said Stubs, pulling my attention back. "Good as new." He'd gotten the last of the egg off and was grinning brightly at me.

"Thanks," I told him. I really wanted to get the hell out of there.

"Hey," Stubs said as I straddled the bike and we set off for home. "You ready for the game on Friday?"

I sighed. It'd been such a bad day that it was hard to focus on something good. "What time are we meeting up?" I asked, still a bit distracted.

"I figure if we get there before seven we can grab a good seat. Unless you want to go to the cheer-off at three?"

I cocked my head at him. "The what?"

Stubs grinned. "The Jupiter cheerleaders challenged our squad to a cheer-off. That's at three."

I couldn't help but laugh. Stubby was so adorably devoted to our cheerleading squad—one of the best in the state—that it cracked me up. I think his unique fascination started when Stubs was younger and he used to sit with his dad on Sunday afternoons and watch football. His dad, who was from Texas, always rooted for the Cowboys, and when the Dallas team wasn't performing well, which was often, his dad would focus on the league's best cheerleaders. Stubs, who was super klutzy, never really got into football, but he had become enamored with all those pretty girls shakin' their moneymakers and doing their flips, twists, and turns. Cheer combined two things Stubs idolized: pretty people and great coordination. He loved it. "I hear Jupiter's got a great squad this year," I said, just to taunt him.

"Yeah, I heard that, too, which is why I want to go. You in?"

I sighed. Ma had been having a really tough time lately with all the stress from the investigation and the worry over money now that I couldn't do readings. "Nah," I finally said. "I should hang out with Ma after school. Why don't you go to the cheer-off and then come pick me up around six thirty?"

When he didn't answer, I looked back and saw that he'd fallen behind and was glancing over his shoulder. "Stubs?"

I got his attention, and he pushed hard on his skateboard to catch up to me again. "I don't want to freak you out or anything, but there's a car following us."

I glanced back so fast that I felt the bike wobble underneath me. Sure enough, a black sedan was cruising slowly down the street. It was too far away to see who was driving, but I had a pretty good idea. "Let's cut through the park," I said. We hurried our pace to the park, where the car couldn't follow us. I felt pretty good about ditching my least-favorite FBI agents until I parted ways with Stubby and came around the corner to my street, only to find that same black sedan sitting at the curb a little bit down from my house.

I was tempted to flip them off, but stopped myself because I didn't know if there was some weird law against giving a fed the finger. Along with not doing any more readings, Donny had also warned me to keep my nose clean.

So over the next couple of days I ignored every teacher who gave me a suspicious look. I also ignored the black sedan that would show up unexpectedly in front of our house or two houses down the street and sit there for hours.

On the night of the game, Ma made dinner, which was huge for her. She surprised me with spaghetti alla carbonara, which had been Dad's favorite.

"I know this has been hard on you," she said as we sat down together. "But I want you to know that I'm very proud of you."

I blinked. Ma's unexpected display of tenderness had caught me off guard. "Thanks," I told her.

She nodded and played with her utensils. She seemed suddenly nervous about something. "You know, though, if you wanted to go back to doing a few readings here or there, I wouldn't mind."

My breath caught. I felt anger rise like heat from my chest to my cheeks. I knew it was Ma's addiction talking, but why did she have to ruin such a sweet moment by being so transparent? "Donny said I couldn't," I reminded her, unable to keep the bitterness out of my tone.

Ma was still playing with her utensils. "I know. But what Donny doesn't know…"

I stared at the plate of pasta, and my appetite vanished.

Ma must've noticed that I was upset because she quickly added, "It's just that the settlement check doesn't quite cover our needs, Maddie. You know we're always short at the end of the month."

I held back the retort that was on the tip of my tongue. I was the one who always made sure the checks got written and sent out the payments, because otherwise Ma would forget and we'd have the lights turned off. I knew as well as she did what came in and what went out, and the thing that always brought us up short was the liquor tab.

I cleared my throat and stared at my plate. "I don't think it's a good idea."

She nodded reluctantly. "Okay, then maybe I'll look for something," she said, but I could tell she was mad. Ma's employment history was spotty at best. And because she'd lost her license, whatever she applied for had to be within walking distance or a short bus ride, which I knew greatly limited what she'd be able to get.

We ate the rest of the meal in relative silence, and I couldn't wait to bolt out the back door and head to the game.

I'd told Stubs to meet me on the block behind my house so we'd avoid the black sedan that might be out front. After cutting through the yard of the people behind us, I came out onto Mt. Clair Street, where I saw Stubby in his mom's minivan a little ways down the block. "Hey!" he said when I got in. "I didn't know which house backed up to yours."

"You did fine," I told him, and we made our way through my neighborhood, careful to keep well away from my street. The route took us a bit out of our way, but worth it if we could avoid the feds.

On the way, Stubby became excited and said, "Ohmigod, Mads! Wait until you see the new girl on Jupiter's squad!"

I laughed. "I take it she's cute?"

"No," he said with a sly grin. "She's *beeeeautiful!*"

I laughed again. Stubby seemed to have a new crush on a different cheerleader every year.

After arriving at school, Stubs parked near a streetlight and we hoofed it over to the gate where we had to show our school IDs to get in. We didn't even bother with the Poplar High bleachers, but aimed our steps toward the visiting team's side.

On our way we passed the concession stand, where there was already a line. I saw kids I'd grown up with: Kristy Junger (1-14-2100), Brady McDonald (3-17-2024), Molly Thompson (10-9-2082), and Tim Goodacre (9-21-2071). I'd ridden the bus to elementary school with Kristy and Brady. I'd been in the same catechism class with Tim, and I'd gone to aftercare with Molly. And yet, when Stubs and I walked by, there was barely a flicker of recognition. I was used to being ignored by my classmates, but with the whole Tevon Tibbolt thing hanging over my head I felt a little more vulnerable and sensitive to it, which made me even more grateful for my friendship with Stubby.

The bleachers on the visiting-team side were fairly full—Jupiter High is our closest rival, and their school always comes out to support the team—but Stubs found us great seats three rows up at the right corner.

I sat down and immediately began to scan the visiting team's bench, which was a mass of light blue and bright white except for three navy rugby shirts. I found who I was looking for right away.

"He's here," Stubby whispered, grinning and nudging his chin toward one of the rugby shirts.

I smiled back, and relished the rapid uptick of my heart while I took in the dark curls and broad shoulders I'd recognize anywhere. Aiden was as beautiful as I remembered. Maybe more so because since the previous spring, when I'd last seen him, he'd grown taller and his shoulders were now even broader.

From freshman year on he'd been the football team's manager, keeping stats for the coaches and rooting hard for Jupiter. I usually only got to see him two or three times a year, when our two football teams played against each other and then during the spring when he played soccer for Jupiter. Our soccer teams always played against each other twice—once during the regular season and once during the playoffs—so I'd see him at those matchups, but it was harder to get near him then because he was always on the field.

As I stared at the back of Aiden's head, that knot that I'd been carrying in my chest since Tevon had been abducted began to loosen. I wanted nothing more than to feel the texture of Aiden's soft curls.

And then, as if sensing that someone was watching him, I saw that head begin to turn. I shifted my gaze away quickly, pretending to focus on the game. But then I snuck another glance and was shocked to see Aiden staring back at me.

For a moment I couldn't breathe or look away. And then he smiled, and my heart stopped. I think it skipped at least three beats before it started pounding again.

Stubby nudged me with his elbow. "He's looking at you!" he whispered.

I felt the corners of my mouth quirk, and my brain felt fuzzy. Could this really be happening? Could this boy who I'd secretly adored for the past two years actually, *really* be smiling at *me*? And then I realized he was. And then, even more miraculously, I was able to smile back at him. In that instant everything else went silent, and it felt like the whole world had paused to allow us a moment of perfection. It was the best I'd ever felt in my whole life.

*Hi,* he mouthed.

My breath came quick and I went light-headed while my hands began to tingle. His smile widened, and somehow I managed to nod and smile back at him, silently thanking God for this small bit of perfect happiness.

In the next second the spell was broken when the crowd erupted in a roar. I jumped as all around me people leaped to their feet and began to cheer and clap. I lost sight of Aiden, and by the time the crowd settled down again, I saw that he was back to scribbling on his clipboard and focusing on the game.

But I'd had that moment—that one, sweet, amazing, perfect moment. I shut my eyes to replay it again in my mind.

"Mads!" Stubby whispered excitedly.

Reluctantly, I opened my eyes. Stubby was pointing to the cheerleading squad now moving down the sidelines. "See her?" he said, nudging me while pointing to an exotically pretty girl with silky black hair, a perky nose, and full lips. Pretty much every high school boy's wet dream.

She was also *way* out of Stubby's league, but as his best friend, I wasn't about to tell him that. "Her name's Payton," Stubs said, and I swear he added a sigh. "Payton Wyly. She's a junior, and she moved here from Colorado three months ago."

I couldn't help but laugh. He was so smitten. "How do you know her name and her history already?"

Stubby blushed. "At the cheer challenge today I pretended I was on Poplar's school newspaper and asked the Jupiter assistant coach about her."

"I'm impressed," I said. Leave it to Stubby to think up something clever to find out about the new girl on the team.

"God, she's *soooo* pretty." He sighed. Next to us one of the Jupiter kids looked at Stubby like he was weird, and Stubby blushed. Clearing his throat, he added, "I mean, go Jupiter!"

I laughed into my hand, and Stubs squared his shoulders, trying to regain his composure, but I saw him continue to sneak glances Payton's way.

Still giggling, I was about to tease him a little when a couple of parents wedged their way to the bleacher just below us and sat down. The man took his seat right in front of me, obscuring the perfect view I'd had of Jupiter's team bench.

"Great," I muttered, leaning to the right and left, trying to see around him, but he was too big.

I started to look for another place to sit, and motioned to Stubby that we had to move. He frowned because he still had a good view of Payton, but then he pointed to a small area in the very front that was dead center to the cheerleaders and even closer to Aiden.

I nodded, and we got up and snaked our way over. While we were moving, I hoped that Aiden wouldn't look up and see me making my way closer to him—I didn't want to be *that* girl.

Still, I felt brave with Stubby next to me. At last we were settled again and we both smiled to each other. Mission accomplished. I felt a warmth bubble up in my middle, and I couldn't seem to stop smiling. "We gotta be cool," Stubby said, clearly fighting a grin of his own.

Nearby the cheerleaders were all chatting and gossiping happily to one another, and much of the attention was centered on Payton. There was a timeout from the Poplar Hollow side, and the teams gathered around their coaches, allowing us to hear some of what the cheer squad was saying.

"You're *so* lucky," said one girl to Payton. "I can't believe you're getting a freaking *car* for your birthday!"

"It's only because the 'rents are feeling guilty about moving me out here right before my junior year," Payton replied, like getting a car for her birthday wasn't a huge deal. "I mean, I love it here and all, but *they* don't have to know that, right?" All the girls laughed.

"When are you getting it?" another girl asked.

"Next Wednesday, on my birthday!" Payton said, so pleased with herself and the attention that I couldn't understand how it didn't turn Stubby off. "I get the keys right after school, and about two seconds after that I'll be picking you bitches up to do some major damage to my dad's credit card!"

The girls all shrieked and giggled, and I couldn't help but feel that if my dad were alive, no way would I say something that stupid and shallow. But when Stubby turned to grin at me, I shoved a smile onto my lips and nodded like I was happy and excited for Payton, too.

A whistle blew then, and the teams broke their huddle and started to head back toward the center of the field. I snuck a peek at Aiden and saw that he was looking and grinning at me again. I felt my cheeks heat, and shyly glanced away, secretly thrilled. Pretending to take an interest in the crowd, I froze when my gaze landed on someone familiar. All those warm, gushy feelings I'd had a moment before vanished, and my blood ran cold. Staring hard at me was none other than Agent Wallace, who was sitting midway up in the stands. Right next to him was Agent Faraday, who was busy looking at the field.

Immediately, I snapped my head to face forward again and slapped a hand on Stubby's arm. "What?" he asked.

But I was too unnerved to speak. I couldn't believe the

two agents had managed to follow us to the game and even stalked us to the visiting team's bleachers. I didn't know what to do.

"Hey, look, they're starting!" Stubs said, his attention already back on Payton.

Sure enough, Jupiter's squad was spreading out in the small section between the stands and the field, and they began to clap their hands and stomp their feet. Meanwhile, my mind was racing, and I felt like I had to get out of there, but wouldn't the feds simply follow me? Wouldn't rushing out of the stands call attention to me? And what if Aiden was watching? Would he see the panicked look on my face? I couldn't risk glancing over at him.

Next to me I heard Stubby's breath catch, and I realized that Payton was still sidestepping to the right, coming nearer and nearer to where we sat. She stopped in front of us. And then the most horrible thing happened. She was maybe four and a half feet away from me—near enough to see the color of her eyes and read the date on her forehead.

For a moment I was so stunned I couldn't even breathe, and then our eyes met and the expression on her face became confused.

But I couldn't look away from her; that date on her forehead lifted off her olive skin and hovered in the air as if to taunt me. "Oh God!" I gasped, and jumped to my feet, bolting to the stairs leading down to the side of the field. I didn't stop until I was out in the parking lot, but from there I didn't quite know where to go. I felt panicked and shaken, and like my whole world was being pulled apart by a black hole of little numbers.

Stubs caught up with me, wheezing and coughing as he pulled out his inhaler. "What's . . . wrong?"

Stubby has bad asthma, and I knew that his attacks were sometimes brought on by stress, but this was too big and I was too freaked out to keep it to myself. "It's Payton," I said, pacing anxiously back and forth in front of him.

"What about her?" Stubby asked, his breathing settling down a little.

I stopped and looked anxiously toward the stands. "Maddie? Come on, tell me."

My gaze shifted back to Stubby. "I saw her deathdate."

He squinted at me. *"Annnnnnd?"*

"It's next week."

Stubby's mouth fell open. "No!"

I could only stand there and hold his gaze. I wasn't wrong. "Eleven-twelve, twenty fourteen," I said.

"You got it wrong," Stubby replied, but then he seemed to reconsider the date. "Wait, Maddie, that's . . . that's next Wednesday—her birthday. Maybe you saw her *birthday* and not her *deathday.*"

I pressed my lips together. I never see birthdays. I only see death.

Stubby turned and eyed the visiting team's side of the field. "We have to warn her," he said, and I could tell he was about to run back and do just that.

I caught his arm and squeezed it hard. "You can't!"

Stubby tried to shake me off, but I wasn't letting go. "Maddie, we *have* to!"

Still, I was determined. "Stubs, please listen to me for a minute, will you?!" Finally he stopped fighting and stared at me expectantly. I pointed toward the bleachers with my free hand. "Faraday and Wallace followed us here. They're up in the stands right now."

Stubby paled even more. "How did they find you?"

I began to pace again. "I don't know. Maybe they saw me leave the house out the back door, or maybe they had a hunch, but they're here. If we go back and tell Payton that she's going to die next week, don't you think that'll look really, *really* bad to them?"

"Then you stay here and I'll go!" Stubby said, turning away from me.

I clamped down on his arm once more and wouldn't let go. Getting right up into his face I said, "Stubs, stop! You have to think! I mean, Faraday and Wallace *know* you. They've even *talked* to you! They also know that we're best friends and we hang out together. If you go back there and say something to Payton and she ends up dying next Wednesday, they'll know it came from me! Remember what Donny said? He said under *no* circumstances can I tell any-body their date!"

Stubby stood back and simply stared at me as if he couldn't believe what was coming out of my mouth. "We're really gonna let her *die*? Mads . . . come *on*! She's getting that new car next week! What if she goes cruising with her friends, and she gets distracted and loses control of the car, and then some of them die, too?"

I hadn't been close enough to the other girls to see their deathdates. There could be more than one casualty next Wednesday. I balled my hands into fists, so frustrated because I didn't know what to do.

"We have to warn her," Stubby repeated more gently this time as he laid a hand on my shoulder. "I mean, we didn't try hard enough with Tevon, and look what happened to him."

I winced as if he'd struck me. "Ouch."

Stubby immediately lifted both hands in surrender. "Sorry, sorry, sorry."

I sighed. "No. You're right. We can't sit back and do nothing. We'll warn her, but not here and not now."

Stubs frowned. He didn't like my answer. "Then when and how?"

"We have a couple of days. I'm pretty sure we can figure out how to get an anonymous message to her."

"She'll think it's a joke," he countered, looking again to the field.

"And what do you think she'll decide if you go marching up to her right now and say, 'Gee, not to upset you or anything, but you're going to die on your birthday. Just thought you should know!'"

Behind us the roar of the crowd erupted again, but this time it was from the Poplar Hollow side.

Stubby stood there looking at the field for a long time, and I could tell he was wavering about what to do. "I promise you," I told him, "we'll figure out a way to warn her, Stubs. On my life I promise you, but please, not here and not now, okay? Let's think of another place and time when there aren't so many people around and in a way that doesn't lead back to us."

Stubby stared hard at me and sighed, then he looked down and kicked at the ground. "She can't die, Maddie. We have to save her."

I didn't immediately reply because I had no idea what to say. If mere words could prevent someone from dying, then my dad would still be alive and so would Tevon Tibbolt. Still, after a long stretch of silence, what I said was, "I know, buddy, I know. But you have to trust me on this. We can't say anything to her tonight."

"Whatever," he grumbled, turning away from me. "Let's get outta here."

I tried not to feel the sting of that cold shoulder, but it was hard. It got harder still when Stubby dropped me off in front of my house and without another word sped away. I knew he wasn't angry with me per se, but it felt like he was, and I wished very much that I'd waited to tell him until after the game. I didn't know how we were going to warn Payton without it coming back to me. I vowed to call Stubs in the morning and talk about it, but when I walked inside I found Ma on the floor, passed out cold. I cried out as I dropped to her side, momentarily panicked by finding her on the floor facedown. Grabbing her wrist, I felt for a pulse, and glimpsed an empty liter of vodka lying under the coffee table.

I closed my eyes in relief as I felt her pulse, which was slow but steady. When I strained, I could hear her breathing rhythmically, too.

With a tired sigh I got to work cleaning up, and then moved Ma to the couch. It took me a while because she was completely limp, but at last I got her situated and covered with the afghan. And then I stood in the doorway of the kitchen looking at her lying there on our beat-up old leather couch in a room that smelled like cigarettes, with dingy blue

walls, and taupe carpeting littered with stains. I shut my eyes
to block out the sight and thought about Aiden and how he'd
smiled at me and mouthed the word *Hi*.

In an instant what'd filled me with such sunny happiness
clouded over with a threatening storm. I opened my eyes
and looked again at Ma and our house, and I knew that no
boy would ever want to get close to a girl like me. A girl
who lived in a house with threadbare carpeting and dingy
walls that smelled like an ashtray. A girl who saw death in
every face. Who was labeled a witch at school. Who had a
drunk for a mother, and a father who'd died in a gunfight
with drug dealers. A girl who was being investigated for
murder by the FBI.

I was like a whirlpool of tragedy, and anybody who dared
to get too close to me could get sucked in and drown. Like
I was drowning right now.

And I knew that it would never be better. Our house
would continue to slowly fall down around us. I would
always see death. People at school would always think I was
a witch. Ma would always be drunk. Tevon Tibbolt would
always be dead, and so would my dad.

For years Aiden had been like the sun to me, shin-
ing brightly from the Jupiter sidelines. Tonight, for a brief
moment, his star had nearly banished all of the misery right
out of my world. But I finally realized that I should probably
let go of living in the fantasy that a boy as beautiful as him
could meet a girl like me and feel anything other than pity.
I needed to accept that this was my reality, and nothing was
ever going to change it.

With a heavy heart, I climbed the stairs to bed.

# 11-08-2014

THAT WEEKEND WAS TERRIBLE. STUBBY REMAINED distant and didn't call or even send a text all day Saturday. Not that I really noticed, because my hands were full with Ma. She had a really bad day looking online, trying to find a job, when there didn't seem to be anything good available.

Then I caught her on the phone with Donny, asking him if I could just do a few readings a month, and he'd blown a gasket. I could hear him yell at her all the way across the room. After a few minutes, she slammed the phone down and headed straight for her stash. "Ma!" I snapped, once I saw her filling the big plastic cup. I couldn't take it anymore. "If you're going to get a job, don't you think you should try and cut back a little?"

She glared hard at me, and before I knew it we were yelling at each other. Getting angry had never gotten Ma off the bottle, but I couldn't help it. I yelled and yelled at her, and then I threw my hands up and headed upstairs. When I came back down a few hours later I realized she'd left.

I checked the pantry, and sure enough, all the vodka was gone, which implied she'd taken off to replenish the stock. But by seven o'clock she still wasn't back, and I had a bad feeling.

I went to the front window and peered out. I hadn't seen that familiar black sedan all day—it seemed that my least-favorite agents took Saturdays off. Next, I checked the garage, and thankfully Dad's vintage T-Bird was still inside. Neither one of us was allowed to drive it because we couldn't afford the insurance after Ma got her second DUI and lost her license, but Ma refused to sell it even though we really needed the money. She and Dad had had their first date in that car, and I think she was convinced that someday she'd get her license back and come up with the money for the insurance and be back to driving it again. Still, I knew that sometimes, when she was really missing Dad, and she was sick of taking the bus everywhere, she would sneak out and take it for a spin. It scared me because Ma was never sober. She woke up and the first thing she did was pour vodka into her morning coffee. All those agents had to do was call the cops, and Ma would go to jail and CPS would be back at our door.

Donny called my cell as I was pedaling up and down the dark streets looking for her. "I can't find Ma," I confessed as soon as I answered the call.

I heard him sigh on the other end of the line. I knew he was pretty tired of conversations like these, and I'd gotten better about not calling him in recent years. "How long has she been gone?"

I blinked hard. It wasn't just the cold misting up my vision. "I'm not exactly sure, but I think she left sometime after one."

"Did she take the car?"

"No. It's still in the garage."

"Where're you?"

I braked and came to a stop. I was near the park about a mile from my house. "I'm out looking for her."

There was a pause, then Donny said, "It's not even eight o'clock, Maddie. She's probably at some bar, and she'll find her way home just like she always does. Go back to the house and get warm."

I looked up and down the street, my eyes searching for Ma in vain. I knew most of the bars she liked to go to, all within a bus stop or two of the house, but I'd been by them and she wasn't there.

"Maddie?" Donny said. "You there?"

"She doesn't have her coat, Donny." I could feel myself getting emotional, and had to swallow hard simply to talk. I felt guilty about our argument, and I was so tired of this. I wanted Ma to see how tired I was. How worried. How afraid. I wanted her to choose to look out for me for a change. I wanted her to stop pulling stunts like this, because I knew that *she* knew they were really hardest on me.

Donny sighed again. "Maddie," he said gently. "I'm more worried about you riding around in the dark than I am about your mom. Go home, sweetheart. I'm all the way over in

Jersey tonight, but I'll drive up in the morning and we'll have a talk, okay?"

I nodded, even though he couldn't see me. I was too choked up to reply.

"I'll be there around ten and we'll grab breakfast," Donny was saying. In the background I heard a woman's voice. "Listen, I gotta go. As long as Cheryl's not behind the wheel, she'll be okay. She always is. Go home, take a bath, and get warm. I can hear your teeth chattering."

And then he was gone. I tucked my phone into my pocket and again looked up and down the street, and that's when I noticed something weird. Far down the street I could hear the faint rumble of an engine, but all the cars parked along the curb had their headlights off. The light from the lone streetlight at my end didn't let me see into any of the cars, so it was impossible to tell if someone was inside one of them, but I had the prickly feeling that I was being watched by someone other than Wallace and Faraday.

When I got to the next intersection, I paused at the stop sign and heard that slight rumble behind me again. A quick backward glance revealed a large pickup truck moving toward me with its lights off. As I stared, the truck pulled over to the curb and sat there idling again, as if the driver didn't want to pass me before seeing which direction I was going to take.

I felt the hairs on the back of my neck stand up on end. Pushing off, I turned right and rode hard up the hilly street. Behind me, I heard the engine rev, and I knew the pickup had pulled away from the curb and was coming after me.

I pumped hard up the hill, and at the intersection I turned the bike around in a tight loop and raced to the right to hop the curb onto the sidewalk. Crouching low, I pedaled for all I was worth and darted past the truck, gaining momentum on the downward slope. I caught only a blur of movement within the cab of the truck as I whizzed by.

Pumping hard again at the bottom of the hill, I rode my bike back across the street, racing through the metal archway that marked the park's entrance.

Looking over my shoulder, I saw the pickup finishing its awkward turn at the top of the hill, and that's when its headlights finally came on.

I knew without a doubt that I was in trouble now, because the truck roared down the hill heading straight for me. I faced forward again and pedaled as fast as I could, at last moving past the concrete barriers that kept vehicles out and marked the beginning of the trail. The ride immediately got bumpy, forcing me to focus in the dim light of my headlamp on the terrain. But I didn't slow down.

Because I had to focus on the dirt path, I couldn't lift my gaze away to look for the truck, so I kept my ears pricked for the roar of its engine, and I could still hear its loud rumble keeping pace with me in the distance. I was certain the driver was tracking my escape—intent on cutting me off at the opposite end of the park.

My mind whirred: what should I do? There was nobody in the park to help me, and if I stopped pedaling to dial the police on my cell, the driver could also stop, race across the lawn, and nab me before I was even done with the call.

Then I had a sudden insight. As I started to pass a large

clump of evergreen trees, I reached down to click off my headlamp. I lost sight of the path and braked slowly until I came to a stop, huddling next to the largest tree in the cluster. Listening hard, I heard the slight squeak of brakes and then the low rumble of the truck in idle. I gathered my courage and stepped off my bike, running it in a straight line directly in front of the trees, keeping them between me and the pickup as I headed through the grass toward the street I'd been on when Donny had called.

It was then that I heard the rumble of the engine pick up and the truck moved on at a rapid pace again. I wanted nothing more than to jump on the bike and pedal for the street, but I couldn't see the ground clearly. If I hit a log or a rock, I'd be toast. I settled for trotting the bike quickly across the open field, stumbling a few times as my feet met with uneven terrain.

At last I came out onto the street and quickly mounted the bike again. At the top of the street, I moved right over to the first house I came to and huddled in the shadows next to a garage. At the entrance to the park the truck appeared again, moving along slowly while the driver hunted for any glimpse of me in the park. After it passed, I stepped out of the shadows and raced in the opposite direction, which was also the way home. Once I was safely up the drive, I didn't even put the bike away; I simply leaned it against the garage and bolted for the back door. I'd left it open because I didn't know if Ma would be able to get her key into the lock if she came home, but once I was through the door I slammed it shut and threw the dead bolt, then I leaned against it and tried to catch my breath.

Finally, I pushed away from the door and was about to head to the front window, when I tripped over something on the kitchen floor. I heard a muffled grunt. Scrambling backward in the dark, my heart racing, I flicked on the lights and saw Ma sprawled out on the floor, her clothes bunched up around her. She mumbled something incoherent, then she settled into a soft snore.

I stared at her for a long moment, waiting to catch my breath. When I wasn't so panicked, I turned off the lights again and made my way to the front window to peek through the curtains. The street was empty—no sign of the truck anywhere—and no black sedans parked on the street, either.

Next, I went into the bathroom and peeked out the small window on the side of our house. There was no one lurking outside, but I could see Mrs. Duncan in her kitchen doing the dishes. Seeing her helped calm me down, and at last I moved back toward the kitchen.

My eyes were adjusted to the darkness by then and I could see Ma's sleeping form on the linoleum floor. I felt a sudden and unexpected surge of anger. I was so sick of all this that I wanted to scream. But I didn't. Instead I dutifully got her to wake up enough to get her to the couch, and I put her to bed. "Luff you, baby," she slurred after I tucked the afghan around her.

"Then why won't you stop drinking?" I whispered. She didn't answer, so I turned to the stairs.

In my room I tried to decide what I should do about the truck. I thought about calling Donny and telling him about it, but he'd only get upset and tell me to call the police. I knew I couldn't do that because they'd come to the house, take one look at Ma, and then we'd have CPS to deal with, and didn't I already have enough trouble on my hands? I shuddered at the memory of being so scared in the park, and not knowing who was after me. Downstairs, Dad's clock began to chime and I sighed, wishing he were here and could chase the bogeyman away.

By the time I crawled into bed, I'd decided to tell Donny about it in the morning when Ma was sober. Maybe he could even be there when the police came to take my statement. That way they'd know there was a responsible adult in the house, and I could report the incident without worry. It seemed like the only way to go without bringing myself a whole lot of extra trouble.

The next morning I met Donny at the curb. I wanted to avoid having him go into the house, but he was onto me. He got out as I was trying to get into his car, and eyed me across the roof. "Where's your mom?"

"She's inside. Asleep."

Donny's lips pressed together, and he marched up the drive. I trailed behind him, wishing I didn't have such a screwed-up life.

I stood in the kitchen by the back door while he had a look at Ma. "Cheryl," I heard him say. I imagined him standing over her, that look of disgust on his face that he didn't even try to hide anymore. I heard Ma mutter something, and I figured she was trying to roll away from Donny.

"Cheryl," Donny repeated, more sternly this time. "We

need to talk." Ma didn't reply, which was typical. "This is getting untenable, Cheryl. Scott would never want Maddie to grow up like this."

I heard Ma then, loud and clear. "Go to hell, Donny."

I bit my lip. I wanted Donny to come out of there. I wanted him to take me to breakfast and to tell me a story about my dad when they were kids. A story that maybe I hadn't heard before. I didn't want him to come back around the corner looking so disgusted and mean that he looked less like my dad and more like a total stranger.

Donny tried to talk to Ma a few more times, but she wasn't taking the bait, and at last he came into the kitchen again.

"Come on," he growled angrily, moving past me and out the door. I hustled after him.

Donny drove in silence to a local breakfast joint in downtown Jupiter. The place was crowded, but Donny flashed his smile at one of the waitresses and she got us a booth. After we took our seats he started in. "I want you to think seriously about coming to live with me."

I stared hard at the menu.

"It's not safe living with her like that," he continued.

With a pang of alarm, I knew right then that I could never tell him anything about what had happened the night before with the truck in the park. "She always has a harder time in the fall," I said defensively.

He didn't say anything, so I finally picked my chin up out of the menu. He was looking at me with a mixture of sadness and determination and something else that looked a lot like guilt. "If your dad were alive today, he'd never let you live like this."

"If Dad were alive today she wouldn't *be* like this."

Donny winced, but I wasn't sorry I'd said it.

And then he seemed to soften. "Kid," he said, reaching out to put a hand over mine, "I only mean that I want you to remember that, when you're ready, my place is your place. Okay?"

I gave him a crooked smile. "That's the last thing you need. What'll all your girlfriends think?"

Donny grinned. "They'll think what a good uncle I am to take care of my brother's kid, and then they'll want to marry me even more."

I rolled my eyes. Donny had a new girlfriend every month, and he was always complaining that they all wanted him to settle down. Donny wasn't the settling down type—even I knew that, and I was only sixteen.

After breakfast Donny dropped me off back at home, and I went in to face the music. Ma was up and filling the living room with smoke. "Why does my face hurt?" she asked, rubbing the side of her cheek where it had been resting on the linoleum when I found her.

"Don't know. Where'd you go last night?"

Ma scowled, scratching her matted hair. "Can't remember. So what'd Donny want to talk to you about?"

I sat down in Dad's old leather chair. Ma didn't like me to sit in it, but I was still pretty mad at her and feeling defiant. She cocked an eyebrow but didn't say anything. "He just wanted to take me to breakfast."

Ma reached out to flick the ashes of her cigarette into the ashtray. "He ask you to move to the city with him?"

I was surprised by the bluntness of her question and the

fact that she knew Donny had asked me that. I decided if Ma wanted to be honest, so could I. "Yeah."

She took a drag on her cigarette. "You'd hate the city. It used to give you panic attacks, you know."

I didn't say anything.

"It's loud and noisy, and you'd have to leave all your friends," Ma continued, like I had a whole horde of people to hang out with.

I also noticed she didn't mention that I'd have to leave her, too.

"And it's dangerous," Ma added, waving her cigarette at me. "We've got no crime here, Maddie. You can leave your doors unlocked and nobody bothers you."

I folded my arms and looked away. "Unless you're a kid named Tevon Tibbolt," I said, thinking again about the truck that had chased me into the park.

It was Ma's turn to be silent, and when I finally turned to her again, I was shocked to see her crying. But these weren't drunk tears. These were real. All of the sudden I felt ashamed. "If you go," she whispered, "I'll never get to see you again."

I shook my head at her. She was talking crazy.

"No," Ma insisted. "It's true. Donny's never forgiven me for Scott's death. He thinks I should've told your dad that day to—" Ma seemed to catch herself, and then her tears took over and she covered her face with her hands. I got out of my chair and moved over to the couch to hug her. I felt the guilt coming off her in waves, they crashed into my own and swirled around us in a riptide that tugged and pulled and threatened to tear out my heart.

Finally, Ma's tears subsided, and I let go of her to grab a tissue. She mopped at her cheeks and smiled hopefully at me. "I know I need to cut back," she said. "And I promise, Maddie. I promise I will." She then reached out and took up my hand. "But I need you here. I can't make it without you. Promise me you'll stay?"

I looked down at our joined hands, and my mind flashed back to a time when I was five and she'd walked me to the bus stop on my first day of school. I'd cried the whole three blocks, and the minute the bus pulled up I'd pressed myself against Ma's legs and I'd sobbed and sobbed. I hadn't stopped until she'd bent down to hug me and I realized the bus had pulled away. "It's okay, baby," she'd said to me. "We'll try again tomorrow."

But the next day was the same. I was terrified to leave her side, and my own petrifying shyness left me feeling like I couldn't possibly board that bus and go off to some faraway place to sit among strangers.

So we tried again on Wednesday, then on Thursday, and finally on Friday, Ma held my hand just like all the days before, but as the bus rolled to a stop she'd squeezed my hand and looked down at me with a bright, hopeful smile. "There's the bus to take you to school, Maddie. You'll have all sorts of adventures, and drink milk and have cookies, and draw pictures, and learn new things. But if you're not brave enough to get on that bus today, then I'll understand and we'll go home and try again next week. But if you *can* do it today, then I'll be prouder of you than you could know." I'd then watched the other kids load onto the bus, and after much hopping from foot to foot, I'd had a moment of rare courage and I'd let go. I remembered so clearly the cold feeling of my palm without Ma's hand to warm it, and still I'd climbed those big steps onto the bus. Avoiding the driver's watchful gaze, I'd moved to the first empty seat I could find and shuffled to the window to see Ma standing there with hands clasped over her heart and tears streaming down her face. She was beaming with pride, so happy I could feel it all the way through the walls of the bus, and I knew I was worthy and brave.

And now Ma was squeezing my hand, asking me to be patient, and I realized that I'd have to hold on until she was brave enough, too.

True to her word, Ma did make an effort. She got up from the couch, took a shower, dried her hair with the blow dryer, and she even put on makeup. She smiled at me as she came downstairs, and I was struck by how beautiful she still was. The premature lines from years of smoking were still there—and there was a slight puffiness to her face from the drinking—but when Ma made an effort, she was stunning.

"You look great," I told her.

"Yeah?" she said, blushing slightly.

My smile widened. "Yeah. You really do, Ma." My gaze drifted to Dad's picture on the mantel. They had been a beautiful couple.

Ma sighed and pressed her hands together like she was making a wish. "I'm heading to the Drug Mart on Pavilion. I saw an ad online that they're looking for part-time help. Wish me luck?"

I swallowed hard, moved that she was trying. "Good luck, Ma."

After she left I called Stubs, but it went right to voice mail. "Hey," I said in my message. "It's me. Call me about Payton, okay?"

I'd been racking my brain trying to come up with a solution that would honor my promise to Donny and still warn Payton in time for her to make another choice. But so far I had no good ideas, and I was also troubled by the possible fact that—no matter what we did—it might not make a difference. I kept returning to the same troubling question: Were the dates fixed? Or could they be changed?

I finally decided that simply because I didn't know the answer didn't mean that Stubs and I still couldn't try to change destiny. And after what had happened to Tevon, I knew we had to try something that would get Payton's attention.

While in my room studying, I was staring up at the bulletin board above my desk—where I'd pinned favorite photos and cards and mementos—and I suddenly had an idea about how to warn Payton. I tried calling Stubs again, but he didn't pick up, so I texted him.

With a sigh I got up and went to the window, noticing with a frown that the familiar black sedan was back at the curb.

Then I saw Ma coming back home, her steps unsteady and clumsy. I knew immediately that she'd found someplace to stop for a few drinks. All that hope that'd risen to the surface earlier when she'd come downstairs looking so good had evaporated. My eyes traveled back to the sedan. Those agents must be having a pretty good laugh at seeing my mom stumble home. It filled me with anger, and I clenched my fists, ready to go out there and yell at them, but stopped myself. Yelling at them wouldn't make things better, and it might actually make things worse.

A minute or two later Ma came into the house. "I got the job!" she announced.

But I was mad enough not to care. "You've been drinking."

Ma shrugged, still happy about her news. "I thought getting a job was worth celebrating," she sang. Then she moved past me toward the stairs like coming home stumbling drunk wasn't a big deal. "I'm going up for a bath. There's leftover spaghetti in the fridge if you're hungry."

Her words were slurred and slow, and my anger deepened. I was about to say something really mean, when I heard my phone ping. Lifting it out of my pocket I saw that Stubs had sent me a text. *Can't make the diner tonight. TTYL.*

After not hearing from him all weekend, his text felt like a snub. He'd never been ticked off at me this long before. I sat down in Dad's chair and stared at my phone, trying to think of the words that would make it better between us, but nothing came to me, so I left it alone and hoped I'd find the right words in the morning.

# 11-10-2014

I FOUND STUBBY AT HIS LOCKER ON MONDAY MORN-
ing with a fresh set of bruises to his right cheek and his hand
in a cast. "Dude!" I said when I saw him. "What happened?"

"It looks worse than it is," he told me.

I took hold of his casted hand. "Yeah, this doesn't look
bad at all. It's only a flesh wound, right?"

Stubby humored me with a grin. "It's a hairline fracture.
I only have to wear the cast for a couple of weeks."

"The half-pipe?" I asked.

Stubby shuffled his books into the crook of his arm and
used his elbow to shut his locker. "I was trying a new trick."

I took his books and helped load them into his backpack.
"Yeah? Well, try harder next time."

He shrugged. "It was worth it. Sorry I didn't make it to
the diner, but I was at the ER until late."

I immediately felt guilty about thinking he'd snubbed

me the night before. We started down the hall together. "I wish I'd known. I would've picked up a slice of pie and brought it to you."

Stubs grinned, and I knew we were okay again. "Next time I'll send you the deets." And then he changed the subject. "Did you come up with a way to warn Payton?"

I sighed. My idea wasn't great, but it was all I could think of given Donny's warning and how Faraday and Wallace were watching nearly my every move. "It's super tricky. The feds have pretty much camped out in front of my house, and they're watching me like a hawk."

"Do you think they're tapping your phones?" Stubs asked.

My eyes widened. I hadn't thought of that. "Don't know. But if they are, they might also try and tap into my e-mail and texts. We can't talk about any of this on the phone." I was suddenly very grateful that Stubs hadn't tried to call or text me about it over the weekend.

"What if I sent her an e-mail or an anonymous text?" Stubby asked. I started to shake my head, but he held up his hand and said, "Wait, before you say no, there're a ton of apps that let you send someone an anonymous e-mail or text, and the sender's info disappears in, like, a minute. They're untraceable."

I sighed. "That could work, but how do we get Payton's e-mail address or her cell number?"

Stubby's face fell. "That, I haven't figured out yet."

And then I offered up my idea—the one that'd formed after looking at the last birthday card I'd received from my Dad, which I had tacked to my bulletin board at home. "I think we should send her a card for her birthday."

"A birthday card?"

I nodded vigorously. "Yeah, Stubs, she'd totally open a birthday card, even if it didn't have a return address, just to see if there was a check inside or to find out who it was from. I'll bet if you dig around on the Web, you could come up with her parents' home address, right?"

"Her last name is Wyly, and she lives in Jupiter. Yeah, I could find it. What would we say in the card?" Looking at him I knew he was intrigued by the idea.

"I don't know, but we'd have to be careful about it. We'd have to say something like, 'We heard you're getting a new car for your birthday, and you need to be really careful driving it.' Maybe we could throw in something like, 'Don't text and drive!' and back it up with a statistic or something."

Stubby eyed me like I was nuts. "She's not going to believe something like that, Mads. Plus, we don't know for sure if that's the way she's going to die."

"Well, then, what would you suggest?" I was a little exasperated. I had no idea how to warn Payton, because, like Stubby pointed out, I had no idea how she was going to die. If I knew that, then I could set something in motion to prevent it, but all I had was the date. That's it. Only a date to indicate that she was a dead girl walking.

"Maybe we could call her parents' house like we called Mrs. Tibbolt?"

I shook my head. "If the feds are tapping my phone, they might also be tapping yours, Stubs. We called her from your phone, remember?"

Stubby frowned, but then he brightened. "Okay, then we'll make the call from a public phone, ask for Payton, and disguise our voices. We could say we know something she doesn't. We know she's in danger, and we're worried that she might die on her birthday."

It was my turn to look at Stubs like he had to be kidding. "If you got a phone call from a total stranger telling you that you were about to die, wouldn't your next call be to the police to report a death threat from a lunatic? She'd dismiss the warning, which wouldn't help her, and report the call, which wouldn't help us. What if a surveillance camera catches us using the phone? Those cameras are everywhere. We can't risk it."

Stubby's gaze dropped. "Well, we have to try something that she'll believe, Mads."

"I agree," I told him, and I meant it. "But you also need to accept that even if we get her attention and she believes us, it might not prevent her death. It could still happen."

Stubby frowned. "But even if there's a chance we can save her, we have to try," he said. I could tell that he was still feeling guilty over not trying harder to save Tevon.

I put a hand on his good arm. "You're right, and we'll warn her with the card. We'll be really careful not to leave our fingerprints on it, and we'll choose the wording so that we don't come off sounding crazy. Hopefully she'll listen and be careful next Wednesday, but that's the most we can do. Anything else is too dangerous for us and could even push her to do something risky simply to prove us wrong."

Stubs sighed and nodded reluctantly. "Yeah, okay," he said. "We'll go with the card."

After school we headed for the Drug Mart, and I almost

came up short when I saw Ma in a blue smock standing next to another employee who was showing her how to organize the developed-photos envelopes. "Hi, you two!" She waved when she spotted us.

"Whoa, Mrs. Fynn!" Stubs said, almost as shocked as I was to see her behind the counter. "When did you start working here?"

"Today is my first day," Ma said proudly.

I smiled encouragingly at her but couldn't help drop my gaze to her hands. If there were tremors, I knew she'd be totally sober. If they were calm, I knew she'd be sneaking sips in the back.

I bit my lip when I saw that there wasn't a hint of a tremor. I could only hope that nobody at the store caught on.

Ma waved us away, saying that she had to focus on her training. We headed to the card rack and picked out one together. Making sure not to handle it with our bare hands, we paid for it and headed across town to the Starbucks next to the Jupiter post office to carefully craft a message.

Stubby wrote the message out using his casted hand, which was a good thing because it altered his handwriting enough to make it nearly illegible. We decided to send Payton a message from a secret admirer (that part was true at least), and told her that we were someone who sometimes had strange visions that came true. We wrote that she needed to be very careful when she drove, especially on her birthday. And in general we told her to be careful on her birthday because the alignment of the stars suggested that it was an unlucky day for her.

As Stubby read it back to me I had to admit that it did sound a little crazy, but it was the best plan we had. "If you got this card, what would you think?" Stubs asked me.

I frowned. "I'd probably think that some wacko had sent it, but I'd probably also listen to the message—just in case."

Stubby then shoved the card into the envelope using his sleeve to cover his hands. Then he used his phone to look up her address. It took a few clicks to get the Wylys' new address in Jupiter, but we were confident our card would find its way to her. Stubs then stood to head next door to mail it and said, "You coming?"

But I was only halfway through my caramel latte, and it was so nice and warm in the Starbucks. "I think I'll stay here and study for a while."

Stubs nodded, looking troubled. I knew he was wishing we had a better plan. With a wave he said, "I'll text ya later," and then he was gone.

I sighed, fighting the feeling that I'd let him down, and poked at my drink with the plastic stirrer, when all of a sudden I heard a voice I'd recognize anywhere, and I felt a jolt of adrenaline stiffen my spine. Slouching down in my seat, I leaned out slightly and saw Aiden standing at the counter joking with two buddies while they waited for the barista to take their orders.

Immediately, I looked around for an escape route, but the only exit was the entrance at the front of the Starbucks. I knew I didn't look my best: I hadn't made a big effort that morning. My hair was pulled back, I wasn't wearing any makeup besides a little mascara, and my hoodie was drab and dark. But I was trapped at the back of the store;

all Aiden had to do was turn his head to the right and he'd see me.

Thinking quickly, I bent over and retrieved my backpack from the floor. I dug through it and pulled out the biggest textbook I had—chemistry—and opened it up on the table to partially conceal my face behind it. Listening intently, I heard Aiden's somewhat husky voice rise and fall as he discussed a chemistry test he'd had that day. He and the two other guys were comparing answers. I smiled when I realized that he and I were basically studying the exact same section of the periodic table.

Then I heard a much more feminine voice say, "Hey, Aiden!"

I stiffened. Gripping the sides of the book tightly, I snuck a peek. A girl with long blond hair stood to the side of the three boys. Twirling a few strands between her fingers she said, "Can I add a caramel macchiato to your order?"

There were a lot of customers waiting behind the guys, and it was obvious the girl was cutting the line. The way she was staring at Aiden made me wonder if they were more than friends.

Aiden looked back at the line, offering an apologetic look to the person behind them before replying, "Sure, Kendra. What size?"

"A tall. I'm watching my weight," she said, reaching out to touch his arm and swish her hips.

I stopped breathing. My insides felt gripped by a vise. The girl was pretty. Very pretty. Her hair was hanging loose in long blond waves, she wore lots of makeup, and her clothes looked soft, stylish, and oh-so-touchable.

I stared at Aiden intently. He added her drink to their order, and then he paid for everything—including hers. I didn't quite know what to make of that. Was he just being generous?

Kendra kept on flirting with Aiden while they waited, and he smiled and nodded as she talked. It was impossible to tell if he was into her or only being polite.

But then, I couldn't think of a reason why a guy *wouldn't* be into someone as pretty as her.

The barista called Aiden's name, and he and one of his buddies gathered the drinks. Aiden handed Kendra's tall macchiato over to her, and in exchange she handed him a cardboard drink sleeve. I was confused—Aiden already had a sleeve attached to his cup—then I noticed a hint of black scrawl on the one she wielded, and realized she'd given him her phone number.

After touching his arm one last time, she was gone. I wanted to die. I felt so queasy and dizzy that I wanted a hole to open up in the middle of the floor and swallow me. But shortly after Kendra left, Aiden tossed the sleeve aside and motioned to his buddies to go.

They were out the door a moment later. I sat up, counted to ten, and left my chair to hurry over to the counter to retrieve the sleeve before someone either used it or tossed it in the trash. Sure enough, Kendra's name and phone number were written in curly script across the middle.

I shut my eyes and held the small bit of cardboard to my chest, so relieved he'd tossed it and any interest in her aside. "Did you need something?" I heard, and my eyes flew open. The barista was leaning over the counter looking at me. She was close enough so that her deathdate read clearly: 3-30-2070. "No," I said quickly, feeling my mouth lift into a jubilant smile. "Thanks, though. I was just leaving."

The next couple of days passed in a bit of a blur. Stubby and I didn't talk again about warning Payton, but that didn't mean we were both happy about how we'd left it. I'd stayed up almost the whole night before trying to come up with a better idea than the birthday card, but nothing came from all that thinking. By Tuesday morning, I decided to let it alone and hope we'd done enough.

As of Wednesday, there were no updates in the Tevon Tibbolt case, and there was no story about a car accident involving Payton Wyly or about her sudden death. I called Stubs the minute the news was over. "I think we did it!" I said the second he answered. "Nothing on the news about Payton."

"I know! I saw it too, and I think you're right! We saved her!" But then he seemed to sober as he added, "We should go to the next Jupiter football game, you know, to make sure she's okay. I'll look online and see who they're playing, but it's probably going to be one of Grand Haven's teams, and since they played us last week, it'll be a home game for them. I'll ask Mom if I can have the van for the night."

"Awesome. I'm in," I said. I was tingly with relief. I couldn't believe we'd actually changed Payton's numbers—I wanted to go to the game to see it for myself. And of course there'd be the added bonus of seeing Aiden again.

Donny called me later on that night to let me know he hadn't heard anything more from the feds, which he thought might be good news, and sure enough, on Thursday when I rode up into my driveway, the familiar black sedan wasn't behind me, and it wasn't parked on the street, either.

Even Ma seemed to be doing better. She was given a few shifts at the Drug Mart, and she'd gotten through thcm okay, but I was still a little worried about her drinking on the job. I knew she was sneaking some liquor into her water bottle, and I was afraid her manager would find out.

Still, it was better than having her sit home and drink alone all day. Her job seemed to be giving her some confidence, and when I came in through the door on Thursday after hanging out at Stubby's for the afternoon, I found her in the kitchen cooking us dinner. "I'm making stir-fry!" she announced proudly.

"Awesome!" I said, feeling that bubble of hope rise in my chest. I had good news to share, too. "I got a hundred on my U.S. History exam."

Ma's face blossomed into a beautiful smile, and she reached out to wrap me in her arms and hug me fiercely. It was the safest I'd felt in a long, long time.

After letting go of me she said, "Let's eat in the living room."

We arranged two TV trays in front of the couch and, after loading up our plates, sat down together. Ma flipped on the TV for the news.

The weatherman came on and waved his hand at the area map to show us that a cold front was moving in over the weekend, bringing rain and hail with it. "We'll have to turn the heat on," Ma said, her eyes glued to screen.

I ate my dinner happily while we sat together. I thought

the stir-fry tasted even better than her spaghetti. I was so lost in thought about how good she was doing that I was hardly listening when the anchorwoman said, "Jupiter police are still puzzled over a missing teen who hasn't been seen since yesterday afternoon. Payton Wyly was last seen on Wednesday around three P.M. when her mother and father handed her the keys to a new car for her birthday." My head snapped up and I dropped my fork. It clanged loudly against the plate, and Ma startled.

"The young teen's car was found only an hour after her parents contacted police, about ten P.M. last evening, parked at the side of the road near Westcott and Terrace Lake," the anchorwoman continued. "The driver's side door was open, the engine was still running, and there was no sign of the missing girl. If you've seen Payton or have any information on her whereabouts, police are asking that you contact a special tip-line they've set up, and that number is . . ."

I was breathing so hard that I was losing oxygen, and the room was starting to spin. I heard Ma calling my name, but my eyes were riveted to the screen, where a picture of Payton Wyly smiled out at me. On her forehead was the same set of numbers I'd seen at the Jupiter game.

"Maddie!" Ma yelled, and I realized she was tugging on my arm. "What is it?"

I shook my head to clear it, and did my best to focus on Ma, but I was way too upset to hide it.

"Do you know that girl?" Ma asked, pointing to the TV. And then she turned back to me and her eyes went wide. "Do you know what's happened to her?" I knew she meant to say, *Do you know if she's dead?*

I shook my head again. Donny's warning came back to me, and I realized that Stubby and I had just involved ourselves in what might be another murder. If the FBI found that birthday card with its cryptic message...

"Maddie," Ma said again, cupping my chin with her hand and looking me in the eye. "Tell me. What's gotten you so upset about that girl?"

I had to move Ma's attention off Payton until I could talk to Stubby and figure out what to do. "It's not the girl," I told her. "It's...I forgot to bring home my algebra book, and I've got a big math assignment due tomorrow. Would it be cool if I went over to Stubby's to borrow his?"

Ma blinked and let go of my chin. I didn't think she believed me, but after a long pause, she didn't push for a confession. "Finish a little more of your dinner first," she said with a frown. "And remember tomorrow is garbage day, so put out the bin before you head over to Stubby's."

A few minutes later I was pedaling hard toward Stubby's house when I rounded the corner to his street and almost immediately had to slam on the brakes. There was a familiar black sedan parked in front of his home.

"Damn it!" I whispered. Had Wallace and Faraday found our birthday card at Payton's? Had they already traced it back to Stubby? We'd been careful to handle the card and the envelope using only our sleeves, but what if Stubby had somehow touched it and left a fingerprint?

I squinted down the street. Faraday and Wallace were still in the car. What they were waiting for I didn't know, but I didn't want them to look in the rearview mirror and see me, so I hustled up the driveway next to me and hid in the shadows. Taking a huge risk, I pulled out my cell and called Stubby.

"Hey," he said jovially. "I was about to text you. My mom said I can have the car for the game tomorrow night."

I sucked in a breath. He didn't know. "Stubs..." I said, but my voice cracked.

"Mads?" Stubby said, alarmed. "Are you okay? What happened?"

I swallowed hard. "It's Payton."

I heard Stubby suck in a breath. "Was she...was she in an accident?"

I closed my eyes. "No, buddy. It's way worse. She's missing."

Stubby sucked in another breath. "How do you know?"

"It was on the news tonight. They found her car late last night, but no sign of her." I hesitated, unsure how to break it to him, but he'd hear about it soon enough. "They showed a picture of her on the news. Her deathdate didn't change, Stubs. Payton died yesterday."

My best friend was silent for so long that I thought my phone had cut out, but then I heard him sniffle. "Oh, honey, I'm so, so sorry," I told him. I wanted nothing more than to go straight to his house to give him a hug. I needed one as much as I suspected he did.

"You're sure?" he asked after a moment, his voice thick with sorrow.

"Yeah. I'm sure." My gaze drifted back to the sedan parked in front of his home. "Listen," I said. "I have something else to tell you—"

"Where are you?" he asked suddenly. I thought he might've heard the wind blowing through the phone.

"I'm down the street from your house."

"Are you coming over?"

I didn't know what to say. The feds would see me, but then I realized that wasn't so abnormal. They already knew that Stubby and I were friends. I was about to tell him yes when the sedan's brake lights went off, and Faraday and Wallace started to get out.

"Stubby!" I hissed.

"What? What?"

"Listen to me! The feds are in front of your house! They're on their way to your door!"

"Oh, man!" Stubby cried, and I thought he might be on the verge of panic. "Maddie, what do we do?"

"I don't know!" I whispered. "Listen, they probably found the card. Maybe..."

At that moment I heard Stubby's doorbell ring through the phone. Wallace and Faraday were standing on the doorstep. In the background I heard Mrs. Schroder call to Stubby to see who was at the door, and I cringed. "I gotta go," he said meekly.

"I'll call my uncle!" I promised. "Don't say anything to them until they tell you why they're there!"

The line was silent and I called out to Stubs, but then I heard a beep and realized he'd already hung up.

Next, I dialed Donny, ready to confess to him what we'd done, but I got his voice mail. "Why don't you *ever* answer my call?!" I snapped when the voice mail kicked in. I took a deep breath and left him an urgent message to call me back. Then I waited in the dark, watching Stubby's house for a long time. At last the door opened and the agents came out.

I stared at my phone display anxiously, and as their car was pulling away, Stubby called me. "I think it'll be okay," he said.

"What happened?"

"They didn't ask about Payton. They just wanted me to go over your alibi again for the day Tevon disappeared. Was I sure we were together? What time did you leave my house? What'd I get on the chem test? That kind of stuff."

My brow furrowed. Why had they asked about all that again?

As I was contemplating that, Stubby added, "Oh, and they wanted to know why we were sitting in the Jupiter team's bleachers last Friday instead of with our school."

That was weird. "What'd you tell them?"

"I said our bleachers were too crowded, and we had a better view of the game from the visitor's side. But then they wanted to know why we left early, and I said because you had a stomachache."

I sighed with relief. "Maybe we're okay."

Stubby was quiet on the other end of the line, and belatedly I realized he was still upset about Payton. "Do you want me to come over?"

Stubby sniffled. "If it's okay with you, Mads, I think I want to be alone for a while."

That took me aback, and I couldn't help but feel hurt. I was upset over Payton, too. "Uh...sure. Okay, Stubs. Call me later, though, if you want to talk?"

"Okay," he said. And then he was gone.

Cold and feeling sad and alone, I began pedaling back home. My cell rang on the way and I answered my uncle's call. "What's happened?" Donny asked sharply, no doubt irritated with me for the voice mail.

For a moment, I didn't know what to tell him. If I came clean about sending Payton a birthday card, warning her of her imminent death, he'd be furious and he might even insist that I move to Brooklyn with him, if only to keep me out of trouble. Then again, if the feds never found the card—if Payton maybe threw it away or we'd been careful enough and they couldn't trace it back to us—we might be worrying over nothing. I decided not to risk angering Donny unnecessarily, and luckily, I now had a pretty good backup excuse for calling him. "The feds were just at Stubby's house," I said. Then I explained what they'd wanted. By the time I was done, I was home, walking my bike up the drive.

On the other end of the call, Donny was quiet for a long time, and that worried me. "Okay," he said at last. "Keep me posted if you hear anything else." With that, he was also gone. Sighing, I headed inside to get warm and tried not to let my thoughts linger too much on Payton Wyly. That proved impossible, though, especially when Stubs didn't text me once the rest of the night.

Friday sucked.

There was no other way to describe it. Stubby texted me that morning that his little sister was sick, and he had to stay home with her because his mom had a meeting she couldn't miss. Not having him next to me in the hallway made me feel small and vulnerable, and at lunch it was even worse. I sat by myself at a table in the cafeteria, eating quickly. The only bright spot was Mr. Pierce, who stopped me again on my way out of class. "You hanging in there, Maddie?" he asked kindly.

I didn't feel like talking, so I merely gave him a half-hearted nod.

"Good," he said with a warm smile. "And great job on the lab experiment today."

I thanked him and hurried to my next class. Still, it was nice to know that all my teachers weren't against me.

Later, when I came out from school to get my bike, I found it once again covered in eggs and shells, but this time Stubs wasn't around with his usual wad of paper towels and sunny disposition. It hit me how much of the sting he managed to take out of all those times I'd been bullied or made fun of.

After cleaning up my bike, I pedaled home. I'd checked the Web at lunch to see if they'd found Payton, or if there were any leads in the investigation, but nothing new was posted. I was anxious to follow the story, and by now I had a terrible suspicion that her abduction and death were somehow linked to Tevon's, which meant that I could indeed be sucked into her murder investigation, too. It would also indicate that there was a serial killer on the loose.

Payton was a sixteen-year-old girl, and Tevon was a thirteen-year-old boy. They weren't very similar as victims except for the fact that they were young. Still, something nagged at me, something dark and scary that again made all of those hairs on the back of my neck stand on end.

When I turned onto my block, I saw Donny's car parked at the curb. "Hey, Maddie," Donny said out the window as I stopped next to the driver's side. "Your mom's at work. Feel like grabbing a bite?"

I looked at the display on my phone. "It's only three," I said.

Donny grinned. "Feel like grabbing a snack, then?"

"What gives?"

"We should talk," he said cryptically.

I waited for him to say more, but he simply sat there looking at me until I gave in.

Donny drove us out of Poplar Hollow all the way to Parkwick. We entered a nice Italian eatery, which barely had any patrons because it was still so early. Sliding into a booth, Donny handed me one of the menus the hostess had given us and said, "Spill it."

At first I didn't know what he meant. "Spill what?"

"Your mom called me today and said that another kid in the area has gone missing. She said that when the girl's photo came up on the news broadcast last night you looked like you were about to faint. She also said that you refused to talk about it, but then you bolted over to Stubby's the first chance you got, so she's wondering if maybe you read for one of the girl's parents and we might have another issue with the FBI on our hands. So come clean, kiddo. What're you hiding?"

I set the menu down. Donny had me and he knew it. "Stubby and I went to the Poplar game against Jupiter last Friday night. We sat on Jupiter's side, and Stubby pointed out this new cheerleader on their squad, Payton Wyly, that he had a crush on. We were near enough to her so that I could read her deathdate."

He went a little pale. "Is she dead?"

I nodded. "Wednesday."

"Son of a bitch," he hissed, closing his own menu and shaking his head. "Please tell me you kept that to yourself."

I took a sip of water but had a hard time swallowing.

"Madelyn?" Donny said sternly. "Please *tell me* you didn't share that with anyone."

I took a deep breath and looked him in the eye. "I told Stubby."

Donny blinked. "And?"

"See, Stubs really did have a huge crush on this girl, so he was really upset—"

Donny buried his face in his hands. "Jesus," he mumbled. "What'd he do?"

I took another sip of water. My hands were shaking like Ma's. "It's what *we* did, Donny."

Donny parted his fingers and looked at me with one eye. "What did the two of you do, Maddie?"

"We sent her a birthday card."

The hands fell away and revealed his slack jaw. "You sent her a *birthday card*? Why the hell would you do *that*?"

"Payton's birthday was Wednesday, the same day as her deathdate. We wanted to warn her, but we didn't know how, and I'd promised you that I wasn't going to tell anybody their deathdate, but we couldn't just let her die without warning her, Donny!" My voice had risen, and my eyes misted. I was starting to get overcome by what'd happened.

Donny laid a hand on my arm and said, "Hey, sweet girl, take a breath. Tell me what happened and we'll figure it out, okay?"

I wiped my eyes and tried to calm myself, feeling embarrassed because we were in a public place and I was sure I'd called attention to us. When I felt calmer, I told him what we'd done. "We took the card to Starbucks, and Stubby wrote out a message. He broke his arm last Sunday, so it disguised his writing pretty good. Anyway, we pretended to be Payton's secret admirer, and we told her that we were someone who sometimes had visions of things before they happened. We said that we'd had a vision of her getting hurt in an accident, and we wanted her to be really careful when she drove her new car—we overheard Payton at the football game telling the other cheerleaders that she was getting a new car for her birthday."

Donny nodded, but his expression was grave. "Okay, so is that all you said in the card?"

"No. We also said that she needed to be careful on her birthday because the stars suggested it wasn't a safe day for her."

Donny closed his eyes as if that was the worst thing we could've written. Finally he said, "Okay . . . is that it?"

"Yeah, mostly. Stubby mailed the card, but we both were careful to handle it using our sleeves. I don't think either one of us ever touched it with our fingers."

"The card went out on what day?"

"Monday. We mailed it from the Jupiter post office so it'd get there by Tuesday."

"What return address did you use?"

"We didn't. We kept it blank."

Donny sighed and shook his head. "Kiddo . . ." he said, and I knew he thought it was bad.

"I'm sorry, Donny!" I told him. "We only wanted to try and save her. We didn't think it'd turn out like it did with Tevon."

Donny reached out again and squeezed my hand. "Well, kiddo," he said, "the feds haven't come around your house holding the card in an evidence bag, so I guess that's a good thing. They would've gone through everything in Payton's room by now, so if it was there and could be traced back to you, they'd have done that by now. Maybe she got it Tuesday, thought it was a joke, and threw it out."

I nodded. I sincerely hoped that's exactly what'd happened.

"So until this becomes an issue, you don't tell anyone about this card, *capisce?*"

"Okay."

"If the feds haul us in and ask us about it, though, you'll have to tell them the truth."

I looked down at the table, dreading that thought. "I know."

"Hopefully, it won't come to that. In the meantime, do me another favor," he said.

"What?"

"The next time you see the deathdate of anybody who's about to die, you call me first before you send them a card or a gift basket or anything else you can think of to get around my direct order."

It was clear that Donny was trying to make light in order

to cheer me up, so I attempted a smile and held up three fingers. "Yes, sir. Scout's honor."

But Donny looked taken aback.

"What?" I asked.

It was his turn to smile sadly. "Nothing," he said. "It's just that your dad used to do that. Three fingers and Scout's honor. It was funny because he got kicked out of the Scouts when he was twelve for being dishonest."

I laughed, surprised by the lightness between us again at the mention of my dad. "I never knew that."

Donny sighed and his gaze dropped to the table again. "I miss him, Maddie."

And just like that all the humor left me. That happened a lot with the memory of my dad. It could make me laugh and cry at the same time.

"Donny?" I asked after a bit, still worrying about the possibility of being accused of Payton's death.

"Yeah?"

"Do you think I'll be okay?"

It was Donny's turn to push a smile onto his face as he held up three fingers. "Sure, kiddo," he said. "Scout's honor."

I didn't have it in me to ask Donny if he'd been kicked out of the Scouts, too.

# 11-15-2014

PAYTON WYLY'S BODY WAS DISCOVERED EARLY THE next morning. I found out when Donny called me after breakfast and said he was headed our way again. The feds were asking us to come back in for another meet and greet, and I felt a terrible foreboding.

Ma had been at work at the Drug Mart until late the night before, and was still in bed by the time Donny arrived, so we left her to sleep and headed to downtown Grand Haven. The bureau offices were again buzzing with activity, and this time when we came through the doors we found Faraday waiting for us. He walked us back to a room with a two-way mirror on the wall, and an overhead fluorescent bulb that gave our skin a sickly hue.

Donny and I sat down and Faraday asked us if we wanted anything to drink. I'd brought my own bottled water this time, and Donny declined, but Faraday left us anyway, saying that he was going for some coffee.

We waited patiently for him, but after twenty minutes it was clear that he was leaving us to sweat. Donny got up to pace and he even went to the door, but he found it locked, and that seemed to infuriate him. After two hours the door opened, and in walked Faraday. He had a records storage box with him and he set it on the table in front of us. My heart was pounding. I knew that whatever was in that box was bad.

"Have a seat," he said to Donny and me.

Donny started in on him right away. "Is my niece under arrest?" he barked, pointing to the door. "Because we came down here, Faraday, on our own good faith, and you locked us up in here without charging her, which is illegal."

Faraday cocked his head, and he wore a mocking sort of smile that I knew only angered Donny more. "Was the door locked? Huh. Sorry about that. Sometimes the door sticks, like at your sister-in-law's house, and it can be a real pain to open."

Donny's fists clenched, and I could tell he wanted to storm right out of there, but Faraday calmly lifted the lid of the box and peered inside like he had a secret treasure he couldn't wait to show us.

Donny looked at me, raising an eyebrow. I shook my head slightly. I had no idea what was in the box. With a sigh, my uncle took his seat and crossed his arms. He'd put up with this little charade only as long as it took for Faraday to deal his hand, then I knew he'd demand to leave.

Faraday sat down, but kept the contents of the box hidden from us. "As you may have heard," he began, "we found Payton Wyly's body early this morning down by the Waliki

River about a half mile from where Tevon Tibbolt's remains were discovered." My mouth went dry. I knew that much, but it was still hard to hear. He then reached into the box and pulled out an evidence bag. Inside was what looked like a torn-up image of a kitten with its paw raised. It'd been taped back together a bit haphazardly, but I recognized it immediately as the card we'd sent to Payton. Donny scowled. My efforts to save Payton had just come back to haunt me.

"Know what this is?" Faraday asked me.

I didn't even have to look at Donny to see if I should answer. He'd already told me at the restaurant the day before. "Yes," I said. "It's a card that Stubs and I sent to Payton Wyly."

Faraday's brow shot up. He seemed surprised by my answer.

I knew I had to tell him why we'd sent it, so I began with the football game, pointing out that I'd seen both him and Wallace there, and while we were in the stands I'd seen Payton's deathdate. "It was coming so soon that I freaked out when I saw it," I explained. "I left the stands, and Stubby came after me, so I told him what I'd seen. He wanted to go back then and there and warn her, but with you guys in the bleachers and all the stuff that happened after I read for Mrs. Tibbolt, I didn't think that was such a good idea."

Donny leaned forward. "I had also told my niece that she was not to verbalize any deathdate she saw to anyone."

I nodded. "Right. But Stubs and I both felt really bad for Payton, and we decided that we had to try *something* to warn her, so we bought that card and wrote out a message to mail to her. I know the message sounds weird, but we didn't know what to say to get her to listen to us. We'd overheard her tell her friends that she was getting a new car for her birthday, and we kind of assumed she was going to be in a car accident. Neither one of us thought it would end like..."

My voice trailed off. It was still hard for me to fathom that Payton had been murdered.

Faraday was eyeing me with intense scrutiny. I couldn't tell if he believed me or not. "You didn't think it would end like what, Maddie? Like this?" And he reached inside his box and pulled out a photograph, slapping it down on the table in front of us.

I looked away. He'd used this tactic before, and I didn't want to go through it again. "Jesus!" Donny hissed. Out of the corner of my eye I saw him flip the photo over. "Really, Faraday? My niece is sixteen! Quit trying to shock a reaction out of her by showing her these crime scene photos!"

Faraday reached out and flipped the picture back over. I didn't look away fast enough, and I caught a glimpse of Payton's face, her eyes open, her cheeks swollen and bruised, a gash on her forehead, and a large open wound at her neck. My eyes watered, and I squeezed them shut. I heard Donny's chair scrape the floor. "Maddie," he said. "We're leaving."

"Oh, I'd advise against that," Faraday said. I peeked out at him, and he was leaning back in his chair as if he double-dog dared Donny to leave. "At least not until you hear me out, Fynn."

Donny picked up the photo and tossed it at the agent. "You have thirty seconds to tell us what you want, Faraday, and then I'm walking Maddie out of here, and if you even think about flashing another gruesome photo at her, I'll be on the phone with the DOJ demanding they investigate your tactics before I'm even out of this building."

Faraday picked up the photo from the floor where it'd fallen and put it back in the box, but he still seemed really angry, and I could understand, because what'd happened to Payton looked worse than any nightmare I could imagine. But I wasn't responsible. He *had* to know that.

Faraday inhaled deeply, and it seemed like he was trying to rein in his anger. He then looked me square in the eye and tapped the evidence bag with the card and said, "Here's the thing, Madelyn. We didn't find this in Payton Wyly's trash." My brow furrowed. "We found it in Arnold Schroder's trash can."

My jaw dropped. That made no sense! "See," Faraday continued, "Agent Wallace and I went over to reconfirm you alibi with Schroder, to check if maybe he wanted to change his story. Your buddy stuck to the facts, but he was so nervous and jumpy that we felt he was hiding something. So, later that night we swung by again and noticed that he'd set out the trash. You don't need a warrant to go through someone's trash, did you know that? We picked up yours, too, by the way. You guys need to recycle more."

I felt the blood drain from my face. Ma hid her empties in the trash because she didn't want our neighbors seeing how many liquor bottles were in the recycle bin.

"So Schroder never mailed the card," Donny said, the vein at his temple noticeably throbbing. I knew he was furious at the agent for that last comment. "Is that a crime now, Agent Faraday?"

Faraday seemed to ignore him and went back to fishing

around inside his box. I felt myself bracing for what might come next. He retrieved a sheet of paper and set it on the table. I was so tense and on edge that I immediately turned away. "Recognize him?" he asked.

I didn't look until I felt Donny's hand on my arm, and then I focused on the piece of paper now on the table. It was an artist's sketch of a man's face, and even though it was a pretty rough sketch, the first person I thought of when I looked at it was Stubby.

My pounding heart was like a wrecking ball in my chest. I knew that Faraday could tell I saw the similarity, but I smelled a trap, so I shook my head. "No," I said, but it came out in a whisper.

"Really?" Faraday said, all shock and awe. "You don't recognize your own best friend, Maddie?"

Donny was looking from me to Faraday. He smelled a trap, too. "You have her answer. What's your point?"

Faraday pulled out another document. It looked like a handwritten letter. Then he pulled out another and another and another. Donny lifted up the papers and began to read, but I was focused on Faraday, who in turn hadn't taken his eyes off me. "Those are witness statements," he said. "From Payton's fellow cheerleaders. They all give pretty much the same story. They say that last Monday afternoon right after cheerleading practice, Payton was approached by the boy in that sketch and he had a pretty amazing story to tell her. He claimed that he was psychic, that he had visions that often came true, and that he'd seen Payton at a football game and was overcome by a vision of her being killed on her birthday. He didn't give her his name, but he warned her not to drive her new car, which he said he'd also seen her getting for her birthday."

I felt my blood turn to ice. I knew instantly what Stubby had done. He'd taken the card after leaving me at Starbucks, and he'd had second thoughts about sending it, knowing it was likely Payton would think it was a joke. He'd probably decided then and there to ignore all my warnings and headed straight to Jupiter High only a few blocks away.

And after I'd told him that Payton had been murdered and the feds had come back to question him about my alibi, he'd panicked by tearing up the card and throwing it out in the trash to get rid of the evidence.

With a sudden horror I knew exactly where the feds were going with this. They thought Stubs had murdered Payton. And since her crime scene photo had resembled Tevon's, it wasn't a leap to think they'd try to pin his death on him, too.

While I was putting all of that together, Faraday reached into his box again and pulled out yet another statement. "Here's a witness statement from Payton's coach, who told us that a boy resembling this sketch approached her and claimed to be from the Poplar High newspaper. He was very interested in the new star on the team, Payton Wyly. This was before the football game, Maddie, when you supposedly saw Payton's deathdate. And we checked with your school's newspaper—Arnold doesn't contribute to it, and he never has."

"He didn't do it!" I blurted out, panic-stricken about where this was heading.

Donny's hand clamped down on my arm, but it was too late.

"Didn't do what?" Faraday asked, leaning forward. "Or maybe I should ask, *who* didn't do what?"

I looked at Donny, practically pleading with him to let me talk, to let me explain it to Faraday, but the warning in my uncle's eyes was clear. I wasn't to say another word until he gave the okay. "What does any of this have to do with my niece?" Donny demanded.

Faraday pulled out a picture of Stubby. It was his sophomore yearbook photo. The agent held it up next to the artist's sketch. "See a resemblance?" he asked.

Donny kept his eyes on Faraday. "Again, what does this have to do with Maddie?"

Faraday set the articles down. "It has everything to do with her, counselor. The boy in the sketch is her best friend—this Stubby character. We've got him here now, and he says it was all Madelyn's idea. He says that she came up with a plan to kidnap and kill Tevon Tibbolt, convinced him to do the dirty work, and they both enjoyed it so much that they went looking for another victim: Payton Wyly."

My mouth fell open and a noise came out from deep inside me, one that was unbidden and primal. Donny's hand squeezed my arm again, and I barely managed to stop and get hold of myself.

"Cut the crap, Faraday," Donny snapped. "Schroder said no such thing! If he had, you would've arrested Maddie by now, but you've got nothing but a torn-up birthday card, a crude sketch, and some witness statements that I will tear holes through in court. You have no proof that the guy in the sketch is Schroder, and no proof that he actually harmed Payton Wyly!"

Faraday seemed unfazed by Donny's outburst. He rubbed his chin before leaning forward even more, his large frame hanging over most of the table. "You know what else I find interesting?" His question was aimed directly at me. I found myself shaking my head, and I couldn't seem to stop myself. I didn't want to hear it, whatever it was, because it was all a lie. "Your best friend's statement is your only alibi for the day Tevon Tibbolt was kidnapped and murdered. We've been looking at the timetable, Madelyn. It seems Tevon may have been abducted later in the day on the twenty-ninth than we thought. We think he was taken anywhere between three and nine P.M. So, I gotta ask you: who's covering for whom?"

An involuntary squeak bubbled up from my throat, and Donny's hand clamped down on my wrist again. "We're going," he said, half lifting me out of my chair.

But Faraday wasn't done with us quite yet. Quick as a flash, he took out a folded piece of paper from inside his coat pocket and snapped it open right in front of Donny.

Donny paused when he saw the paper—it looked official. Snatching it out of Faraday's hand, he started to read it.

"We've served out a search warrant," Faraday said casually, and from the box came something else that froze me in place and turned my cold blood to ice. "This we found hidden in Maddie's nightstand," he said, holding up my death-date notebook and wiggling it back and forth. "It makes for really interesting reading, if you like names and dates. So many names and dates, Madelyn."

My breath started to come in short little pants, and the world began to spin.

"Here's a name and a date that's pretty interesting," Faraday said, thumbing to one of the last pages. "Tevon Tibbolt, ten twenty-nine, two thousand fourteen."

Donny's face drained of color, and he looked at me with a mixture of shock and horror. I'd never told him I kept the notebook. I'd never told anybody. Well, except Stubby.

Faraday flipped the page. "And here, in one of the last entries, we have the name Payton Wyly. Next to that is the date eleven twelve, twenty fourteen."

For a long moment nobody spoke. Faraday continued to thumb through my notebook while Donny clenched and unclenched his jaw. Finally, he said, "Is my niece under arrest?"

My knees threatened to give out from underneath me, but Donny held my arm firmly, supporting me. Faraday took his time answering, but finally he said, "Not yet, Fynn. But soon." Switching his focus back to me he added, "Don't leave town, Madelyn."

Donny moved me toward the door, but Faraday stuck his leg out, blocking us. "The warrant extends to her phone," he said, his voice hard as steel.

I looked at Donny, who eyed the search warrant in his hand and nodded for me to comply. With trembling fingers I removed my phone from my pocket and set it gently on the table. I tried to think what texts might be on the phone that could incriminate me, but my mind was a jumble of panicked thoughts, and I couldn't remember.

We exited the room, and Donny held on to me the whole way. "Look straight ahead," he whispered as he moved us steadily down the hallway. As we were nearing the exit, though, from around a corner came Agent Wallace and another agent, and between them was Stubby, his arms bound behind him.

"Say nothing!" Donny whispered harshly into my ear.

I was so stunned to see Stubs handcuffed and being escorted by two agents that I was at a loss for words anyway. But Stubby lifted his chin when he saw me. His looked terrified. "Maddie!" he cried out. "Tell them! Tell them it wasn't me!"

A sob formed in my throat, and as we passed each other I tried to reach out to him, but Wallace glared and blocked me with his body while Donny pulled on my arm to keep me away, but then he leaned over and said to Stubby, "Do you want my help?" Stubby nodded desperately, and Donny said, "Don't say a word until I get back, Arnold; do you understand?" And then to Wallace he said, "Mr. Schroder is now represented by counsel. You cannot interview him until I get back; got that, Wallace?"

Wallace made a face like Donny could suck it, which prompted Donny to shout back at Stubby as the three moved past us, "Don't say a word, Arnold! *Nothing*, you hear me?"

I craned my neck to look back at Stubby. He was openly weeping, and he was now slumped between the two agents, who were holding him up and moving him along while Stubby's feet practically dragged on the ground.

"Stubby!" I cried out to him, and Donny's grip on my arm got even tighter, but I didn't care. I wanted him to know he wasn't alone. I'd do whatever I could to help him.

By the time we made it to Donny's car, I was crying so hard that I couldn't catch my breath. It was a while before I realized that Donny had driven us a few blocks away and had parked on the side of the road. He was rubbing my back and waiting for me to get it together.

At last I lifted my chin and pleaded with him. "You have to help him, Donny! He didn't do anything! He only wanted to warn her! That's all! It was all because of me. I told him about her numbers. It's *my* fault, not his!"

Donny rubbed my back again and squeezed my hands. When I could look at him without sobbing he said, "Kiddo, none of this is your fault. I promise you that I'll help Stubs, but you have to be straight with me first."

I sniffled and wiped my cheeks. "I have been straight with you. I told you all about the card."

Donny eyed me critically. "Did you know that Stubs went to that high school to warn Payton?"

I shook my head vigorously. "No! I swear! He never told me. I thought he'd just mailed her the card. I had no idea he'd done that."

"What about what her assistant coach said? That Stubby had an interest in her even before you saw her at the game?"

I shut my lids and put a hand on my forehead, so exhausted and distraught that I felt hot and feverish. "You know how much Stubs likes to watch the cheerleaders, right?" Donny nodded. "He heard that the Jupiter squad had challenged our squad to a matchup before the football game, so he went to watch. That's when he saw Payton for the first time, and I don't know . . . She was such a pretty girl and I guess he started crushing on her right away. He was curious, so he asked the coach a little bit about her. It was harmless, Donny, I swear!"

"I believe you," he said. "But it doesn't help us that he scoped her out before you saw her deathdate, Maddie."

My eyes welled again, and I wanted to curl into a ball. It was my fault. If I'd never said anything to Stubby about Payton's deathdate, then nobody would've ever heard about his casual conversation with her coach.

Then Donny said, "What's the deal with the notebook?"

I shook my head and dropped my gaze to my lap, so ashamed to have him learn that I kept something like that. I knew how morbid it made me look. "It helps me cope," I whispered. "I need to do something with all those numbers, Donny. They're everywhere I look, and writing them down helps me deal. I see so many people who think they've got another fifty or sixty years ahead of them; they have no idea that death is so close. It breaks my heart all the time to think about that moment when they'll know that they have way less time than they thought, how hard that must be for them to realize they're about to lose everything and leave everybody they love behind." What I didn't say was that I thought it'd been that way for my dad, but I had a feeling that Donny knew exactly what I meant.

When Donny didn't say anything I picked my gaze back up and saw his eyes were moist. He lifted his hand and cupped the side of my cheek. "I can't even imagine how hard it must be for you, kiddo," he said. "I'm sorry you have to deal with that. And I'm sorry you have to deal with all this. I'll do everything I can to help you, though, okay?"

I nodded, and without another word he drove us home. When we pulled onto my street we could see it crowded with vehicles and vans. Then I saw a few men and women wearing dark blue Windbreakers with FBI stenciled in yellow on the back. Our front door was open and the feds were walking in and out of it, carrying paper bags and my MacBook, which Donny had given me for Christmas the year before.

I cried out, and Donny pulled over in front of Mrs. Duncan's house. As he got out to go confront the agents invading our house, I saw Ma dressed in her Drug Mart smock and standing with Mrs. Duncan. Ma's whole body was shaking; she'd been crying, too. When she saw Donny she let out a sob and ran to catch up with him.

Part of me wanted to go comfort her, but I found that I couldn't bring myself to move. I wanted to blame so much of this on Ma. If she hadn't practically forced me to do those readings for strangers, we wouldn't be in this mess. If she didn't drink away all our money every month, we wouldn't need the extra cash. If she hadn't moved us here in the first place. If she'd known what the numbers meant when I was little. If she'd put it together sooner and had warned Dad . . .

If.

If.

If.

If I had never been born . . .

Except . . .

Except that Tevon would still be dead.

So would Payton.

And my dad . . .

Ma finally caught up to Donny, but her hysterics forced him to lead her away from the cluster of agents, and he walked with her back toward Mrs. Duncan's. Across the street I saw Cathy and the rest of the Hutchinson family out on their front porch, openly gaping at the scene unfolding on our lawn.

Ignoring them, I got out of the car and headed up the walk toward our kindly old neighbor. "Oh dear," Mrs. Duncan said, when she caught sight of me. "You look a fright, Maddie. Why don't you come inside and I'll fix you some tea?"

I sniffled and glanced at Donny. He had Ma wrapped in a hug while she cried on his shoulder, but he nodded at me and said, "I'll be in soon. Go with Mrs. Duncan while I take care of your mom."

I lowered my head, trying to hide my tears. Mrs. Duncan's kindness touched me deeply. Once inside, she put me in her cozy kitchen, which was a bright yellow with gleaming white trim. It smelled like cinnamon. "Are you hungry, Maddie?" she asked.

I shook my head.

Mrs. Duncan filled a kettle and placed it on the stove to heat up before she set down a plate of chocolate cookies in front of me and smoothed out my hair. It was such a tender gesture that it nearly undid me. Mrs. Duncan moved to a cabinet and brought out a box of tissues. She set that down next to the plate of cookies, and pulled out a chair next to me and held my hand, repeating over and over again that I'd be okay.

I appreciated her calm, grandmotherly demeanor more than I could say. By the time she set down the steaming cup of tea, I had wiped my eyes and gotten myself together. Ma and Donny still hadn't come in, but I could see through Mrs. Duncan's front window that the street was still lined with spectators and cars.

To distract myself, I cupped my hands around the mug and let the warmth seep into me.

Mrs. Duncan brewed herself a cup as well before settling across from me. "How're you doing in school?" she asked.

The fact that she was making an effort not to ask me about what was happening next door wasn't lost on me. I looked up at her forehead, and felt a wave of sadness. She'd be gone by the end of February. "I'm doing okay, I guess," I told her, my voice hoarse. I cleared my throat and added, "I should make the honor roll again this semester."

Mrs. Duncan beamed proudly at me. "I always knew you were such a bright child, Maddie, but the honor roll? That's wonderful!"

I worked hard in school. I really wanted to go to Cornell, but Donny had flat out told me that there wasn't enough money left in the trust to support four years at an Ivy League school. If I got in, I'd have to do it on what he could manage to give me from the trust, and scholarships and student loans and maybe even part-time work. "I'm trying to get into Cornell," I told Mrs. Duncan.

She blinked in surprise. "You are? Oh my, Maddie! That was *my* alma mater!"

I sucked in a breath. I'd never pegged Mrs. Duncan for an Ivy Leaguer. In fact, I'd never pegged her for anything more than a sweet old lady. "You went to Cornell?"

"I sure did. Class of fifty-four. That's where I met Mr. Duncan. He was an assistant professor and we weren't supposed to date, but we did. We were married a week after I graduated."

Mrs. Duncan's eyes had a shiny faraway cast to them, and I could see how much she missed her husband. Then she focused on me again. "You would've liked Mr. Duncan," she said. "He was a lovely man. And so smart! He was always downstairs in the basement, tinkering with some new invention."

"He sounds nice," I said, taking up one of the cookies.

"He was wonderful," she told me. "I miss him terribly."

At that moment there was a knock on the front door, and Donny entered. "Hey," he said when he saw us at the kitchen table. "The feds left. You can go back home, Maddie."

"Where's Ma?" I asked.

"She's inside. She's had as bad a day as we have. The feds went down to her work to serve the search warrant, and then her boss came by with the stuff from her locker. He fired her."

"Why?" I demanded. "He can't do that, Donny! It's not her fault the feds came to search our house!"

Donny shifted uncomfortably and eyed Mrs. Duncan. "Her manager didn't fire her for that, Maddie. Your mom had something she shouldn't have had in her locker. It wasn't anything illegal, but it was against company policy."

And then I knew what'd happened. Ma's manager had found open liquor in her locker.

"Oh," I said, and got up quickly. Mrs. Duncan stood, too. She reached out and took hold of my wrist and said, "Wait one moment, Maddie." She then moved to the refrigerator and pulled out a large casserole dish. "I made this lasagna last night, and of course I made too much. Why don't you take it for you and your mother to heat up tonight?"

I started to shake my head, feeling uncomfortable with the thought of accepting so much kindness, but she wouldn't take no for an answer. "Yes, yes," she insisted, putting the heavy dish into my hands. "You eat it all up now, Maddie. You're far too skinny for your own good!"

Donny wrapped an arm around my shoulders. "Thank you, Mrs. Duncan," he said. "We really appreciate it, and Maddie will return the dish in the next few days."

I nodded, and Mrs. Duncan smiled and walked us to the door. Once we were outside and headed over to my house, he said, "Make sure you clean that really good before you give it back to her, okay?"

I nodded dully; my attention was now focused on the trash left behind by the FBI agents. There were small plastic evidence bags blowing around on our lawn, and a set of discarded black rubber gloves had been tossed onto the driveway. I looked around at the other houses and found the lawns empty of people. The curtains at the Hutchinson household caught my eye—they were pulled back, and I could see Cathy's mom staring at us. The venom in her gaze sent a chill up my spine.

Shrugging deeper into my coat, I walked a little faster, until we'd rounded the corner to the back door. "Ma?" I called.

"She's upstairs," Donny told me, taking the casserole dish out of my hands and moving with it to the fridge. Opening the door, he stared at the inside for a sec before setting the big dish in it. The fridge was mostly empty, so I knew there'd be room.

"How can you live like this?" he asked me, once he'd shut the door.

"We buy only what we need," I said defensively, only then noticing that much of the kitchen was in disarray. Cupboards had been opened and rummaged through, and the contents of several drawers had been emptied and refilled, but there was still a lot of clutter on the counters.

I hastened to start cleaning up, but then remembered Stubby still all alone at the FBI offices. "Are you going to go help Stubby?" I asked when Donny continued to stand there and look around at the mess in the kitchen.

His gaze moved to me, and something in his eyes hardened. "Maddie, sit down for a minute, okay? Let's talk."

Obediently, I moved to the kitchen table and took a seat. Donny took up the chair across from me, and for a long moment he simply stared intently at me. "I need to ask you something that I know is going to upset you, but before you answer, I need you to really think about it. Because if I'm going to represent Stubby, then I need to know what I'm up against, do you understand?"

My brow furrowed. I couldn't imagine what he was about to ask me. "Okay," I said.

Donny took a deep breath. "Are you positive that Stubby didn't have anything to do with either Tevon Tibbolt or Payton Wyly's murder?"

I was so stunned that for nearly a full minute I could barely form words. "Are you *kidding*?" I finally managed.

Donny knew Stubby. He knew how kind and sweet he was, how awkward and geeky, too. Stubby didn't have a mean bone in his body. And he certainly could never torture and kill two kids.

But Donny's face was dead serious. "Did Stubby know about your notebook?"

I blinked. "Yes."

"So . . . think about it, Maddie," he said softly.

"Think about *what*, Donny?" I demanded. "Stubby couldn't hurt a fly! You *know* he would never intentionally hurt anyone!"

Donny inhaled deeply again and sat back in his chair, still looking doubtful. "Maybe you don't know Stubby as well as you think you do."

I shook my head, staring at him in disbelief. "Why would you think he could have anything to do with this?"

Donny tapped the tabletop with his index finger. "Because you're the perfect foil," he said simply. I didn't know what the hell he was talking about until he started to explain. "If I were a kid as smart as Stubby—but with a screw loose—and I knew you and what you could do, I could take advantage of it. You say that some other kid is about to die on such and such date, and maybe that kid's going to die of natural causes or in a car accident, but I get to him or her first. Maybe I make sure they die on that date, and maybe I make sure lots of stuff points back to you. Maybe when the heat comes down I start to say that *you* did it. I tell the feds about your notebook. I tell them that you're the sick one."

I began to shake my head, slowly at first then more vigorously. "How can you say that?" I whispered. "Donny, you *know* Stubby! And you also know Faraday was lying! Stubby would never accuse me!"

But Donny only frowned and dropped his gaze to the table. "I haven't talked to him yet, Maddie," he reminded me. "And you're right, I do think Faraday was lying. But I also know the law, and that's why I don't honestly think it's a good idea for me to represent Stubby."

"*What?*" I nearly shouted. "Donny! You *have* to help him!"

Donny sighed and drew a small circle on the table with his finger. "Hear me out for a second, will ya?" he asked. I glared at him, refusing to answer. He continued anyway. "Anybody who's ever watched a crime show could figure out that this scenario sets up a solid case for reasonable doubt. It could turn into a classic case of he said/she said. I could head over there right now, sit with Stubby while he's interviewed by the feds, and during that whole time I would advise him not to say much of anything. Even less than I've let you say, actually. And then I could leave, and the second I'm gone he could start blabbing. He could tell the feds that he's waiving his right to counsel and that he wants to confess. He could say that you're the crazy one. *You're* the one who kept notebooks on when people were going to die. *You're* the one who told Tevon's mother that her kid was going to be murdered. *You're* the one who said she saw the date when Payton Wyly was going to die. *You're* the one who came up with the plan to send Stubby to talk to her and tell her that she was going to die on her birthday. And guess what, Maddie? The second he points the finger at *you*, I won't be able to help you. I could recuse myself from representing Stubby, sure, but I'd be barred from representing you—because the courts would view it as a conflict of interest—having already represented the guy who's now accusing my niece. They'd say that I had inside information or knowledge that might make Stubby's defense vulnerable."

I was shaking my head, hard. "Stubby wouldn't do that!" I insisted. "Donny, please! You gotta trust me! He's my best friend in the whole world. He's the most loyal, honest, sweet, kind person on the planet! He couldn't hurt anybody, and besides, he *liked* Payton. He was trying to save her. And he was the one who made me call Tevon's mom before he went missing to try and get her to listen. He even told me that he'd wished he'd called her himself to vouch for me! It bothered him so much that her kid might die, that he was willing to do anything to try and save him!"

Donny's expression became alarmed. "*Did* he contact Mrs. Tibbolt directly?" he asked.

I shook my head, but then I stopped and realized we'd called her on his phone. "No, but it might look like he did."

"Explain," Donny ordered.

"He looked up her information on his phone, and we called her on his cell," I confessed.

Donny pressed his lips together and shook his head. "So he had her information?" he asked. I nodded. "Then he knew where Tevon lived."

"Donny, I swear, we only called her! He'd never go to her house after she threatened to call the police on me." When his eyes widened I added, "I tried to explain to her that I was for real, but she wouldn't let me talk, and she threatened to call the cops if I ever called her again."

Donny frowned. "See, this is the problem I have with what you've just told me, Maddie. You didn't know Stubs had gone to see Payton until the feds told you about it, and now I learn that he looked up the Tibbolt's info on his cell? You may not know your best friend as well as you think you do."

"Donny, he *didn't* do it! Before their bodies were found, he had no idea that Payton and Tevon were going to end up missing! *I* didn't even know Payton was missing until I saw it on the news, and I didn't know that Tevon had been abducted until Wallace and Faraday came to the school!"

Donny stood up and paced the kitchen floor for a minute or two until he seemed to come to a conclusion. "Okay, Maddie. I trust you, and I'm sorry if I upset you, but I had to play devil's advocate to find out how much you really trust Stubby. I've seen way too many of these cases where a defendant suddenly points the finger at his innocent best friend to risk having that scenario happen to my niece. Still, I think you're right about Stubs, and I promise I'll do my best to represent him. But if either of you two lies to me ever again, all bets are off, got it?"

I swallowed hard, both hugely relieved and guilt-ridden. Sighing with relief, I said, "Got it, Donny. Thank you for helping him. I'm really sorry about lying to you."

He nodded and reached into his pocket. He shocked me even more when he pulled out a large wad of cash. "Here," he said, shoving the bills into my hand.

"What's this?" I asked, staring at the money, which I knew we could use, but couldn't accept.

"Your mom lost her job," he said. "And I'm keeping you

from making money on readings. Cheryl refuses my offer to help every time I ask, so I'm bypassing her and giving you a little nest egg."

I shook my head, trying to hand back the cash. Ma would totally freak if she found out I'd accepted the cash. "Donny, I—"

Donny pushed the cash more firmly into my palm. "I'm not taking no for an answer," he insisted, finally letting go to walk to the door. "Hide that somewhere your mom won't find it," he added. And I knew he meant that I should keep it away from her so it didn't go for booze. "I gotta go back and see about Stubby. Do me a favor, though; don't write down any deathdates until we get this cleared up, okay?"

I hung my head. "I will. Sorry. I should've told you."

Donny came back to the chair and kissed the top of my head. "It's okay, kiddo. I have to figure out a way to convince the feds to lay off you two and start looking in another direction."

I thought back to the accusing look in Faraday's eyes as he held my deathdate notebook. "How're you gonna do that?"

Donny moved once again toward the door. "I'll need to reach out to one of my contacts to do some research. I don't know if it'll pay off, but if it does, it'll hopefully take the focus off you two."

"What is it?" I was desperate to know—or, more accurately, I was desperate for some kind of hope.

Donny's face softened. "Let me worry about it, okay? I gotta go see Stubby, and then I'll come back and we can heat up Mrs. Duncan's lasagna. After dinner we'll go out and get you a new cell phone. I want to be able to get ahold of you if something develops."

Then he was gone, and I was left alone with Donny's wad of cash still in my hand. I looked around the cluttered kitchen for a hiding place, and my eye landed on the Garfield cookie jar. We hadn't used it in years. I went over and lifted the ceramic lid. Inside were several stale-looking Double Stuf Oreos. Ma kept the jar only because my grandma had given it to us one Christmas. I knew she'd never think to look inside, so I stashed the cash under the Oreos. After that, I got busy putting the house back together, periodically checking on Ma, who was nursing her wounds with a fresh bottle of vodka and the TV.

It took me several hours to get the house straightened up, and during much of that time, Donny's devil's advocate argument filled my thoughts with ever darkening storm clouds.

# 11-18-2014

THE NEXT TWO DAYS WERE TERRIBLE. THE LOCAL news media had run a story that Stubby had been arrested for Payton's murder, and there were unconfirmed reports of a female accomplice. I knew that everyone at school would know the reporter was referring to me. When I got to school Monday morning the rumors were flying, and I started to notice that more and more kids were looking at me with real fear in their eyes.

I couldn't believe my life was starting to spin so out of control. And the teachers weren't immune to the affects of all those swirling rumors, either. By fourth period I was asked to sit at the back of the class, well away from the other kids, because I was "causing a disturbance." If by that, Mrs. Napier (5-23-2036) meant that I'd come into class, slunk down in my seat, and hid behind my textbook while all the kids in class whispered, then yeah, I was causing a huge disturbance.

Things got worse the next day. Tuesday morning I tried to go to Principal Harris for help when I found my locker had been filled with shaving cream, but he wouldn't even come out of his office. I overheard one of the secretaries say that if I wanted the principal's help, next time maybe I shouldn't have my uncle call and threaten to sue him.

That shocked me. I hadn't realized Donny had called Principal Harris, but he had been furious when he found out that Harris had let the feds talk to me in his office.

Later on, I was even given detention by Mr. Chavez for walking into his class right as the bell sounded. Never mind that Stephanie Corbin (11-4-2080) walked in behind me and didn't get in trouble.

At three thirty when I came out of detention, I found that all the spokes on both wheels of my bike had been cut and the frame and the seat were covered in ketchup, mustard, and toilet paper.

It was all a little much for me, so I left the bike and walked home. Once I got there I found Ma upstairs, sprawled out on the bathroom tile. I felt that familiar jolt of alarm like I did every time I found her facedown on the floor, but when I bent to roll her on her side, I saw that she was breathing normally.

It took a while, but eventually I managed to move her over to the bed and cover her with the blanket. On the nightstand were two empty bottles of vodka, and a third, half full. I took it to the sink and poured the clear liquid down the drain, knowing full well that it wouldn't change anything.

Still irritated, I headed downstairs and found Mrs.

Duncan's casserole dish soaking in the sink. I scrubbed it until it gleamed, and by the time I finished, I was a little less angry. As I was drying the dish, my thoughts drifted to Stubby. I felt so guilty for getting him involved, and I wanted to help him so bad, but how?

Lost in thought, I moved to the kitchen table and sat down, thinking and thinking about any way I might be able to help him. I sat there for a very long time, wondering how I could convince the feds that I was telling the truth. Finally, the thread of an idea floated up in my mind, and I wondered if it was worth a try. Pulling out my new cell I called Donny, but as usual it went straight to voice mail.

After leaving him a message to call me, I grabbed my coat and the casserole dish and headed over to Mrs. Duncan's.

It was starting to get dark, and when I reached the part in the driveway where I could cut over I heard a low rumble that reverberated somewhere down the street.

I squinted into the darkness—I could faintly see the outline of a large pickup truck, parked at the side of the road in the cul-de-sac at the end of the street. The truck's engine was running, but the lights were off. My breath caught, and I held perfectly still. I wasn't sure if the driver could see me in the dark because I was well out of the glow of the streetlight, but I had a sneaking suspicion that I was being watched.

Remembering the truck that'd chased me into the park, I turned toward Mrs. Duncan's house and dashed up her drive to the back door, knocking loudly as I peered over my shoulder. Even before she answered it I saw a flash of black pass by, and I knew the truck had sped off.

She greeted me warmly and invited me inside. "Oh my,

Maddie!" she exclaimed, taking a good look at my face. "Are you all right?"

I nodded and squared my shoulders. I didn't want to worry Mrs. Duncan, especially since she lived alone. "Yes, ma'am," I said, offering her the casserole dish. I really wanted to race back home and lock myself in my room until Donny called me back. "Everything's fine. And thank you so much for the lasagna. It was awesome."

She smiled proudly and put up her index finger. "Before you go running off," she said, disappearing into her kitchen only to return a moment later with several Tupperware containers. "I made you and your mom some chicken, mashed potatoes, and green beans," she said. I was moved by her continuing kindness toward us.

"Mrs. Duncan," I said, ready to refuse her offerings, because what could we give to her in return? "Thank you so much but—"

"Oh, and there's some peanut butter cheesecake, too," she said before I had a chance to say more. "Mr. Duncan used to rave about my cheesecakes!"

Her eyes sparkled every time she mentioned her late husband, and I realized that she missed taking care of someone. So I accepted the dinner as graciously as I could. "Thank you so much, Mrs. Duncan. Ma and I really appreciate it, and I'll bring your containers back tomorrow."

She beamed at me and waved as I left her house and ran straight across back to my own door, banging through it because I was still a little spooked. I tried to tell myself that it was a coincidence, but what if it wasn't? What if the driver had somehow found out where I lived?

I shuddered as I set the containers on the kitchen counter, grateful to have something warm and delicious to eat for dinner. My phone rang as I was getting down a plate. Donny's name flashed on the screen.

"Hey, there," he said when I picked up. "What's wrong?"

"Nothing. I just . . . I have an idea that might help Stubby."

"Kiddo," he said with a tired sigh. "I know this is hard for you, but anything you say or do can be used against you by the feds, so for now, let me worry about Stubs, okay?"

"Donny, please? Listen to my idea."

My uncle sighed again. "Fine. Tell me what it is."

"I want to give Wallace and Faraday a demonstration. If I can convince them that I really can see deathdates, maybe they'll believe I'm telling the truth about everything else, and they'll see that Stubby was only trying to help me warn Payton. I thought about it, and if we ask them to show me some photos of people who've already died and I prove to them that I can read deathdates in the past as easily as I can see them in the future, that might be a way to convince them I really see what I see."

On the other end of the line Donny was quiet for a long time. Finally he said, "Listen, sweetheart, I don't think it's a good idea. It could backfire on us."

"Donny," I whispered, so frustrated and desperate I didn't think I could stand it. "Stubby's in jail with bad men. They could hurt him just for being weaker than they are."

Donny was quiet for a bit. Then he said, "Maddie, I hate to break this to you, but Stubby may be in the safest place for him right now."

My brow furrowed and I felt my temper flare, because Donny wasn't listening. "What does that even mean, Donny? You think it's safe for him *in jail*? Are you kidding?"

"He's been getting death threats," he said.

"Death threats?" I repeated. Was he serious?

"I've had a few come into my office, and his mother's gotten one or two at her work. People are really angry about Tevon's and Payton's deaths. The media has hyped this whole thing up, and I've been worried as hell that soon they'll get your name and we'll have to move you out of there. All it takes is one unbalanced idiot who decides to turn himself into a vigilante."

I felt sick to my stomach. "Do you think that'll happen?" I asked, sinking down in a chair.

"I hope not," Donny said. "But for now, it's important for you to stay as far away from Stubby as possible. The feds are looking for ways to connect you two, and the media is trying to figure out if the feds are serious about bringing charges against this unnamed female accomplice. The minute they figure out you're a person of interest, Maddie, I don't even want to think about how bad it could get."

"So I can't even go visit him?" I asked, because that'd been a question I'd wanted to ask after telling Donny my idea. Stubby needed me, if only for moral support.

"No way in hell can you go see him," Donny said. I blinked hard because I started to get a little emotional again, and I didn't want Donny to know. This whole thing seemed so hopeless.

"Hey," Donny said, probably hearing my sniffles. "I

might have something that could help. I've got a private investigator working on something for me, and I don't have all the facts yet, but I'm working another angle that could push the case in a new direction."

I shook my head. *Working another angle* didn't feel like enough. "Donny, please? Please let me try my idea?"

"No, Maddie," he said. "Be patient and let me run this my way for now." When I didn't say anything, Donny added, "Maddie?"

"I'm here."

Donny sighed heavily. I knew he was as frustrated as I was. "Kiddo, you need to cooperate with me on this. I need you to tell me you understand."

"I understand," I muttered, even though it was a lie.

It was Donny's turn to be quiet. "Okay. For now, go to school, keep your nose clean and your grades up. The best defense we have is to show what a good kid you are, so keep being that good kid, you hear?"

"Whatever." I knew I was being a brat, but I couldn't help it. I was stuck between a rock and a hard place, and feeling like the life was getting squished right out of me. "Listen, I gotta go," I said, wanting nothing more than to get off the phone with him.

"Okay," Donny said. "But remember what I said."

As I hung up, I wondered how he thought I could ever forget.

# 11-20-2014

TWO DAYS LATER DONNY STOOD NEXT TO ME IN THE parking lot of Poplar High, armed with his camera phone and a simmering anger that pulsed through the vein at his temple.

I'd never in my life seen him so angry.

"Show me," he said, his voice flat and purposely quiet.

I cleared my throat and resisted the urge to put a hand to my eye, which throbbed in rhythm with Donny's temple. "Over there, at the back entrance," I said.

Donny took my hand, gripping it with great care. It was a cold day and I was grateful for the warmth of his palm.

We walked silently across the nearly empty parking lot. It was past five o'clock and most after-school athletic practices had already let out. I led him in a straight line, dreading his reaction. When we got to the bike rack he kept silent, but I saw the muscles in his jaw clench.

He took a picture of what had once been my bike and was now a ruined mass of metal, toilet paper, eggs, ketchup, mustard, and shaving cream. On the seat there was a smear of something brown and smelly, and it didn't take a genius to guess that someone had found some dog shit and made use of it.

After photographing my bike, Donny nodded and we went inside. I led him silently down the empty halls, feeling anxious and jumpy. He seemed to notice, because he squeezed my hand, letting me know I was safe.

We stopped in front of my locker, which was slimed with bits of eggshells and more shaving cream. A foul odor emanated from inside. Donny got out his phone and snapped a few pictures. Then he said, "Now show me where you were attacked."

I walked him back down the hall we'd just come from, but took a right at the second corridor. At the end was a set of stairs leading down a half flight to the boys' locker room. I pointed to it. "They grabbed me from behind and took me down there," I said, my voice wavering.

"Walk me through exactly what happened," Donny said, his jaw clenching and unclenching.

"Eric and Mario grabbed me from over there," I said, pointing now to a water fountain at the entrance to the corridor.

"Did you have a class around here?" Donny asked.

I shook my head. "I was coming back from Principal Harris's office after he met with me, and one of the secretaries was nice enough to let me have a hall pass 'cause it was after the bell rang. I was getting scared to walk the hallways, and you saw what they did to my locker."

Donny closed his eyes, and I could see he was trying very hard to keep calm. "So, Harris essentially tells you that you're on your own, and you come back down this hallway and stop for a drink and then what?"

"Mario and Eric must've skipped their last class, because I didn't even know they were behind me until they'd grabbed me. Mario had me in a chokehold, and he covered my mouth so I couldn't scream. Eric grabbed my legs and they took me to the stairwell."

Donny swiveled slightly to stare at the steps leading down to the locker room. Turning back to me, he asked, "Were there any teachers around? Any other kids who witnessed it?"

"Yeah. I saw Jacob Guttman walk by. I know he saw what was going on."

"Did he say or do anything to help you?"

I shook my head. I'd seen with my own eyes while I was kicking and struggling with Mario and Eric how Jacob (5-25-2081) had snickered and kept on walking.

"Then what happened?" Donny asked.

I put a hand up to my swollen eye to cool it. I'd had ice packs on it off and on since the day before. "While they were dragging me down the steps I got a leg free and kicked Eric in the groin. He doubled over, and Mario let go of me. That's when Eric got really mad and slapped me. I hit my head on the railing and went down."

Donny's lips thinned again, and he looked murderous. I saw him breathe in deeply and let it out slowly, but it still took him a minute before he could speak again. "Who found you?"

"Mr. Pierce," I said. "I think he had hall duty, and he found me and helped me to the nurse."

Eric had hit me hard enough to slam my head into the railing, which had nearly knocked me out. I was discovered, dizzy and disoriented, by my chemistry teacher, who helped me to the school nurse, who'd then called my mom. She and Mrs. Duncan had come to pick me up in Mrs. Duncan's car, and they'd taken me to the doctor. While I was in with him, Ma called Donny and he'd walked right out on a client and driven two hours at rush hour to see me. He'd spent the night with us, and he'd been on the phone raising hell all morning and afternoon. That's what had led to the late afternoon meeting with the superintendent.

"Okay," Donny said, snapping another photo. "I think I've got it." Then he took my hand again and said, "We're meeting Mrs. Matsuda in the principal's office. Can you take me there?"

I stared down at my feet. We were at the school to meet with the superintendent, but I didn't want to explain to anybody but Donny what'd been happening to me over the course of the last few days. It was too overwhelming.

Donny squeezed my hand encouragingly. "Listen, kiddo, I know this is hard, but you have to speak up and tell the superintendent what happened. If you don't, then not only will Anderson and Rossi get away without much more than a slap on the wrist, but Principal Harris won't get reprimanded, either. Poplar High is supposed to have a no-bullying tolerance, and any reports of bullying are required by the school's own charter to be acted upon immediately. You reported several incidents to Harris, and in your last effort to notify him, he told you that if you didn't like it, you could leave. And the guy was dumb enough to say it in front of one of his secretaries, which means he thinks he's above the school's policy. Don't you see how unacceptable that is?"

I did see, but I didn't think I could bring myself to walk these halls during the day ever again. "I can't come back here, Donny. Everybody's against me."

"That's because no one's telling them they can't be," Donny said. I frowned at him. He didn't understand. "What're you gonna do, Maddie? Drop out of school? Cornell doesn't take dropouts."

"I could go to another high school," I told him.

"You want to come live with me?" he asked.

I dropped my gaze. He knew I couldn't. "Maybe I could go to Jupiter or Willow Mill?"

Donny sighed. "Getting you into their school system would be tricky. This county doesn't like students crossing residential lines to attend other schools, and frankly, as long as this murder investigation hangs over your head, you're going to have issues no matter where you go."

I shuffled my feet, still undecided.

Then Donny said, "Plus, what's Stubby going to do once we get him cleared of all charges? You think he'll want to come back to school without you?"

My head snapped up. "You found something that'll clear Stubby?"

Donny shrugged. "Maybe. It's something that I still need to look at, but there could be something that shifts the investigation away from both of you. At the very least I intend to present it at Stubby's pretrial hearing next week. With any luck, the judge will see it our way."

I felt a seed of hope begin to spring up inside me, but Donny held up a hand of caution. "Don't set your hopes too high, Maddie. The feds have been busy building their case, and I won't see much of what they have until the pretrial. There might be enough circumstantial evidence to convince the judge to hold Stubby over for trial. I hope there isn't, but I want to warn you that I might not be able to clear him this early."

Still, it was at least a ray of hope and I clung to it. "Will I have to testify?"

Donny shook his head. "No way am I gonna put you on that stand. At least not for the pretrial. It's too risky. The DA knows the feds are trying to link you to the murders. If you get on that stand, they'll do their best to insinuate that you were involved too so they can use your testimony against you later, if the case goes to trial. We'll wait until then to get you up there."

I breathed a sigh of relief. I'd been terrified of going on the witness stand and being identified by the DA as Stubby's female accomplice. But then another dark thought entered my mind. "Donny? If the jury from Stubby's pretrial hearing rules that the case should move forward to an actual trial, does that mean that the feds will arrest me next?"

Donny sighed and I could see in his eyes that he was worried. "I hope not, but they could."

"What are they waiting for?" I asked. The anxiety was killing me.

Donny smiled like he thought I'd asked a naive question, and he cupped my chin fondly. "Because you don't look like someone who'd torture and kill two kids, Maddie. You look like the sweet girl next door, which is exactly what you are, but from the DA's perspective, so many of these cases are won in the court of public opinion that, unless they find you with a smoking gun, or Stubby implicates you directly, the feds know that with only the notebook and Mrs. Tibbolt's flimsy testimony, they're fighting an uphill battle."

His explanation didn't make me feel better, because in my world here at Poplar Hollow High, the public had already found me guilty and I was paying the price for it. "Oh," was all I could say.

Donny took up my hand again and swung it back and forth. "Hey," he said. "Buck up, li'l camper. Let's have our talk with the superintendent, and then let's see about chasing down that lead that'll help Stubs."

When we got to the principal's office, I noticed that all but one of the secretaries had gone home. The woman who remained was Miss Langley (7-22-2076), and when she saw me, she offered me a nervous smile. She'd been the witness to Mr. Harris's last, dismissive conversation with me.

"You can go right in," she told us, and Donny led the way into Principal Harris's office.

I was surprised to find a petite Asian woman with shiny black hair and knobby jewelry sitting there. "Mr. Fynn," she said warmly, getting to her feet to come around and shake his hand. "Thank you for coming on such short notice."

She then introduced herself to me. "You must be Madelyn."

I shook her hand and nodded. "I'm Mrs. Matsuda, the super-intendent of schools."

Mrs. Matsuda (1-15-2056) then pointed to the two chairs in front of the desk, and we all took our seats. For the next hour, I was asked to tell her exactly what'd been happening at the school since word got out that my best friend had been arrested for the murder of Payton Wyly and my house had been searched by the FBI. After that, Donny showed her the picture of my bike, my locker, and the stairwell where Mario and Eric had jumped me. She remained silent as I told her what'd been going on, and her face betrayed nothing of what she might be thinking—not even when she saw the image of the garbage heap that'd once been my bike.

At last I was done, and she started to ask me questions. She'd been taking notes all along, and I realized some of what she'd been jotting down were questions that she wanted to ask me. They weren't all about the bullying in the hall-ways or the hard time Mr. Harris and a few of the teachers were giving me, but things like how long had Stubby and I been friends? Did I like going to school at Poplar Hollow High? And, most interesting of all, she said that she'd heard about my special ability and found it very intriguing. "Can you see everyone's deathdate, Maddie?" she asked me.

I nodded.

"Really?" She didn't seem doubtful so much as surprised.

"Yes, ma'am. I can see them on anyone as long as I'm within about four or five feet of them. I can also see them on a person in a photograph as long as it's not taken from too far away."

"What if the person is already dead?"

I shrugged. "It doesn't matter. Their deathdate still shows up even if it's in the past."

Donny sat forward, but he didn't comment. I could tell that he was prepared to stop me from answering any question she might ask that could be used against me later.

Mrs. Matsuda stood up and moved over to a row of books. I saw that they were all the textbooks we used here at the high school. Taking one down she thumbed through it. "This is the senior history book," she said. And then she paused about the middle of the book and turned it toward me. On the page was a black and white photo of a bearded man in period attire. "Do you know who this is?" she said, careful to hold her hand over the caption underneath the photo.

I leaned forward to really look at the picture, then shook my head. "No, ma'am."

"Can you see his deathdate?"

"December tenth, eighteen ninety-six, ma'am."

Mrs. Matsuda's brow shot up. "You're correct, Maddie," she told me, turning the book back toward her. "That is Alfred Nobel. He invented dynamite."

I looked at Donny, but he seemed focused on Mrs. Matsuda. The superintendent then thumbed a few more pages and swiveled the book toward me again. "How about this woman. Do you know her?"

That photo was far more contemporary, but I still didn't recognize the woman. "No, ma'am. I don't know her."

"What about her deathdate?"

"March twenty-sixth, twenty eleven."

Mrs. Matsuda sat down and stared at me with a mixture

of wonder and disbelief. "You really don't know who she was?" she pressed.

I shook my head. "No, ma'am. I'm sorry."

Mrs. Matsuda chuckled. "There's no need to be sorry. That's a photo of Geraldine Ferraro. She was the first female candidate for vice president of the United States. She was a personal hero of mine, and she died of cancer a few years ago. I don't know the exact date, but I'll bet if I look it up you'll be right."

And then Mrs. Matsuda reached down to her pocketbook and pulled out her iPhone. Thumbing through it she finally turned it toward me. Pictured there was the superintendent with her arm around an older woman who bore a slight resemblance to her. "Can you tell me the deathdate for the woman sitting next to me?" she asked.

I squinted and bit my lip when I saw the numbers. "She died last month, ma'am. The twentieth of October. I'm really sorry."

Mrs. Matsuda's eyes misted, and she put the phone to her chest. "It's okay, Maddie. My mom was sick for a long time."

After tucking her phone back into her purse, Mrs. Matsuda moved a manila file from the right of the desk over to the center and opened it. She then ran her fingers down the side of the top page, and I wondered what was in the folder, and then she began to read from it. "Madelyn Fynn; junior; cumulative GPA of three-point-eight-five. Fourth in your class with an excellent attendance record." I realized then that she was reading from my student file. "Last summer, you contributed one hundred and sixty hours of community service to Habitat for Humanity; you are a member of the Concerned Students for Animal Welfare; and your PSAT scores from last year put you in the ninety-seventh percentile overall."

Donny reached out and squeezed my hand. I knew he was proud of me, but I was still focused on Mrs. Matsuda. She closed the folder and gave me a thoughtful look. "You say that Mrs. Wilson gave your paper on *Catcher in the Rye* a D minus?"

I nodded as my face flushed with heat. I felt like I was ratting out Mrs. Wilson.

"May I see that paper?"

I dug through my backpack and fished it out. Mrs. Matsuda took it and began to read. It took her a few minutes because it was about five pages, but at the end she folded it up and set it on top of the manila folder. "Maddie, I must apologize to you. It seems that you have not been afforded the standard that all people in this country have as their right, which is the assumption of innocence until proven otherwise in a court of law, not the court of public opinion. I don't know if you had anything to do with the death of those two young people, but I'm inclined to believe that you didn't. It's clear to me that you have a special and incredible talent, and that talent has brought you a world of hurt and misjudgment. Bullying at this high school— or at any school within my jurisdiction—is intolerable. And anyone who actively ignores—or through inaction promotes—such behavior will be swiftly dealt with.

"It's clear to me that you've been bullied. What isn't clear is who's responsible. I've heard your claims that Principal Harris knew of the extent of this behavior and did nothing about it, and I've already discussed the matter with Miss Langley, but I would like to take tomorrow to interview a few of your other teachers, including Mrs. Wilson. While I'm conducting my investigation, I'd like for you to take the day off from school. I'll make sure your assignments are delivered to your home tomorrow evening with specific instructions from all your teachers, and I will be reviewing your work along with your teachers to ensure that you are fairly graded."

I felt as if a heavy weight had been lifted off my shoulders. Mrs. Matsuda was going to help me. Donny squeezed my hand again and offered me an encouraging smile. He was pleased, too.

Shifting her gaze to Donny, Mrs. Matsuda added, "And I will be suspending Mr. Anderson and Mr. Rossi, and I'll also give Mr. Guttman a stern warning and two weeks' detention so that the next time he sees something like that going on, he'll think twice about not reporting it.

"Additionally, Mr. Fynn, at this time I am not going to grant your request to bring suit against the school, but I will make sure that Maddie is reimbursed for her bicycle. And when she returns to school, her safety and well-being will be given the highest importance."

Donny nodded and stood up to shake her hand. "Thank you, Mrs. Matsuda. I appreciate your time, and I think your solution is a good one. Please let us know what your investigation turns up."

And then we were leaving. It took me several minutes to process what Mrs. Matsuda had said. "She's going to give me money for my bike?"

Donny nodded. "Yeah. I'll take you to the bike shop tomorrow to pick out a new one, and we'll keep the receipt to make sure they reimburse you."

When we got to the car I said, "What'd she mean, you couldn't sue the school?"

"In this country you have to get permission to sue the government," Donny explained. "I had to submit a motion to sue through the superintendent."

"That's crazy," I said. "Why would they ever give you permission to sue them?"

Donny grinned. "They almost never do, but they also realize that we could take all this to the press and things could get ugly for them, so they pay attention to stuff like this."

"The bike store should still be open," I mentioned, excited by my sudden change of fortune.

"We can't. We have another appointment with a colleague of mine."

"Who?"

"You'll see," Donny said, and I could tell he wasn't going to elaborate.

I sat back in my seat, still thinking about my change of luck, which is why I didn't press him on it. As Donny was backing up the car I happened to catch a glimpse of Mr. Chavez walking through the parking lot. I saw him stop at a pickup and pull out his keys. I blinked. The truck was one of those big, older models, the kind that makes a lot of noise when it's moving.

A tickle of fear snaked its way through my stomach as I watched Chavez unlock the door and prepare to get in. And then, as if sensing he was being watched, he paused, turned toward Donny's car, and stared hard at me. I saw his shoulders stiffen along with his expression, and I knew he could see me driving away in my uncle's BMW. The tickle of fear grew tentacles that inched up my chest and spine, and I pulled my face away from the window, slumping down to hide in my seat.

Donny was too busy trying to dial his phone and drive at the same time to notice me. And I didn't know what to say to him even if he had been paying attention. I'd already mentioned how mean Mr. Chavez had been toward me to both Donny and Mrs. Matsudo, and I hadn't actually seen Mr. Chavez in that truck sitting idle outside my house— the same one that I was convinced had tried to follow me around the park. But Chavez scared me. There was something dark about him. Something mean. It wasn't anything I could point out directly other than what I'd already said to Donny and the superintendent, but I did wonder if he was capable of chasing me into the park after dark. And yet he was a respected teacher. Was I was wrong to suspect him?

Still, I was happy that, for the next few days, I didn't have to see him.

"Okay, we'll be there in ten," Donny said, nudging me in the arm and pulling my attention back to him. "This could be good news."

"What?"

"Remember I told you I was having someone check something out for me?"

I thought back. "Vaguely."

"Well, that was my private investigator. He found something that he thinks might help us."

"What'd he find?"

Donny smiled sideways at me. "Dunno, kiddo, that's why we're going to meet him."

We met with the PI at McDonald's. He was a grungy-looking guy named Greg DeWitt (8-17-2041). He wore a coffee-stained sweatshirt, dirty jeans, and a beard that looked like it still had some of his breakfast in it. Also, his breath could've peeled paint. He was so repugnant that I offered to stand in the long line to get us all dinner simply to get some space from him. By the time I returned with the tray of food, DeWitt was gone and Donny was peering into a large manila envelope.

"Where'd he go?" I asked, setting the tray carefully on the table.

Donny looked up at me. "Huh? Oh, he had another assignment."

"What's in the envelope?"

Donny tucked it down at his side protectively. "Nothing I want you looking at."

I scowled. "That's nice."

From the tray Donny picked up the burger I'd gotten for him. "It's not like that. I just don't want to upset you."

"Yeah, because I haven't been upset by any of this so far."

Donny rolled his eyes but grinned. "DeWitt found a case that might help us. I want to take it over to the feds tomorrow, and I'd like you to come with me."

"What's the case?" I asked.

But Donny shook his head. "You'll hear about it tomorrow. Tonight, I want you to relax. You've been through enough the past couple of days."

I frowned hard at him, but he wasn't budging.

We ate together in silence. His evasiveness put me right out of the mood for casual conversation. As soon as we finished up, Donny drove me home. "I'll try to get a morning appointment with Faraday and Wallace, and I'll call you when I'm on my way. After we talk with them, we'll see about getting your bike replaced." I nodded and climbed out of the car, but Donny called me back. "Maddie," he said, and I could feel a lecture coming on. "Do me a favor, okay? Try and dress up a little tomorrow. No hoodie and jeans combo," he said, motioning at my outfit. "Try a sweater and a skirt. And do something with your hair. Every time I see you, you've got your hair in a ponytail."

I clenched my jaw, my cheeks burning. All of a sudden I was acutely aware of my appearance.

Donny's features softened. "You're a pretty girl, Madelyn Fynn," he said gently. "You've got your mom's cheekbones, your grandma's nose, and your dad's eyes—and that's a killer combo. Your dad always used to kid around that he was gonna have to invest in a bat-making factory to beat off the guys."

I opened my mouth, but Donny wasn't finished. "And today you proved to the superintendent of all Grand Haven schools that you're also smart as a whip. Meanwhile, you walk around trying not to get noticed . . . and I get it, I really do. I can't imagine what it's like to see what you see, or have people know you can tell them the exact date they're going to die—but, kiddo, if your dad were alive today, he'd never put up with this shrinking violet act. You've been trying to turn invisible for too long. Guess what: you're not invisible anymore. And like I said back at the school, looking like the gorgeous girl next door can only help us when the feds try to make you out as a villain. So, it's time to stand up to all these people who want to label you as weird or a psycho or weak or dumb or a witch or whatever, and show them what you're made of. You're a Fynn, Maddie. And Fynns don't hide. We stand up and we stand out. Period."

I could feel a retort forming, but Donny didn't wait for a reply; he offered me a three-finger Scout's-honor salute and drove off. I watched his flashy car cruise down the street, and had no choice but to consider what he'd said.

The next morning, Donny called to say that he couldn't get a meeting with the feds until after three, but he'd be by a little after noon to take me to lunch and pick out a new bike.

He showed up at twelve thirty, took one look at me, and broke into a sideways grin. "Afternoon, gorgeous," he said.

I'd paired my nicest skinny jeans with a camel cashmere hoodie from J. Crew, which Ma had given me last year for Christmas. I'd also blown out my long hair and dabbed on some mascara and lip gloss. Finally, I'd substituted leather booties for my usual sneakers. I figured it was as close to meeting Donny halfway as I was going to get for now.

We had lunch at a sandwich shop in Grand Haven that Donny liked, then headed to the bike shop. And after much debate, I finally got to pick out a new road bike that was light as air and fast as lightning. I was dying to hop right on and take it for a spin, but we needed to get to our appointment with the feds.

We arrived at the bureau a little before three, and Agent

Wallace came to the lobby to escort us to Faraday's office. As we entered, Faraday's back was to us and he was speaking angrily into his cell. "Jenny, if he wants to try out for the team, then I say he can." There was a pause, then, "You know what? I can't listen to this right now. He's got my okay. Sorry you don't like it, but what else is new? I'll expect a call from your attorney."

Wallace cleared his throat loudly, and Faraday registered our presence. "I gotta go," he muttered, jabbing at the END button with his thumb. We took our seats, and as we did, I saw Faraday and Wallace exchange a knowing look that seemed to be about the call.

Wallace pulled his chair in from the glass office behind Faraday, and they adopted identical expressions of *Yeah?*

Donny cleared his throat and reached into his briefcase. He extracted the same envelope he'd been so careful to hide from me, and handed it over to the agents. Faraday took it and opened the flap to peer inside. I saw his eyes widen, and then he dumped out the contents on his desk. Even upside down I could tell that the envelope contained some gruesome crime scene photos. My breath caught, and Donny laid a reassuring hand on my arm.

"What's this?" Faraday asked, sifting through the contents while Wallace scooted his chair over for a better look.

"That's a copy of a police file," Donny said. "A kid named Robert Carter from Willow Mill went missing last August, and his body was found on the banks of the Waliki River about three and a half miles south of where Payton Wyly's body was found."

I had to swallow the bit of bile that came up when one of

the photos that Faraday was spreading out on his desk caught my eye. A close-up of the young man's face had landed near me, and I could see his deathdate imprinted on his forehead. 8-19-2014.

"He'd been stabbed, tortured with cigarette butts, and had his throat slashed," Donny continued. "The MO is exactly the same as the guy who killed Wyly and Tibbolt."

"You mean Arnold Schroder," Wallace said. With a sneer he added, "And your niece."

"No," Donny said, reaching down into his bag to pull up another set of photos and papers. "It couldn't have been Stubby or Maddie, because they were both with me in Florida at Disney World at the time. Here are the photos and ticket confirmations to prove it."

Donny tossed them onto the desk, and they fanned out with all the other documentation. Faraday pursed his lips and reached for the photos that Donny had tossed while Wallace picked up the Carter file and some of the crime scene photos. After a few seconds of silence as they sorted through the new evidence, Wallace said, "None of this proves that Schroder and your niece didn't murder Tibbolt and Wyly."

My jaw dropped. Was he kidding?

Donny pointed angrily to the file. "What I've just delivered to you is reasonable doubt, gentlemen. You want to take this to trial? I'll make sure the jury hears all about the similarities between the cases."

Wallace glared hard at him, and Faraday lifted the file out of Wallace's hands and skimmed the pages. "Why the hell didn't we hear about this?" he muttered to his partner.

Donny answered for him. "Because Carter was eighteen. He wasn't a minor, so when he went missing it was handled by the local Willow Mill police department."

Wallace waved his hand as if that explained it. "Well. There you go, then," he said. "Different MOs, Fynn. If Carter was eighteen, then he doesn't fit the victim profile of the other murders. Your niece and Schroder could've heard about Carter's murder and committed a couple of copycat killings."

"Oh, come on, Wallace!" Donny snapped. "The longer you try to pin this on Maddie and Arnold, the more time you waste getting the real killer off the street. *Look* at Carter, for Christ's sake. He may have been eighteen, but he was only five foot six and a hundred forty pounds. He didn't look a day over sixteen, and you know it!"

But Wallace's expression clearly implied that he wasn't buying it. And Faraday set down the file and nodded, too. "Sorry, Fynn," he said. "This doesn't prove anything."

Wallace began to gather all of the documentation into a neat stack. "But, hey, thanks for bringing all this to our attention, counselor. Maybe we can find a name in Maddie's little death book that matches up with Carter."

My heart started thudding in my chest. I didn't think there would be a match in my notebook to Carter, but I also didn't think that made any difference. If there was anything even close to matching either his initials or his deathdate, they'd twist it to say that I'd planned it.

Next to me Donny was quietly seething. It seemed like this had all been a mistake, but I couldn't blame him for trying. My gaze drifted to the mug shots on Faraday's wall of CAPTURED felons. Was my mug shot eventually going to end up there, too?

And then that idea I'd run by Donny from a few nights before came to me along with Donny's speech about how I was a Fynn, and Fynns didn't back down; they stood up and stood out. I got to my feet while I still had the courage. Lifting a felt pen out of Faraday's pencil holder, I moved to the corner behind his desk. "What's she doing?" I heard him ask Donny. I knew that I'd probably startled them, but I didn't care. Swiftly, I began to mark the photos that stood out to me. "Hey!" Faraday snapped. "Cut that out!"

But I didn't. I noted six photos out of about twenty in total that could help make my case. I went to those six and quickly and methodically marked the foreheads of each and every one. As I jotted down the last digit, I felt Donny's hand on my wrist.

"Maddie!" he whispered harshly. "What the hell are you doing?"

I handed him the pen. "Proving that I can see what I say I can see. Like yesterday with Mrs. Matsuda."

Donny stared at me, his eyes wide, then he looked at the wall of mug shots and his brow went up.

Over my shoulder I saw Faraday and Wallace both standing with their hands on their hips, and I almost laughed because I could imagine that they were trying to think up a law I might've broken. "These are right," I said to them. "You can double-check if you want."

I'd written the deathdate for all six mug shots. Some had died as far back as two years before, and the most recent had been about a week earlier. Donny walked me back to my chair and I sat down, waiting on the two rather stunned agents to say or do something, but for a long time they simply stared at the wall.

Then Wallace pointed to the most recently deceased felon. "That guy's not dead," he said. "I personally sent him to Sing Sing last year, and as far as I know, he's still alive and well, enjoying a ten-by-ten cell and three squares a day."

I turned to Donny. "I'm not wrong."

Donny lifted his chin toward Wallace. "Check it out. We'll wait."

Wallace and Faraday exchanged another look, but finally Wallace shrugged and moved to Faraday's phone. We waited while he was patched through to the warden. "Warden Thomas," Wallace said, all smiles and confidence. "It's Kevin Wallace." There was a pause, then, "I'm good, sir, and you?"

I tapped my foot with impatience while Wallace exchanged pleasantries. "Listen, the reason I'm calling is to check in on Javier Martinez. I wanted to make sure he's enjoying his—" Wallace's voice cut off, and that smug expression he'd worn since picking up the phone fell away like shattered glass. "What?" he said, turning slightly away from us to stare at the mug shot of Martinez. "When?" Faraday leaned forward in his chair, his focus intent on Wallace, who was now asking, "Why wasn't I informed?"

I dropped my chin and took a relieved breath. Maybe now they'd listen.

Wallace hung up, his lips pressed tightly together. "She's right," he said. "Martinez was stabbed with a shiv last week. He died a day later, the same date she wrote up there."

For a long time no one spoke, but I could practically see

Faraday's wheels turning, and I didn't like it. "Still doesn't prove anything," he said to Donny, with only a fraction less conviction than he'd had at the start of our meeting.

"You're kidding, right?" my uncle shot back.

"Listen, Fynn, both of you have been in this office before." Waving at the mug shots Faraday added, "How do we know that you two didn't write down the names of all these bastards and hit the Internet to research them and find out who was dead? If these guys are in the prison system, then anybody with a computer could look up their info. Even Martinez's information would have been posted online."

Donny glared hard at him. "Maddie doesn't have a computer, remember? You took it."

Faraday rolled his eyes. "Yeah, but I'm betting you've got a laptop in that briefcase."

Donny reached for my hand. "We're done here," he said.

"Thanks again for the file," Wallace said as we got up and headed toward the door.

Donny didn't say a word as we stormed out. At last we reached his car, and he opened my door for me, his anger evident by the set of his jaw. When I hesitated he said, "You getting in?"

"It's so unfair," I started.

Donny sighed and his expression softened. "It is," he agreed. "But, Maddie, you have to realize that people like Wallace and Faraday get tunnel vision when it comes to stuff like this. They get so focused on trying to make all the jigsaw puzzle pieces fit that they lose sight of the big picture. With the Robert Carter murder we've got a solid case for reasonable doubt, and the district attorney's bound to realize that. All they've got is flimsy circumstantial evidence right now. And there's nothing to tie you or Stubby directly to the murders."

I nodded and reluctantly slid into the car. Still, I didn't like the lines of worry at the edges of Donny's eyes. If Wallace and Faraday couldn't be convinced I was telling the truth after what I'd shown them with the mug shots, then how would a jury ever believe me?

# 11-24-2014

I COULDN'T GET OUT OF SCHOOL FAST ENOUGH ON Monday. There'd been big changes waiting for me when I arrived that morning: Principal Harris had been suspended, my American Lit paper had been upgraded to a B, and I was now being escorted from class to class by the teacher assigned to monitor the hallways for that period.

I should have been glad for all of that, and I was to a degree, but everything that was being done to help me feel safe actually made me feel even more exposed and uncomfortable. There was a kind of tension around me from students and teachers alike, like a bubble of unease and hostility that I couldn't get away from until I was out of the building.

So, the second the final bell rang, I bolted for the door. I had to get home and call Donny about Stubby's pretrial. To my surprise, when I rounded the corner to my street, I saw my uncle sitting in his car parked in the driveway. "Hey!" I said when I came up next to him.

"Hey," he replied tiredly. It was then that I noticed he looked like hell.

I knew immediately the pretrial hadn't gone well. Tensing, I asked, "What happened?"

Donny didn't answer. Instead he rolled up the window and opened the car door. After getting out and locking it, he wrapped an arm around my shoulders and said, "Come on. Let's go inside and I'll explain."

Once we were inside, Donny called out for Ma. She came into the kitchen warily, as if she sensed he was the bearer of bad news. "What's happened?" she asked.

Donny motioned for us both to sit down. Ma took ahold of my hand once we were seated, and we waited for Donny to talk. He didn't sit down. Instead he got himself a drink of water and leaned against the kitchen sink. "I have a lot to tell you. Most of it's bad. You should brace yourself, Maddie."

I swallowed hard and Ma squeezed my hand. I could feel my breath coming quicker. I wanted Donny to blurt it out so that I could begin to process the bad news. "Tell us," I begged.

Donny sighed and set his water glass down. "Stubby's being held over for trial. His bond has been set at five hundred thousand dollars. I've talked to his mom and she doesn't have the fifty grand it would take to secure a loan from a bondsman, so she's trying to get ahold of his dad in California, but it's not looking good. Stubby may have to remain in jail until the trial."

I sucked in a breath. "How long until the trial?" I asked.

"A year," Donny said. "Maybe eighteen months."

I shook my head in disbelief. "Isn't there anything you can do?" How would my friend survive a year in prison?

"I did everything I could for him today, Maddie, I swear, but the feds have dug up some compelling evidence."

"What evidence?" I demanded. "All they had was that birthday card and my notebook and some witnesses who said they saw Stubs talking to Payton. How could they keep him in jail for *that?*"

Donny leaned over to grab a box of tissues, and he brought it to the table. I was having a tough time. "Here," he said, offering me the box. Ma got up and went to the cabinet to get a glass, which she filled with water and brought it back for me. She stroked my hair while Donny told me the rest.

"The search warrant at the Schroder house produced some circumstantial evidence that the jury found compelling. In Stubby's nightstand they found a hunting knife with a blade sharp enough to inflict the wounds found on Payton Wyly's body. The knife also had dried blood on it with the same blood type as the victim."

I gasped, shocked to my core that Stubby had something like that in his nightstand.

Donny held up his hand. "Stubs told me the knife was a present from his dad and the dried blood is his. He'd accidentally cut himself with it, and his blood type is O positive, the same as Payton's. The feds should've run a simple test to determine if the blood is male or female, but they claim that they haven't gotten to that yet, and running a DNA test will take months because the labs are so backed up."

A memory floated up from years ago, and I said, "Donny,

Stubs is telling the truth! His dad walked out a week after Stubby's twelfth birthday. That knife was the last present he ever gave him. That summer Stubs got it into his head that he wanted to make himself a walking staff like the one Gandalf used in Lord of the Rings, and while he was working on it, the knife slipped and he cut his hand really bad. If you look at his left palm you'll see the scar."

Donny nodded and put up his hand again. "I saw the scar, kiddo and I'm going to subpoena his medical records to show he got stitches for it, but still, this is all evidence the DA is presenting simply to move the case to trial. They didn't have to prove that the knife was *the* murder weapon today. They only had to prove that it *could* be the murder weapon."

I wiped at my cheeks with the tissue. I hated what was happening to Stubs.

"There was more evidence that was a little harder to explain, though," Donny went on.

"Like what?" Ma asked.

"They found some hiking boots in Mrs. Schroder's closet with a tread pattern similar to the footprints found at the murder scene. I saw the boots and they're two sizes too big for Stubs. His mom says they were her ex-husband's, and she's kept them all these years because they were like new and she was waiting to see if Stubby would grow into them before she gave them away to Goodwill."

I shook my head, feeling bitter. "They'll try to make anything fit, won't they?"

Donny pressed his lips together. "Some stuff they didn't have to work too hard at."

"Like what?" I asked.

"On the day of Payton's murder, Stubby was seen by the Wyly's neighbor, skateboarding up and down her street. The neighbor is a retired cop who happened to be working at his computer, which faces the road. He had a good view of Stubby and picked Stubby's photo out of a six pack—a set of photos of random people including the suspect, similar to a police lineup," he explained. "He says that Stubs cruised up and down her street for a good half hour between three and three thirty P.M. That not only puts him at her home but within a half mile of her abandoned car."

"Why was he at her house?" I asked, wondering why Stubby would do something so dumb.

"He says he was worried about her and wanted to keep an eye out from a distance. He'd been hoping that she'd stay in on her birthday and take the new car out the next day, so he was waiting and watching for any sign of that. He swears he thought that's exactly what'd happened, because other than a brief interruption to take a whiz in the woods, Stubby watched her house until about four and never saw her leave. We now know she left while he was in the woods."

"But if he was in front of her house during that time, then he couldn't have abducted her!" I pointed out.

"That's the thing, Maddie," Donny said. "No one knows exactly what time Payton was abducted. She was due at her friend's house at three forty-five. Her car was found half a mile away from her home, and she left her house sometime between three and three thirty. The timeline is tricky and no one saw her leave, not her parents and not even the retired cop, because after watching Stubby head toward the woods down the street, he got a phone call and claims he was distracted for the next hour."

"Is there any good news?" Ma asked.

Donny shook his head. "Not really. In fact, it gets worse."

"How much worse?" I whispered. I didn't know how much more bad news I could take.

Donny sighed again. "As you know, Stubs had run a search on his phone of the Tibbolt's address and phone number the night you called Mrs. Tibbolt. For whatever reason, he bookmarked the search. The feds presented a screenshot of the search on Stubby's phone in court, along with several other screenshots of other searches he'd done in the days after Tevon went missing but hadn't yet been found murdered. All those searches were the same. Stubby had Googled the words *Tevon Tibbolt death*. The second those searches went up on the screen, the court collectively gasped. It was incredibly powerful."

"Donny," I said, knowing the way Stubby's mind worked almost as well as my own. "Stubs was upset about the fact that Tevon was missing, and he believed me when I told him that Tevon was dead. He was only trying to do a search to see if Tevon's body had been found. He had no idea he'd been murdered!"

Donny sighed heavily, like he carried the weight of the world on his shoulders. "I know, Maddie, but there was no way I could defend against that today. Especially since the DA also presented evidence from the coroner that Tevon was likely murdered by the same blade that killed Payton, and that Tevon's blood type was also O positive."

I knew from freshman biology that O positive was the most common blood type. But still, why did Tevon and Payton have to share Stubby's blood type?

Donny rubbed his temples like he had a headache. "Basically, the pretrial was all downhill from there. And there was another detail the DA brought up, and that's that they also found an empty box of Marlboro Lights in his trash can."

Ma's gaze flickered to the ashtray on the table. There was a used Marlboro Light butt in it. "Why was that relevant?" she asked him.

"The killer tortured both Payton and Tevon by burning them with a Marlboro Light cigarette butt. Again, they're testing the DNA against Stubs, but it'll take months."

In an instant I knew exactly where that box of smokes had come from. "No, Donny," I said. "They've got it all wrong! Stubby got that cigarette box from me. He dressed up like James Dean for Halloween, and he needed the pack to roll up into his shirtsleeve. He's never even smoked a cigarette in his life!"

Donny nodded, like he'd heard that already from Stubs, but then his gaze dropped to the table and I knew there was more he wasn't telling us.

"What?" I demanded. This was all so damaging; I didn't know how much worse it could get.

"The DA officially filed additional charges today, Maddie. They want Stubs for Tevon's murder, too. And because there's some evidence linking you to Tevon, it's likely that you'll be named as a coconspirator before this is all over."

I felt the blood drain from my face so fast that I became dizzy and light-headed. "Wha... what?" I whispered.

"It's the notebook," Donny said. "The DA is claiming it was the playbook Stubby was using to choose his next victims."

Ma put a hand over her mouth and stared at Donny like she couldn't believe it. "Are they going to arrest her?" she asked.

Donny shook his head. "Not right away. They're trying to build a strong case against Stubby. If they feel they have a good, solid case, one that they can definitely win, then they'll go after Maddie. He's the linchpin. If they nail him to the cross, then it'll make their case against her that much stronger."

The dizziness persisted, and I realized my breathing was coming in great big gulps. I couldn't get enough air, yet I was sucking in oxygen as fast as I could. The edges of my vision started to get fuzzy, and Ma and Donny's voice sounded far away. I knew from experience that I was having a panic attack, but knowing what was happening didn't help lessen the attack. As I was gasping for air, Ma pulled out my chair and pushed on the back of my neck to get me to bend over at the waist. I was starting to black out. Then Donny put a brown paper bag up to my mouth, and I shut my eyes and tried to focus on Ma, who was gently telling me to keep breathing in and out as slowly as I could manage.

After what felt like forever, I started to breathe more normally. And then the dizziness faded and I pushed the bag away. "I'm okay," I said, and Ma let me sit up.

Donny tucked my hair back behind my ears and said, "I'm sorry, kiddo. Maybe I shouldn't have told you."

The tenderness in his voice was so sincere. It almost made

what he'd said bearable. "No. I needed to know. How long do you think I have before they arrest me?"

"A few weeks at least," he said. I didn't know if I felt relieved or even more scared. "Hey," he said, cupping my chin. "That's time, Maddie, and it may be all we need to clear this whole thing up. While the feds are focused on you and Stubby, I'm going to focus on building the case for someone else as the killer. I've got my PI back on the case, and I've also sent out the blood from the knife they took from Stubby's nightstand to my own lab for analysis. We'll work this until the feds are forced to consider someone else as the killer. Until we make it clear to them, you gotta have hope, okay?"

I nodded, but I didn't feel very optimistic.

Donny stood, and after looking at his watch he said, "I gotta go. I've had a hell of a day and it's a long drive back to Brooklyn. I'll call you if anything new develops."

Later, while Ma and I ate dinner, we watched the evening news together. The lead story was about Stubby, and the anchor told the audience about the results of the pretrial.

While the reporter covering the story talked, the broadcast flashed images of Payton's car, her class picture, and finally a photo of the woods where her body was found. Then the shot moved back to the reporter, who talked about Stubby arriving in court. Two policemen escorted him into the courthouse—only the person being escorted looked nothing like Stubs.

He was wearing an orange jumpsuit and shackles. His hair was a shaggy mess, and he appeared to be much thinner than the last time I'd seen him. His face lifted toward the camera and my breath caught. Looking back at me wasn't the chubby-cheeked, baby-faced kid I'd grown up with. Instead I saw someone with vacant eyes and a hardened expression. In that moment I saw him as the entire television viewing audience must have seen him—guilty.

I set aside my dinner and stood up. "You okay, sweetie?" Ma asked me.

I shook my head. "I need some air."

She started to say something more, but I shook my head and she fell silent. Moving to the door I tugged it open and stepped out onto the front porch to let the cold night air wash over me. Stubby's image had rattled me for so many reasons.

My gaze landed on the mailbox at the bottom of the drive. Ma never got the mail, and I knew I hadn't retrieved it in several days. I stepped out from the porch and began to walk toward it, and that's when I saw a car drive past. It was a dark SUV, and as it cruised in front of me, the light from the streetlamp sent a beam across the interior. I came up short. My principal, Mr. Harris, was behind the wheel.

For the briefest of moments, our eyes met. His registered surprise at the sight of me, and then they turned dark. Angry. Murderous. But he didn't stop. Shaken, I turned on my heel and ran back inside without bothering to collect the mail.

# 11-25-2014

TUESDAY I COULD HARDLY CONCENTRATE AT school. Nobody bothered or bullied me, but there was an underlying tension all around me in the halls and in class. I was like that guest who stays too long at the party— everybody just wanted me to leave. The atmosphere was made all the worse when it was announced at the end of seventh period that Mr. Harris would no longer be our principal, and for the time being, the vice principal would be taking over as head of the school. All eyes in my ceramics class had turned to look at me, and it was obvious that everyone believed I was responsible for getting Harris fired.

After school I wanted to be alone—but not holed up in my room hiding from Ma, who was so upset and worried, too, that she'd been hitting the bottle hard again. I decided to head to the park where Stubs and I often hung out. It was over in Jupiter, and there was a half-pipe there. Kids were boarding all over it, and I grinned at the memory of Stubs

trying to hang with them when he really was the clumsi-
est kid ever. I missed him so much; it physically hurt. I sat
feeling helpless on a park bench for a long time, all the hope
draining out of me like a slow, painful leak.

When I was good and numb with cold, I pushed myself
up from the bench and reached for my bike. "Hey!" someone called.

The voice that had called out was familiar. I froze for a
second before turning to see Aiden make his way toward me
with a friendly wave. My heart started hammering. I was
acutely aware of the moisture that coated my palms. I didn't
know what to say or do. There was a part of me that wanted
to get on my bike and ride away, because the second Aiden
figured out who I was, he'd never smile or wave at me again.

But I couldn't move. I was rooted to the spot. "I didn't
know you came here," he said, like we were old friends. I
drank in the sight of him as he approached. He wore faded
jeans and a letter jacket with a bright white *J* on it. The color
of the jacket matched his eyes. He'd strung his cleats around
his neck, and a soccer ball was tucked under his arm. "I saw
you sitting over here while I was practicing," he added, ges-
turing toward the large field next to the half-pipe, where a
group of guys was still playing soccer.

I felt myself nodding, but speaking was proving to be a
little more difficult.

"Cool bike," he added.

I looked down. My knuckles were white against the handlebars. "Thanks," I said, trying to find my voice. "It's new."

"I saw you in the stands at the Poplar game a couple
of weeks ago," he added, grinning at me. His grin was

adorable—broad and welcoming. It lit up his whole face. "You go there, right?"

I swallowed hard and nodded again. What if he knew someone from Poplar High and asked about me? Oh, God, I couldn't bear the thought of seeing him look at me like all the other kids did.

Aiden didn't seem to notice my anxiety. His smile remained fixed and friendly and so beautifully inviting. "You left the game before we had a chance to talk," he said with a wink.

"Yeah, sorry," I said, finally finding my voice. "I . . . I had to get home. My mom wasn't feeling good." Such a lame excuse, but he nodded as though he totally understood. I dropped my chin again and found myself fixating on his feet. He was wearing tan work boots. They looked big, but not out of place on him.

"I'm Aiden, by the way," he said into the awkward silence that followed—and I realized he was sticking out his hand, waiting for me to shake it and introduce myself.

"Hi, Aiden," I said taking his hand, which was warm and smooth. He closed his fingers around my palm, and I thought I'd never felt such raw energy. Heat practically pulsed between us. I was pretty sure I was lighting up like the Fourth of July. "I'm—"

"Aiden!" we heard someone shout from across the lot. Aiden turned, and a soft breeze lifted a few of his dark curls.

There was a woman in the parking lot, waving to him— and she didn't look happy. Aiden made a face and turned back to me. "That's my mom," he said, turning his hand, which still held mine, to eye his watch. "I have a dentist appointment and we're already late."

I smiled slyly. "You shouldn't keep the dentist waiting," I said. "That's *his* job." I'd never had a dental appointment that'd started on time.

Aiden seemed to get the joke, because he laughed and swung our hands back and forth flirtatiously. "Maybe we have the same dentist."

*"Aiden!"* his mom yelled again. "Right now, young man!"

With a sigh, Aiden let go of my hand and began to back away from me. "See you around here again sometime?" he asked. "We practice here on Tuesdays and Thursdays."

I nodded, but suddenly I realized that I could never go looking for Aiden again. Not at football games, soccer matches, or here at this park. He'd learn soon enough who I was, and that smile he wore when he looked at me would fade to a look of judgment. I knew I could take that look from everyone else—the whole world in fact—but not from him.

*"Aiden, this instant!"* his mom shouted while he continued to walk backward away from me. He rolled his eyes, shrugging playfully before he flashed me one last smile and jogged over to her car. As the car backed up, he sent me another little wave. I stood there for a long time. Part of me couldn't believe it. Aiden had come over to *me*. He'd smiled at *me*. He'd talked to *me*. At that moment a large cloud moved across the sky to hide the sun, and I shivered with cold again and something more . . . something sad. I knew it was time to let the Aiden fantasy go. But it hurt.

The next day was a half day, and third period had just started when Mr. Chavez got a call on the phone next to the whiteboard. The room fell silent—the phones never rang unless something awful had happened.

I knew that from personal experience.

After answering, Mr. Chavez muttered softly into the phone, his back to us; then he turned and surveyed the room, his dark gaze stopping on me. With a mocking smile he pointed at me, then toward the door. "Go to the principal's office, Fynn. There's a police officer waiting for you." I could tell he took some pleasure in saying that to me in front of the whole class.

I felt the blood drain from my face. I was so stunned that for several seconds I couldn't move. "Fynn," Chavez repeated, his eyes narrowing to slits. "Did you hear me? Get your butt out of that chair and down to the office."

I could feel all eyes on me, and I knew exactly what they were thinking. I was finally being arrested. I'd be spending Thanksgiving in jail, but I was terrified that the police could also be here to tell me something bad about Ma.

As fast as I could I gathered up my things and hustled out the door. The officer met me at the principal's office and Mrs. Richardson (2-29-2050), the vice principal, was standing next to him. "Maddie," she said softly as I hurried over to her. "This is Officer Bigelow. Dear, your mother has been in an accident."

I looked at the officer (1-17-2062) and cried out, "Is she hurt? Is my mom hurt?!" I was shaking head to toe and I felt like I was about to pass out. I knew Ma wasn't going to die for another six years, but what if she was injured so bad that she ended up a vegetable or paralyzed or something equally awful?

Officer Bigelow laid a hand on my arm to calm me. "She's bruised but not broken," he assured me.

I blinked hard, but the tears still came. God, I was crying at everything these days. "Can I see her?" I asked in a squeaky voice.

"That's why I'm here," he said. "Come on. I'll take you to her."

Officer Bigelow drove me to the police station, which, ironically, was only a bit down from the FBI offices. Once we were out of the patrol car, he walked me to the elevator and we took that up to the fourth floor. Stepping out into a crowded hallway, I followed him until we reached a wooden door. He opened it and motioned me through. I came out onto an open floor with half a dozen cubicles that looked a lot like the setup at the bureau. "Over here," he said, leading me over to another door. He opened it for me and allowed me to enter first.

The room was spacious, with a square oak table and several chairs. Sitting in one of them was a female officer, and next to her was my mom, slumped in her chair with her head on her arms, sobbing.

I blinked. This hadn't been what I'd been expecting. "Ma!" I called out, rushing to her side. But she was so drunk and distraught that she could barely speak.

Belatedly, I noticed that she was in handcuffs. "Madelyn?" the female officer asked me, getting to her feet. "I'm Officer Dunn. I had my partner pick you up. Cheryl says she's your mom . . . Is that true?"

"Yes. What happened?"

"She ran a stop sign, and before we could pull her over, she plowed her car into a tree."

"She was *driving?*" I'd had no idea she'd taken the car.

Officer Dunn (6-3-2054) nodded. "She was behind the wheel of a black Thunderbird, registered to her and a Scott Fynn." I winced. That car had been my dad's pride and joy. "She was muttering when we pulled her from the car," Dunn continued. "Something about finding money in the cookie jar, and taking the car out to celebrate."

I put a hand over my mouth. Ma had found the money Donny had given me. "How bad is the car?"

Officer Dunn shook her head. "I'm no insurance adjuster, but I'd say it's totaled."

She didn't have to be an expert. We had no insurance, because with Ma's record, we couldn't afford even the most basic policy. "Can you let me take her home?" I thought I might be able to coax Ma onto the bus if Officer Dunn would take pity on us and let Ma go.

"Afraid not," said Dunn. "Your mom's going to be staying with us for quite a while."

I bit my lip and looked at the officer. She had such a look of compassion on her face that it hurt. "It was my fault," I told her. "Ma never drives, and I was the one who hid the money in the cookie jar."

The officer shook her head sadly. "Madelyn," she said, "I'm the daughter of an alcoholic, too. It took me years of therapy and two failed marriages to realize that it's *never* our fault. Your mom's sick. She has a disease, and she needs help."

I felt a lump form in my throat. "Then let me take her home! I promise, I'll get her some help!"

But Dunn wasn't budging. "I've asked your mom for your dad's number, but all she'd give me was your name and where you went to school."

"My dad's dead. He died in two thousand four."

Dunn winced. "Oh," she said. "Sorry, honey, I didn't know."

I wanted so bad for her to give us a break and let Ma go, and I thought maybe she'd feel extra sorry for me if she knew that Dad had also worn blue. "He was Brooklyn PD. He died in a shootout with some drug dealers."

Officer Dunn eyed me sadly, then turned to look at Ma, who muttered something and shifted in her seat. I could see she had a fat lip and a cut above her cheek, but otherwise she didn't seem to be physically hurt. Just very, very drunk. Turning back to me, Dunn said, "Yeah, I think I remember that. Let me guess, though: your mom started drinking after your dad died?"

I nodded.

"Mine started right after my grandmother died. They were really close and Mom didn't know how to deal."

"There's nobody else besides us," I told her, pointing back and forth between me and Ma.

"No grandparents?" she asked.

I shook my head.

"Aunts? Uncles?"

"My Uncle Donny. But he lives all the way in Brooklyn."

"Can he take you in?"

And then I knew. I knew they weren't going to let Ma

go, no matter what I said. "No," I said. "I'm not supposed to leave town."

Her brow furrowed and then she really seemed to look at me. "Hold on," she said. "*You're* the girl the feds have been looking at along with that Schroder kid, right?"

I hung my head in shame. Now she knew everything. Now she would judge me, too, and next she'd probably be on the phone to CPS setting up some foster care for me. But when I looked up she was eyeing me curiously. "I've heard about you," she said. "My best friend went to see you about a year ago. She was worried about her dad. He was sick in the hospital, and the doctors were telling her to prepare for the worst. They said he wouldn't make it through the night. You told her that her dad was going to live another ten years. Damn if that old man didn't make a full recovery, and he's been running circles around the rest of us ever since."

"I didn't do it," I whispered. For some reason I was desperate for her to believe me. The rest came out in a rush. "I didn't hurt anybody, and neither did Stubby—Arnold. Mrs. Tibbolt came to see me, and she showed me her kids, and I only tried to warn her. And then we saw Payton at a football game, and I saw her deathdate, and I told Stubby about it, and he wanted to save her. That's why he tried to talk to her. He was trying to save her. He wouldn't hurt a fly, and neither would I. I swear!"

Dunn's eyes widened a little at the tumble of words, but she was nodding. "I haven't worked the case, but from what I hear, the feds are far from having an airtight case. How old are you, Madelyn?"

I swallowed hard and wiped my eyes. "Sixteen."

The officer sighed. "Well, technically, you're old enough to be on your own with a guardian's consent, but personally, I think it'd be better for you to stay with someone else." I stared at her in disbelief. Could that really be true? Had all my worry over CPS taking me away been for no reason? "Do you have any friends who might take you in while we get this sorted out with your mom?" Officer Dunn continued.

"Not really," I said. I knew that Stubby's mom would let me stay with her if I asked, but I hated to be a burden on her now that her son was in jail because of me.

Dunn sighed and stood up, hooking an arm under Ma's shoulder she lifted her to her feet and managed to get Ma to shuffle toward the door. "Call your uncle, honey, and tell him you'll be home alone and that your mom needs a lawyer. A good lawyer because this is her third DUI, and she'll be facing some serious jail time. Then tell him to move here if he can. You need support and probably some good counseling. Leaving you on your own while you're trying to juggle the investigation and school is a little much, and I'd hate to see you end up like your mom someday."

She moved Ma out the door, and I had to suppress a shudder. I'd never end up like Ma. Never.

But then, did Ma ever think she'd end up like this?

I called Donny and got his voice mail. I tried his office, and his secretary told me he was in court. She promised to get the message to him the moment he checked in, and I was left to pace the floor. And then I couldn't take it anymore. I called Mrs. Duncan, and she told me she'd be right there. True to her word, she arrived at the police station within twenty minutes, carrying a brown paper lunch bag and a thermos. She'd made me a meatloaf sandwich and hot chocolate. I wanted to hug her.

Midway through lunch, Donny called me back. When I told him about Ma, he hit the roof. I'd never heard him so angry, and even though I knew he wasn't mad at me, I found myself getting defensive. Finally, he seemed to rein in his temper and he told me to sit tight, that he'd get to the station as soon as he could.

Donny arrived around three, and then we waited some more while he dealt with Ma. He came into the conference room looking stressed out to the max. "With the holiday, I can't get her out until next week," he said, sitting down and yanking at his tie to loosen it. "But truthfully, Maddie, I don't know that I want to."

*"What?"* I cried. "Donny, we have to get her out!"

But Donny only shook his head. "Maddie, given your mom's blood alcohol content and the fact that this is her third strike, the judge might not even set bond. He's far more likely to keep her in jail and force her to dry out until her trial, at which point I'll be lucky to get her sentence down to under five years."

I felt like I couldn't breathe. Mrs. Duncan took my hand and squeezed it tight. "Let's focus on staying positive, shall we?" she said.

Donny's gaze flickered to her and he sighed. "You're right, Cora. But Maddie needs to know that her mom's not going to be coming home anytime soon. Which means she'll have to move in with me. I'll clear it with Faraday the day after tomorrow."

I shook my head. "No."

"What do you mean, no?" Donny asked sternly. "Maddie, you can't stay here on your own."

"Why not?" I challenged. "Donny, I've been taking care of Ma for the past couple of years. I'm the one who gets the groceries, does the laundry, makes sure Ma gets something to eat! I can manage okay."

Donny tapped his fingers on the table. "What's wrong with moving to the city?"

I sighed and stared down at my hands. "I can't go back there, Donny. I can't breathe when I'm there."

Donny was silent for a long moment. I knew he understood. And then Mrs. Duncan spoke. "I could look in on her," she said. "I live right next door and could easily make sure Maddie's getting enough to eat and being taken care of."

I eyed her hopefully, but Donny was shaking his head. "Thank you, Cora, that's very kind of you, but we couldn't."

"Why not?" I snapped. My uncle could be such a stubborn pain in the butt sometimes.

Donny looked sharply at me. "We don't impose, Maddie."

"Oh, but it's no imposition!" Mrs. Duncan insisted. "Maddie's a lovely girl, and frankly, I'm an old woman who could very much use a bit of company and a reason to get out of my old house."

I smiled gratefully at her before turning back to Donny. "Please, Donny? I'll call you every day to let you know I'm okay."

Donny tugged again at his tie. "I still feel like it would be too much of an imposition."

"Oh, bah," Mrs. Duncan said with a wave of her hand. "Maddie's a wonderful girl. She's no trouble."

I almost laughed. I'd been nothing *but* trouble the past few weeks.

Donny sighed, then nodded and tried to put on a good face. "All right, Cora. Thank you. Thank you very much. I'll take Maddie for Thanksgiving and bring her back on Monday morning."

"You'll do no such thing!" Mrs. Duncan said, clapping the table with her fingertips and giving him a broad smile. "You'll come to my house for Thanksgiving. I insist."

"Aren't you going to your daughter's house?" I asked. Mrs. Duncan always spent Thanksgiving with one of her daughters.

"No," she said, lifting her chin a little, and I could see it was to cover the hurt in her eyes. "Janet's not very happy with me at the moment. We've decided to spend the holidays apart and give each other some space. And Liz is spending the day with her in-laws, so unless you two want to let an old woman spend Thanksgiving alone, you'll come over and keep me company."

I turned back to Donny. I knew that without the invitation from Mrs. Duncan, Donny and I would spend the next day at some restaurant where the turkey was dry, the stuffing tasteless, and the mashed potatoes lumpy.

"Okay," Donny relented with a smile of his own. "But I'm paying for the groceries."

# 11-28-2014

MRS. DUNCAN COOKED ENOUGH FOOD TO FEED AN army, and we ate like kings. It was the best Thanksgiving I could remember since before my grandma died. Well, besides the fact that I tried to call Ma at the jail, but I was told she wasn't feeling well enough to come to the phone. That really bummed me out, but Mrs. Duncan assured me that once my mom had a few days of rest we'd be able to talk. I knew she really meant once Ma got all the alcohol out of her system, she'd be well enough to come to the phone.

Donny spent the holiday with us, but early Friday morning he told me he had to get back to the city for an emergency with one of his clients, leaving me with a day to fill the best I could.

Feeling bored, I looked out the window and saw that Mrs. Duncan's yard was still covered with leaves. Wanting to pay her back for all the kindness she'd offered us, I headed downstairs and rummaged around in the garage for a rake and one of the big plastic garbage cans that we used to put the leaves into when we used to care about having a neat and tidy lawn.

Pulling the rake and the bin over to Mrs. Duncan's house, I got to work. She came out after about a half hour. "Oh, my!" she said from her front porch, her hands clasped together over her chest as she beamed at me. "Maddie, what're you up to?"

"I'm getting up some of these leaves for you, Mrs. Duncan," I said.

"Well, aren't you sweet?! Have you had lunch?"

"I'm not hungry, ma'am," I told her. I didn't want to stop. I wanted to rake every single last leaf up off that lawn and make it look pristine.

"When you're ready for a break, dear, come inside and I'll fix you a hot turkey sandwich, all right?"

I nodded and kept raking. I was a raking machine.

"I'm expecting some furniture today," Mrs. Duncan added before going back inside. "The truck should be here soon. Tap on the window when you see them, will you, dear?"

"Yes, ma'am," I promised.

The furniture truck rumbled up shortly after that, and by then I'd cleared a nice path to the front door.

Rick Kane got down off the truck and came over to me with a broad smile. "Hey, there, Maddie," he said. "Happy Thanksgiving to you."

I stopped and wiped my brow. "Thanks, Mr. Kane. You, too."

He gave me a friendly pat on the shoulder. "Hey, call

me Rick," he said, and put his hands on his hips, surveying my efforts. After giving the lawn an appreciative whistle he said, "You're hauling some major butt here, girl. You on a mission?"

I grinned. "Mrs. Duncan's been really nice to us lately, and I wanted to pay her back some for looking out for me."

Rick cocked his head at me. "You okay, sweetie?"

There was something in his kind face that undid me a little. "Yeah," I said, quickly looking away. "Ma's been having a tough time, and Mrs. Duncan's been watching out for me while Ma gets herself together."

I bit the inside of my cheek before I could say anything more. Why I was telling this total stranger all our troubles, I didn't know. Rick was simply a really nice guy. The kind of guy I imagined my dad would've been if he lived to be Rick's age. Also, Rick didn't have long to live—maybe that's why I'd confided in him. All my secrets would die with him.

He squeezed my shoulder again. "That's rough, Maddie. I'm sorry."

I swallowed hard and shrugged. "It's okay."

"Rick!" his partner called. I saw that he'd already opened up the back of the truck.

"Yeah, yeah," Rick said, his voice thick with irritation. "Coming, *Wesley.*" Thumbing over his shoulder he said to me, "Wes gets his panties in a wad if he thinks he's gonna have to lift something heavy by himself."

That made me smile.

"How about *today*, Rick?" Wes complained, disappearing into the back of the truck.

Rick rolled his eyes. "That kid's a pain in the butt and

always in trouble. I'd get rid of him, but he's my wife's cousin and he needed the job, so what're you gonna do? It's family, you know?"

I nodded because I really did know, and with one last squeeze, Rick let go of my shoulder and moved off to help Wes while I got back to raking.

I kept out of their way as they carried in Mrs. Duncan's items. She seemed so pleased by the new furniture that it warmed my heart to see her so excited.

As I was loading a big bundle of leaves into the garbage bin, however, I felt a prickly sensation on the back of my neck, and I glanced up to see Wes coming toward me, carrying a small chair. He was staring straight at me. And it wasn't a nice stare. It was a leer. He licked his lips as he passed by in a way that made my stomach turn.

But what caught me even more off guard was the date on his forehead. I moved to the edge of the lawn then, well away from the truck, and kept a wary eye on him while the rest of the furniture was unloaded. I saw him glancing over at me quite often, and I didn't at all like the smirk he wore. Finally, Rick had Mrs. Duncan sign the receipt and wished her a happy holiday. Before I could second-guess myself, I motioned him over. He approached with a smile and a curious look. "What's up, honey?"

I bit my lip nervously. I didn't know how to tell him, and I knew I was violating Donny's orders, but this was an extenuating circumstance and I felt I had to take a chance. "Rick, there's something you should know...." My voice trailed off as I struggled to find the words.

"What is it, doll?"

I cast a nervous glance toward the truck. Wes had reemerged and was pulling on the handle to lower the back hatch.

"It's Wes...."

Rick immediately stiffened. "Did he give you any trouble?"

I shook my head, deciding not to tell Rick about the leering and simply confess my real concern. "He has the same date as you."

Rick blinked. "The same...?"

I pointed to my forehead. "His deathdate. It's the same as yours."

Rick paled and he turned to stare at his partner. It was a long time before he said anything. "Whoa."

Wes had now finished locking up the truck, and he was eyeing us warily. I could tell he knew we were talking about him. "What if you didn't go to work that day?" I asked. "What if you both took the day off?"

Rick turned to look at me again. "You think maybe there'll be an accident?"

I nodded. That was exactly what I thought might happen. "Maybe you two should avoid hanging out together that day?"

He glanced again at Wes. "Yeah," he said. "Yeah, okay, honey. I'll do that."

I peered at his forehead, willing that deathdate to change, but it remained stubbornly fixed.

"You coming?" Wes snapped when it was obvious his cousin was taking longer than usual to wrap it up.

Rick frowned at him, then turned to me and tried to

smile, but it failed to reach his eyes. "Thanks, Maddie. For telling me. I appreciate it."

And then he headed back to the truck, got in, and started up the engine. From the passenger side I saw Wes turn and stare at me, and this time it wasn't a leer. This time it was full-on sinister.

Donny was still caught up with his client in the city, so I slept in the house alone that night, which I'd done on a few occasions when Ma was out on a bender, but this time it felt different. I knew there was no chance she'd come back into the house at three or four o'clock in the morning, so I was able to fall into a deeper sleep, but then I woke with a start. My heart was pounding as I looked around the room. The digital clock next to my bed read four A.M. Something had woken me up. Something out of place. Had it been a noise?

Taking great care to be as quiet as possible, I got up and crept to the doorway. I peered into the darkness, but I didn't see anything amiss. I held my breath and listened. Faintly, I could hear the ticktock of my dad's clock downstairs, but nothing else. I counted to ten. Then to twenty. Nothing.

With a sigh of relief, I turned back toward the bed, and that's when I heard a rumble outside. A low, familiar rumble. My breath caught, and I darted to the window. I craned my neck to catch sight of a large pickup cruising to a stop before turning the corner.

I stood there for a long time with my nose pressed to the cold glass. It was then that I realized my arms were covered in goose bumps. It was unquestionably time to tell someone about that truck, no matter how resistant I felt.

The next morning I called the jail and said that I wanted to speak to my mom, but they told me that Ma had been taken off phone privileges. When I asked why, they told me they couldn't give out that information.

I called Donny and told him about it, and he said he'd see what was up. He called back about a half hour later. "She's been acting up and throwing her food at the guards," he said. He sounded really tired.

"She *what?*" That seemed so out of character for Ma, I thought maybe the guards were lying.

"Kiddo," Donny said, "you gotta understand. This is the first time your mom's been sober in a very long time. She's going through a nasty withdrawal, and it's making her act out. We gotta be patient and let her get the alcohol completely out of her system."

"Well, when can I talk to her?"

"I don't know, Maddie. Hopefully tomorrow, if she calms down and behaves herself."

I felt a rush of anger. Ma wasn't some animal at the zoo. "When are you getting her out?" I demanded.

"Her pretrial is set for Wednesday. They'll try her in drug court."

"Drug court?" I repeated. "She wasn't on drugs, Donny. She just had a little too much to drink."

Donny barked out a laugh. "Kiddo, both legally and scientifically alcohol *is* a drug, and your mom had quite a bit more than, 'a little too much to drink.'"

I felt like Donny was rebuking me, and it ticked me off, and then, suddenly, all of the anxiety and tension I'd felt the past several weeks came bubbling up, and I began to yell angrily at him. "It's like you're happy she's in jail!" I told him. "And why wouldn't you be? You never cut her a break, Donny. You always give her a hard time about everything! There's nothing she can do that's good enough for you! Even when she tries, you put her down!" I railed some more insults at my uncle, accusing him of never liking Ma, of wanting to get me away from her just to hurt her, of never being there for us. All lies, and I knew it, but I couldn't stop. At last I fell silent, squeezing the phone, not sure if he'd hung up or not.

"You done?" he said curtly.

My lower lip trembled. I knew I'd gone way over the line and I should apologize, but I couldn't bring myself to do it. So I didn't say anything, and the silence stretched out between us.

At last Donny said, "I'll be up on Wednesday. We'll talk then." There was a click, and he was gone.

I moped on the couch after that, trying to work up the courage to call Donny back and tell him that I was sorry, but I didn't. Belatedly, I realized I'd forgotten to tell him about the truck. That seemed a stupid thing to bring up now in light of our fight.

I went out to the kitchen and rummaged around in the fridge for something to eat. Mrs. Duncan had sent me home with so many leftovers that I wouldn't need to go shopping for anything more than milk for at least a week. And while I was taking out a container of leftover turkey, I noticed the pecan pie she'd given me as I was leaving her house the day before.

It was encased in plastic wrap, and Mrs. Duncan had tied a sweet plaid bow around it to make it look like a gift.

Stubby loved pecan pie, and in that moment I missed him so much that I could barely stand it. I knew I couldn't visit him, but maybe I could visit his mom and his brother and sister. Maybe hanging out with them would take a little of the guilt I felt for yelling at Donny away.

A few minutes later, I was out the door, pecan pie in hand.

Mrs. Schroder (5-11-2052) answered the doorbell before the echo had faded away. "Maddie!" she said when she took me in. Before I knew it I was wrapped in her arms and she was squeezing me tightly. "Oh, Maddie. I've missed you so much!" And then she was crying. Like, seriously crying. I felt so bad for staying away as long as I had. After pulling me inside, she cupped my face and said, "I'm so glad to see you!"

I held up the pie. "My neighbor baked it," I told her. Then I noticed how puffy Mrs. Schroder's face was and how swollen her eyes were. She'd been crying for some time.

"It's beautiful, sweetie," she said, accepting the pie. "Come in, come in!"

I followed her into the kitchen, and through a doorway that led to the playroom I could hear Stubby's younger twin brother and sister arguing over a video game they were playing. "I thought about calling you so many times," Mrs. Schroder said, putting the pie on the counter at the same time she reached for her coat and purse. "I'm so sorry I didn't. But you're here exactly when I needed someone, like an angel sent to me this morning."

I was super confused. "Did something happen?" I asked.

Mrs. Schroder shrugged into her coat. "An officer from the jail called me fifteen minutes ago."

I sucked in a breath. "What's happened?"

"He said that Arnold has been involved in some sort of disturbance, and they'd like me to come down there." Her voice became hoarse as she said the words.

I bit my lip. "Disturbance? What does that mean?"

Stubby's mom wiped her eyes. "I'm not sure. I've called your uncle several times, but it keeps rolling right to voice mail. So I'm heading downtown to see if I can find out what happened. I didn't have anyone to watch Sam and Grace; would you mind staying with them for a bit?"

I blinked, "Oh! Sure, I'll watch them, Mrs. Schroder, don't worry. Please go see Stubs and tell him that I said hi and I miss him, okay?"

Mrs. Schroder stepped forward to hug me again. "Thank you. I will." And then she was rushing out the door.

I spent most of the afternoon with Stubby's younger brother and sister. Sam (4-25-2092) and Grace (3-17-2048) were nice enough kids, but they were also a little bit of a handful. By the time Mrs. Schroder got home I was pretty relieved. Until I saw her face. "Is it bad?" I gasped.

Stubby's mom was crying, but trying to turn her face away from Sam and Grace so they wouldn't see how upset she was. I had the sense that she'd held it together until she walked through her own door, and it all came crashing down on her. I coaxed her to a chair, got her a box of Kleenex, and waited for her to collect herself. Finally, she seemed to settle down, and I asked, "Can you tell me what happened?"

"Arnold was taken to the hospital," she said, her voice cracking with emotion. "The disturbance was that his cellmate assaulted him. He broke his nose, re-fractured his hand, and he has a severe concussion. Enough that they're keeping him overnight for observation."

I bit my lip, near tears myself. "Did Donny call you back?"

Mrs. Schroder nodded. "He's trying to get Stubby moved to solitary confinement—which sounds awful and extreme, but it would keep him separated from the general population and he'd be safe there. Still, your uncle says the warden is in tight with the FBI, and they're pushing to keep him in that same cell block with all those murderers and drug dealers."

Mrs. Schroder's voice pitched up high again, and she had to reach for another tissue. "Donny thinks they want to make Arnold as miserable as possible so that he'll eventually point the finger at you."

I sucked in a breath. All of this was my fault. Stubby was in the hospital because of me, and he'd be thrown back to the wolves again because he was my best friend and he wouldn't lie and say I had something to do with Tevon and Payton's murders.

"It's the notebook, Maddie. They can't seem to get past it. They really believe you're involved."

I dropped my chin. Stubby's mom hadn't been accusing me, but I still knew that I had to shoulder all of the blame. "I'm so sorry, Mrs. Schroder, but I *swear*: neither of us had anything to do with the murders."

I felt her reach out and pat my shoulder. "I know, honey," she said, and I wondered if she really did. She was quiet for a bit, and then I heard her get up and move away. When I looked up she was bringing me a small frame. "Will you look for me?" she whispered.

My brow furrowed. "At what?"

She put the frame into my hands, and I realized it was a photo of Stubby. "Has his... has his date changed?"

I stared down at the round pudgy-cheeked image of Stubby grinning ear to ear. He was always happy. Always looking at the bright side. I missed him so much in that moment that for a time I couldn't see the photo through my tears. Wiping at my eyes I focused on his forehead. "He'll be okay, Mrs. Schroder."

But she wasn't going to let me off the hook that easily. "What's the date, Maddie?"

I lifted my gaze back to her. Did she really want to know?

"Please tell me," she begged, and looking into her pleading eyes, I couldn't deny her.

"Eight nineteen, twenty ninety-four."

I was hoping that would bring her some comfort, but Mrs. Schroder only bit her lip and turned away. "The DA told your uncle that they intend to pursue a life sentence without the possibility of parole. That means Arnold could spend the next eighty years in prison. That's no life for my son, Maddie. No life at all."

# 12-02-2014

THE FOLLOWING TUESDAY I FEIGNED A STOMACH-
ache and cut my last two classes. I was so depressed and sad
about Stubby and Ma that I couldn't concentrate; all I wanted
to do was go home and curl up into a ball.

As I was pulling my bike out of the rack to head home, I
saw a gleam of black out of the corner of my eye. The next
thing I knew, Donny's BMW had pulled up next to me.
"Oh, good, you got my message," he said, getting out of the
car to come over to me.

I was so surprised to see him that I simply stood there
stupidly. "Message?" We weren't allowed to have our cell
phones on in school, and I'd forgotten to turn mine on
when I left.

Donny took hold of the handlebars and began to push
the bike toward the car. "Come on, kiddo. Traffic was bad,
and we're gonna be late as it is."

I shook off my surprise and moved to his car. As we set off I asked, "What's up?"

"It's your mom."

I stiffened. "What happened?"

"She collapsed this morning at the jail. I tried to get them to put her through a detox, but nobody over there wanted to listen to me, and now she's in the hospital. Her liver and kidney functions aren't good."

I was so stunned and afraid for Ma that for several seconds all I could do was stare at him.

Donny put his free hand over mine. "Hey," he said. "Don't look so scared. She'll be okay, Maddie. But I wanted to take you to see her before her court date."

We parked in the garage across the street from the hospital, and I followed dully behind Donny as he led me inside. We paused at information before heading up to the fourth floor and inquiring at the nurse's station. From there we walked the length of the corridor and stopped in front of an armed guard, stationed outside Ma's room. He held the door open for us and came inside to stand with arms folded across his chest. The message was clear: we'd have an audience for the visit, like it or not.

Ma was so pale she looked gray. There were tubes snaking down from IV stands into her right wrist, and the sharp edges of her collarbone were sticking out. She looked so thin and frail. It was hard to believe this was my mom lying there.

There were also straps across her body, tethering her to the bed, but she seemed so frail and sick that I doubted she'd be able to fight her way out of bed, much less out of the room and past the guard.

As we stood there and took stock of Ma, a nurse came in, nodded to us, then went over to change a bag on the IV stand.

"Why do they have her strapped down like that?" I asked Donny.

"It's to help with the seizures," the nurse answered for him.

*"Seizures?"*

"Maddie," my uncle cautioned as Ma stirred but didn't open her eyes. "Keep your voice down, kiddo."

I lowered my voice to a whisper. "Why is she having seizures?"

The nurse looked to my uncle first before answering. He nodded, and she focused on me. "Your mother is going through alcohol withdrawal. When long-term addicts are forced to go cold turkey, their bodies often can't handle it. Your mom should've been admitted to a detox facility instead of a jail cell."

The nurse shifted her gaze to send an angry look at the cop guarding her, and he in turn rolled his eyes and looked away.

"Will she get better?" I asked.

The nurse collected the old IV bag. "She should. We'll need to keep her here for at least the next forty-eight hours to make sure her kidney and liver functions come back to normal, but she should be well enough to be released back to the county in another day or two."

"I'd like to speak to her doctor, if that's okay?" Donny

asked, smiling at the nurse. I could tell he thought she was cute.

"Sure," she said, with a hint of a smile in return. She apparently thought he was cute, too. "Come on. Doctor Aruben is on rounds right now. I'll take you to him."

"Stay here till I get back," Donny said to me. I nodded, and he kissed the side of my head and followed after the nurse. The guard didn't budge from his post right inside the door, so I did my best to ignore him.

I moved to the bedside in order to hold Ma's hand, but it was twitching so much that it scared me, so I set it back down. "Ma?"

Her eyelids fluttered.

"It's me." She didn't respond. "It's Maddie." Still nothing. I bit my lip, trying hard not to cry, but she looked so bad lying there all pale and clammy and twitchy. Even when she was in her worst blackouts she didn't look this bad. "Ma," I said again. "You gotta fight, okay? You gotta get better so you can come home."

Ma's eyelids fluttered again and then they flew open, as if suddenly being released from a latch. "What're you doing here?" she demanded, her voice rough as sandpaper.

"I . . . I came to see you."

"I don't want you here."

I reached for her hand again, but she pulled it away. "Get out, Maddie."

Her words hit me like a slap. "Ma—"

"Get out!"

I backed up from the bed but didn't leave the room. "Ma," I tried again. I couldn't keep the waver out of my voice.

"Go!" she snapped, her eyes black and hard as iron.

Still I stood there for another few seconds, waiting for her to tell me it was all a joke, that of course she wanted to see me, that she was happy I was there. But her hard expression never softened. Finally, I turned and left the room.

I walked fast down the hallway without a thought or a care for where I was going. I only wanted to get away. And that's when I walked right into Agent Faraday. "What're you doing here?" he asked, when I backed away muttering apologies.

I looked up and realized who I'd crashed into. "I . . . my mom . . ." I pointed down the hall at a loss for words.

Faraday's eyes scanned the corridor behind me, and I turned to look over my shoulder, too. The guard was just coming out of Ma's room and taking his seat on the folding chair in the hallway. "Oh, yeah," Faraday said. "I heard she got picked up the other day. Guess you won't be using her as a character witness, huh?"

He said it with such cold-hearted callousness, I felt something inside me give way, and then the dam broke. I moved toward the wall and rested my forehead against it, wrapping my arms tightly around myself as a huge wave of despair surged its way up from inside me. I fought hard, but I couldn't keep it down. I began to weep, then sob, and all the anguish I felt over my dad, my mom, and Stubby came tumbling out in a long, heartbreaking wail. I crumpled to the floor, hugging myself tighter and tighter, but I couldn't hold it in.

"Hey," I heard. "Hey, Madelyn," Faraday said. I felt his cold fingers on my shoulder. "Come on, girl, pull it together."

But I couldn't stop and I couldn't catch my breath and soon I started to see stars. I heard a call for a nurse, and then I was being picked up, shouldered between people, and carried along to a gurney. The sobs kept coming: an ocean of grief, fear, and worry pounding me into the surf. I felt hands all over me and chatter around me, but I couldn't pick anything distinctive out. And then I felt a pinprick and I took three short breaths, forcing myself to focus. I saw a needle slide into the vein of my right arm, and then the world spun. I caught sight of Faraday's face right before the lights went out. His expression had changed. I could've sworn that now he was the guilty one.

I woke up feeling very disconnected—as if my mind had been pushed to the very back of my head behind a layer of cotton balls, and all my other senses and functions were simply going through the motions—void of any will or desire on my part.

Slowly, I became aware of voices, angry but hushed. "What'd you say to her?" Donny demanded.

"Nothing, Fynn," Faraday said. "She bumped into me, and then she just lost it."

Liar, I thought, without any emotion at all.

"The nurse saw you say something to her," Donny growled. Now *he* sounded angry.

"Listen, counselor," Faraday told him, "I'd love to stand here and argue with you, but I gotta get back to the office. I hope your niece is okay, but seriously, bringing her here with everything that's going on—do you really think that was a good idea?"

"What the hell do *you* know?!" Donny was shouting now.

"I got a kid, Fynn," Faraday said. "If his mom was a drunk and she'd been picked up and brought here for detox, I'd *never* let him see her until she was back on her feet."

"Go to hell, Faraday!" Donny spat. And then he was next to me and I heard Faraday's footsteps clicking loudly down the hall. "Hey, kiddo," Donny said, lines of worry etched onto his forehead. "You okay?"

I nodded. I was fine. At least my mind was fine. It felt tucked into the back of my head where it didn't have to think or worry. I didn't know about my body, though. It felt sluggish and heavy.

Donny stroked my hair and kissed my forehead. "The doc says that you need to stay here until that IV finishes, then I can take you home."

I nodded again, but I was suddenly so tired. Nodding was like moving a big ball of lead up and down. My lids slid closed and I heard Donny say something more, but it didn't register. My mind was shutting off, and it was a relief.

I woke up in Donny's car. Sitting up, I looked around dully. We were almost home. "Hey there, sleepy," he said.

I tried to open my mouth to reply, but it felt sticky and way too difficult.

"I'm going to drop you at home, Maddie," Donny said. "Mrs. Duncan's meeting us there, and she's going to look after you while I go meet with the drug court advocate. I'll be back in time for dinner and then we'll talk, okay?"

I blinked at him. I hope he understood that was a sign for yes. He grinned sideways at me. "Man, they gave you some really good drugs, huh?"

Good? No. Nothing about this was good, but at least I had an excuse not to talk. I laid my head back and shut my eyes. I was asleep again in seconds.

The next time I woke up was in the dark. I sat up, completely disoriented. It took me a minute to figure out that I was in my room. I looked toward the nightstand—the clock read seven thirty, and I couldn't tell if it was morning or night. But then I realized that it was usually light out by seven thirty A.M. Swinging my legs out of bed I had a moment of dizziness, and I gripped the edge of the mattress tightly. As I was trying to get my balance, the scene at the hospital came back to me. How Ma had ordered me out. How Agent Faraday had been so mean. How I'd collapsed in a puddle of tears.

I felt my cheeks heat. It was all so embarrassing. At last I felt okay enough to get off the bed and shuffle to the door. Pulling it open, I heard voices downstairs. I rubbed my temples. I could hear Donny and Mrs. Duncan talking, but I couldn't quite make out what they were saying.

The smell of something delicious wafted up from the kitchen. Careful to grip the banister, I headed down the stairs and rounded the corner into the kitchen. Mrs. Duncan sat at the table with Donny, who was eating a chicken potpie so creamy and mouthwateringly delectable that it could have graced the cover of a cooking magazine.

"Oh, Maddie!" Mrs. Duncan said, hurrying out of her seat to come put her arm around me and guide me to the table. "How're you feeling?"

I wiped the sleep from my eyes. "A little groggy."

"Are you hungry, kiddo?" Donny asked, offering me his fork.

I nodded, and Mrs. Duncan said, "Donny, you eat that. I've got one warming in the oven for Maddie."

A minute later she'd placed my dinner in front of me with a tall glass of milk, and I dove in.

"Careful!" she warned as she took her seat again. "That's hot."

I blew on the forkful of creamy chicken and pastry and popped it into my mouth too soon. It burned the roof of my mouth a little, but it was so good.

"I talked to the drug court advocate," Donny said, eyeing me sideways as if to see if I was coherent enough to talk.

I blinked. "Who?"

"The drug court advocate. They assess the cases of people like your mom and make recommendations to the judge who has the authority to send those people either to rehab or jail, depending."

"Depending on what?"

"Well, on lots of things actually," Donny said. "Whether or not the accused has an extended history of drug or alcohol abuse, if the accused has ever had treatment before... stuff like that."

I nodded. I understood. "What'd he say?"

"She," he said. "She said that she'll suggest a plea agreement that'll keep your mom out of jail, if Cheryl enters a four-month alcohol treatment program."

I took a sip of milk, trying to figure out if that was good news or bad. "What does that mean?"

Donny wiped the corners of his mouth with his napkin. "It means that she agrees that your mom is sick, not irresponsible. She looked at Cheryl's history and the fact that your mom was a nurse with a master's degree and a great job until Scott's death. It means that she understands that Cheryl's not some lowlife who's made poor choices her whole life. So your mom will go to rehab, and then she'll have a few hundred hours of community service to complete along with court-mandated blood tests and AA meetings, and hopefully we'll be able to keep her out of jail this time. But, Maddie, if she fails even a single blood test, they'll put her in jail and she'll have to serve out a five-year term."

"She can do it, Donny. If she gets help, I know she can do it."

He nodded. "I know, too, kiddo. That's why I pushed for it."

And then I thought of something that made me worry. "What if she says no to the rehab?" Ma had said no to getting help plenty of times in the past. She was the only one who didn't think she had a problem she couldn't overcome on her own.

"She's doesn't have much choice. It'll be part of the plea agreement. Either she takes the four months in rehab, or she'll face a trial where she could do serious time."

I pulled at my napkin. Ma could be so stubborn. I worried that she'd say no to the rehab and want to go to trial, thinking that she'd beat the charges.

Donny seemed to read my mind. "Hey," he said. "Don't worry. I'll talk her into it."

I nodded and ate some more of my dinner. "She was so mean to me," I said after a bit.

"Mean to you?" Mrs. Duncan asked.

I kept my eyes averted, feeling shame for no reason I

could name. "She woke up after Donny left the room. She told me to get out, that she didn't want me there."

"Oh, Maddie," Mrs. Duncan said, reaching across the table to squeeze my hand. "I had a brother who struggled with alcohol. He was terrible to us when he was sober and sweet as punch when he had a few in him. They're not really themselves in this state, honey. Your mom just needs some time and you'll see. She'll be the mother she used to be again."

I hoped Mrs. Duncan was right, but the truth was I barely remembered who Ma used to be. "Will she have to go far away?" I asked Donny.

He shook his head. "There's a state-funded rehab center up in Whitcomb." Whitcomb was about forty-five minutes away by car. "I'll come up on the weekends, and we can go visit her once her counselors feel she's ready."

My brow furrowed. "How long will that take?"

"It depends on your mom, Maddie," Donny said, avoiding my eyes. "At least a few weeks. She's going to have to face her problem and take responsibility for it. The only way she'll get better is to accept that she's really messed up her life."

I tugged on my napkin some more. "It's my fault she drinks," I whispered.

Donny eyed me sharply. "*Your* fault? Maddie, how can you think that?"

And then all that anguish I'd felt in the hospital returned, and with a trembling voice, I confessed to him my deepest shame. "She drinks because she blames me for Dad. She doesn't want to blame me, but I know she does. And that's my fault, too. I should've told him, Donny. I should've figured out what the numbers meant, and I should've told him."

Mrs. Duncan reached out to squeeze my hand while Donny stared at me openmouthed. "Kiddo . . ." he said, shaking his head like he couldn't believe what I'd said. "Cheryl does *not* blame you. And I know that for a fact."

I shook *my* head, so ashamed I had to stare at my lap. "She does blame me," I insisted. "But I know she doesn't want to."

Donny reached out and lifted my chin, forcing me to look at him. "Maddie," he said gently, "I'm going to share something with you that your mom made me promise never to tell you, but in light of what you've just said, I think I have to."

I sniffled. "What?"

Donny took a deep breath, and dove in. "Do you remember that drawing you made of your mom, dad, and you? The one you insisted Scott hang on the fridge in your old apartment?"

Immediately, I knew he was talking about the drawing Ma still kept hidden upstairs. "Yeah."

"The day you brought that home your mom and dad had me over for dinner. While we were all in the kitchen you brought in a drawing you made of me. You gave it to me, and I saw that you'd written in my numbers, too. After you went to bed the three of us were hanging out, and Scott mentioned the drawings. Your mom thought you were quite the little artist, but Scott was focused on the numbers you'd drawn on everybody's forehead. We didn't know why you kept insisting that you saw them on every face you looked at, and Scott was convinced there was some meaning there.

"The three of us tossed out theories about what the sequence might mean, and your dad was the one who suggested that maybe you were some sort of gifted intuitive and the numbers were like birthdays but in reverse. He thought maybe the numbers were a date, and that you were seeing the date the person was going to die."

Donny paused and his lower lip trembled. He dropped his gaze to the table, as if he were ashamed to continue. Finally, he cleared his throat, and with an unsteady voice he said, "Your mom laughed at the idea. She said that Scott's theory was ridiculous; no one could know that. She thought you simply loved to count and assigned everyone random numbers because you were creative and smart and thought it was a fun game. She talked your dad right out of the idea. A year later, we knew that Scott was right all along."

Donny then lifted his gaze back to me. A tear escaped him and he wiped it away quickly. "So, Maddie, both me and your mom know it's not your fault. She doesn't blame you, kiddo. She blames herself, and she drinks because of that and the fact that she's terrified that someday I'll tell you what happened that night, and you'll blame her, too."

I sat in my chair so stunned I could hardly think. I didn't know what to say or even how to feel. I'd carried the burden of blame for my dad's death for more than half my life and it'd never occurred to me that he might've guessed long before his death what the numbers meant. I turned to look toward the mantel in the living room where his picture was.

If he knew, or even if he'd suspected, why had he gone into that building?

Donny seemed to read my mind. "Your dad never mentioned the theory again," he said. "But I knew him better than anybody. On the day he died it had to have been a thought in the back of his mind, but he was never the kind of guy who would turn his back on his brothers in blue. I think he went into that building knowing there was a good chance he wouldn't come out alive, and he made the hardest choice there is to make, because deep down, Scott was a guy with the heart of a hero."

Mrs. Duncan moved her chair to hug me tightly while Donny squeezed my hand. This time, my tears were cleansing. When I was done I felt lighter. And prouder of my dad than I could say.

Donny stayed the night, sleeping in Ma's room. The next morning he had to get back to the city, but before he left, he was nice enough to call and get me out of school for the day. I still felt shaky and emotional from the day before, and I couldn't face the accusing stares and comments from the kids and teachers. He promised to call me later in the evening to check on me, and I knew that Mrs. Duncan would be over at some point, too.

I sat around for a couple of hours, restless and anxious while I channel surfed, but I couldn't seem to get into anything on TV.

I kept thinking about what Donny had said about my dad. He never turned his back on his brothers in blue, and he had the heart of a hero. I sat for a while in his recliner, staring at his photo. He hadn't ignored the call for help when it came. He'd taken action. He'd made the hardest of choices. And I didn't think he'd approve of the fact that I was sitting here doing nothing when I could take action, too.

With new resolve, I went upstairs to shower and change, and I even did my hair. Then I went back downstairs, left a note on the back door for Mrs. Duncan in case she came by to check on me, and headed out.

I rode to the bus stop and took the 110 bus to downtown Grand Haven. After the driver helped me get my bike down from the rack in the front of the bus, I rode to the bureau offices. Locking my bike to a small tree, I walked inside, but I had to pause on the first floor to collect myself. My heart was hammering, and I was shaking with nerves. I had to take a couple of deep breaths before I could go up the stairs and into the offices. The receptionist behind the desk was very nice, and after I told her who I wanted to see, she pointed me to a chair and I waited.

After about two minutes, Agent Faraday came to the front, wearing a curious expression. "Madelyn?" he said, looking around the lobby. "Where's your uncle?"

"He's not here."

Faraday frowned. "I can't talk to you without your uncle present."

I squared my shoulders. "Yes, you can."

He squinted at me. "Oh? Are you waiving your right to counsel?"

I shook my head. "I'm not here to talk about the case, Agent Faraday. I'm here to talk about something else."

Faraday studied me, and I could feel the receptionist sneaking surreptitious glances at us over the top of her computer monitor. "Okay," he agreed. "Come on back."

I followed behind him and reminded myself to breathe. I'd asked to speak to Agent Faraday because, between him and Wallace, I thought Faraday might be the more open-minded.

I knew that Donny would be furious with me for coming here, and I also knew that I might be risking my own freedom by entering the lion's den, but Stubby needed me, and I knew I had to convince Faraday that I was telling the truth about seeing deathdates. If I could get him to believe me about that, then maybe I could get him to believe me about Stubby. It was a long shot, I knew, but it was the only thing I could think of that might help my best friend.

Faraday led the way to his office, and we took our seats— him on one side of the desk, me on the other. "You feeling better?" he asked, and I could detect a note of guilt. It made me feel a little more secure about deciding to ask for him instead of Wallace.

"I'm okay."

Faraday nodded and leaned back in his chair. I could tell I'd sort of thrown him by coming here. "So what brings you by, Madelyn?"

"Will you do me a favor, Agent Faraday?"

"Depends on what the favor is."

I sighed wearily. Why were adults so exhausting? "Can you please call me Maddie?"

His eyes narrowed, his guard never really coming down.

"I think I can grant that favor," he said after a moment. "So, what brings you by, Maddie?"

I looked at the mug shots on his wall. The ones I'd written on were still there. "I want you to test me."

Faraday stopped rocking in his chair, and those eyes narrowed again. "Test you?"

"You don't believe that I can see what I can see, right?"

Faraday tapped the arm of the chair. "You mean about the deathdates?"

I nodded.

"No," he said bluntly. "I think you're full of it." Glancing over his shoulder to the wall behind him he added, "I think that was a neat trick, though. What I can't figure out is if your uncle put you up to it, or if you came up with it on your own."

I smiled. It was good to have that out in the open. "Okay. You don't trust me or believe me. Then how about if *you* design the test? That way you'd see I'm telling the truth."

"Test you?"

"Yes, sir."

Faraday snorted. "And how can I test you, Maddie? Until someone dies, there's no way to prove you see what you say you can."

"Sure there is. Show me any photograph of any person you know who's died, and I'll tell you the exact day they passed away. And make sure the photos don't come from anybody famous or that you think I could access online. Make me look at only those photos of people you're sure I couldn't know. And time me."

# 12-03-2014

I HUNG OUT AT THE GRAND HAVEN LIBRARY FOR A few hours, then at a coffee shop down the street from the bureau offices, my knee bouncing the whole time. I was anxious to get the test over with, and as customers came in, I found myself staring at their foreheads, making sure I could see every single deathdate. I could, of course, but it still reassured me in spite of the macabre nature of it all.

At two forty-five I left the coffee shop and headed back to the bureau. The receptionist told me that Faraday had told her to walk me back when I arrived, so I followed behind, even though by now I knew the way. Faraday was on the phone, his back to us, and from his posture, I could tell he was angry. "Jenny," he growled, "if he wants to live with me, then he can live with me!"

The receptionist came up short and looked around uncomfortably. She cleared her throat, but Faraday didn't seem to hear her. "Then I'll get a bigger place," he barked.

Faraday pursed his lips. I could tell he was intrigued. "Time you?"

"Yeah. Give me a nice, thick stack of photos, and only, like . . . five minutes to get through them all."

Faraday seemed to think on that for a bit. "I'd want to watch you while you went through them," he said, as if that was something I'd balk at.

I made sure to look him in the eye. "No problem."

"And you'd have to give me all your electronics," he added.

I reached into my back pocket and pulled out the new cell phone Donny had gotten for me. Placing that on his desk in a silent challenge, I sat back in the chair and waited for him to decide.

"I'll want to film it, too, and if you get one date wrong, Maddie, you lose and I get to use this little demo in court."

I held his gaze. "Deal."

Faraday sat forward. "Okay," he said, and I could see that he thought he finally had me exactly where he wanted me. It made me a little nervous, because I didn't know what tricks the feds could pull to make me look guilty, but I was in it now, and no way was I backing out. "Give me until this afternoon to pull it all together. Let's say around three."

I reached out for my phone to check the time. It was ten A.M. "See you at three o'clock, Agent Faraday." And then I left him to his task.

"The custody agreement says we have *joint* physical custody, and if he no longer finds living with you to be the *pleasurable* experience I remember, then of course he can move in with me!"

I glanced around. From what I saw, everyone within twenty feet of us could hear Faraday going off on what appeared to be his ex-wife, and they were all carefully keeping their gazes averted, pretending not to hear. It was a joke.

The receptionist cleared her throat very loudly once more, and Faraday's posture stiffened. He peeked over his shoulder at us and said, "I gotta go. We'll talk about this later." As he was setting the phone down in the cradle I could hear the high-pitched voice of his ex yelling at him through the receiver. I felt sorry for their kid caught in the middle.

"You're back," he said as if he hadn't been expecting me to be on time.

The receptionist smiled awkwardly and said, "Agent Faraday will take it from here." She then made a hasty retreat back down the corridor.

"If you're not ready . . ." I said.

"It's fine. Come in." Faraday motioned me forward, and I walked into his office, noticing that most of the items on his desk had been removed. What had been a surface cluttered with paper and files and picture frames was now clear of everything except the computer monitor and a stack of papers about a quarter-inch thick. On the top sheet of paper was a color copy of an old man, surrounded by balloons. He seemed to have a slight resemblance to Faraday.

On the far side of the room were several photo albums, some looked quite old, and on a tripod was a camera aimed right at the desk. I ignored the camera and started for the chair but Faraday held up his hand. "Your phone, Maddie?"

I pulled it out of my back pocket and handed it to him. Then I stood with raised eyebrows until he motioned for me to sit down. Once I took my seat I looked around the desk. "I need something to write on. And something to write with."

Faraday turned his computer screen all the way around so that the back was facing me before he reached into his desk and pulled out a set of sticky notes and a pen. "Write the date on the sticky note and put it on the photo," he instructed. He then held up his phone and said, "Do you want me to count it down?"

Taking up the pen and setting the pad of stickies in front of me, I couldn't help but smile a little. "Sure."

"Three . . . two . . . one."

I got to work.

The stack was interesting. Most of the pages were color copies of what I assumed were family photos. Some of them contained more than one person, but within that group there was always at least one person circled, and I knew that was who Faraday wanted me to focus on. I didn't spend more than five seconds per photo—that's all it took. I simply looked and wrote down the date. Toward the middle, I saw that Faraday had tried to trip me up by circling the photo of a mature woman—taken at least several decades before—who was still alive. And would be for three more years. I wrote down her date, and next to it I also scribbled *Nice try*.

Other than that, only one photo really stood out. It was the image of a boy around ten or eleven with a big gap between his two front teeth. He was grinning ear to ear and wore a shirt with an oversized collar. His deathdate was 1-21-1974. There was something eerily familiar about him, but I couldn't put my finger on it, and as I was worried about the time, I forced myself to move on.

After clearing through the deck I set the pen down and stood up. Faraday seemed surprised. He looked down at his phone. "You still have two minutes."

I shrugged. "Don't need them."

He eyed the stack of photos with sticky notes neatly attached, like he didn't quite know what to do next.

"I'll wait in the lobby while you grade the photos." And without another word I moved out of his office and headed to reception.

Faraday left me to sit there for a very long time; nearly an hour and fifteen minutes went by before he came down the hall looking for me, and when he did, he seemed stunned. I had to be very careful to hide the satisfied smirk that wanted to work its way onto my lips.

He crooked his finger at me, and I followed him once more to his office. There he shut the door and sat down. I noticed at the top of the stack of photos was the picture of the young boy with the gap in his teeth. "How're you doing it?" Faraday asked after a long pause.

I shrugged. "It's something I've always been able to see."

He squinted at me, those eyes so focused, like he wanted to figure out the magic trick.

"It's not a trick," I told him. "It's real."

Faraday sat back in his chair and ran a hand through his hair. "I've been over it and over it, and there's no way you could know these dates," he said. "I mean, some of these family members died eighty years ago in Ireland."

I shrugged. "I've been trying to tell you."

Faraday picked up the photo of the young boy. "Know who this is?"

I shook my head.

"He's my little brother."

That shocked me.

"He drowned when I was thirteen. We didn't even know he'd gone to the pond that day. He wanted to play hockey like me. He got onto some thin ice and fell through. I was the one who found him."

I squirmed in my chair. "I'm sorry."

He nodded absently and set that photo aside only to pick up the next, which was the photo I'd called him out for—the one of the woman who hadn't died yet. "This is my great-aunt Ginny. She lives in Dublin. She's ninety-seven, and she's always said she wants to live to see a hundred. You have her dying on the eighteenth of March, twenty seventeen. That's the day after her one hundredth birthday, and it'd be exactly like Aunt Gin to check out the second she's made an appearance. She does that at parties, too."

I couldn't help give into the smile that quirked at the edges of my lips. "So now you believe me, right?"

Faraday scratched his head, still staring at the two photos on his desk—the ones of his brother and his aunt. "I watched you like a hawk," he said softly. "You never even looked up. You went through a stack of forty photos of people I *know* you've never heard of or seen before, and you couldn't possibly have researched any of them, and still you didn't miss a single photo. Ginny was supposed to trip you up, Maddie. And if she didn't, then I pulled pictures out of other agents' family photo albums, too. Even if you had researched my entire family, I know you couldn't have randomly guessed the dates of these other people."

Faraday then pointed to the camera. "We had an expert in body language watching you, too," he said. "An FBI profiler in D.C. who's the best in the business says he can't explain how you could do that, but your body language suggests you're not writing down these dates from memory. He says there would have been a momentary pause as you went through each photo to recall the face and the date from your memory—and you didn't pause once except with Aunt Gin, and he thinks that's because you realized I'd tried to trip you up."

Faraday reached down to pull out a folder and laid it on the desk. Flipping it open I could see several photographs— many of them were of Stubby and me from the Jupiter game. "It's never quite fit," he said, scratching his chin. "Agent Wallace and I have been round and round on this. From the first interview with Mrs. Tibbolt, she claimed that you never actually came out and threatened her or her son, only that you had predicted he'd die the following week.

"And we interviewed several other clients of yours, too, Maddie. It's taken us a few weeks to compile a list of them, but the one that really bugged us was Pat Kelly. Remember him?"

I nodded. He was a man I'd read for only a few days before all of this started. He'd been very nice to me, even after I'd given him the bad news.

"He says that he'd come to see you on the twelfth of October. His name was right before the Tibbolts' in your notebook, which is why we were interested in talking to him. We asked him what you'd said, and he told us how you'd predicted he'd die in May. He then told us that he'd just come from his doctor who'd given him six months to live. Kelly swore he didn't tell you or in any way hint to you that he had pancreatic cancer. I looked him over real good, Maddie, and I couldn't tell that he was sick. The guy seemed healthy as a horse."

As Faraday spoke, I didn't interrupt. I simply let him work through it, waiting for the moment when he'd finally tell me that he believed me.

Faraday pivoted a picture to me, and I saw it was of me and Stubs, sitting in the stands at the Jupiter game, both of us smiling broadly and looking so happy. I realized either Wallace or Faraday had taken the photo from their seats in the stands, and they'd inadvertently captured the last time Stubby or I had been that carefree.

"Truthfully, Maddie," Faraday continued, "you and Arnold don't fit the profile for two serial killers."

Faraday's admission left me stunned. "Then why have you been so focused on us?" I demanded.

He sighed heavily and ran a hand through his hair. "We have to follow the evidence," he said. "And there was a lot that pointed to the two of you."

"But there has to be stuff that points away from us, too," I insisted, and for emphasis I waved my hand at the stack of photos that proved I'd been telling the truth all along.

Faraday shrugged, then nodded. "The same guy in D.C.

who watched you zip through the photos sent me the psychiatric profile this afternoon of the person he thinks killed Payton Wyly and Tevon Tibbolt, and I've just had a chance to read it," Faraday continued, and he reached for a manila folder at the side of his desk and opened it. "The report says that Wyly and Tibbolt were definitely killed by the same person, and that person was likely to be a lone white male between thirty and fifty-five. A guy with a whole lot of repressed rage. A guy with sick fantasies but above-average intelligence. He's likely to be adept at keeping secrets, and is very good about hiding in plain sight. He likely has a good steady job, one he's had for years but secretly hates. He's someone who has a distorted view of himself, a guy who thinks he's above most people, and he has a hard time making lasting social connections. He takes his rage out on kids in their teens because he seems to have some sort of sick vendetta against them. They represent some sort of trigger for his anger, and he vents that anger at them by torturing and killing them. My profiler ends the report by saying that it's highly unlikely either you or Arnold is the murderer."

I felt rush of relief, but I didn't want to say anything more to stop the momentum Faraday was building, so I simply let him continue.

Faraday put the file down and lifted another photo. "I keep coming back to this," he said. The image showed me squinting at Payton, a look of shock on my face, and next to me, Stubby was gazing at the pretty cheerleader with shy fascination and adoration. His cheeks were flushed, and he had this hopeful smile on his face. He looked boyish and sweet—not sick in the head. Faraday tapped Stubby's image.

"He doesn't look like anything but a love-struck kid," he said, mirroring my thoughts. "We had a psychologist sit with him, and nothing about that interview came back with any hint of violence or repressed rage. Just the opposite, actually. According to our guy, Arnold's IQ is at genius level, but he's humble about his intelligence. And although he struggles a little socially, he doesn't seem to hold it against anyone. So either Schroder's the greatest young con man we've ever met, or he really is a shy, smart kid who tried to warn a pretty girl that she had a date with death on her birthday. And maybe he's also a good friend who wants people to believe in you so that mothers don't have to bury their sons."

I found myself nodding. "I swear," I told him. "That's all it was, Agent Faraday. Stubby would *never* hurt Payton or Tevon. He's the nicest kid you've ever met. He was trying to find a way to save them both."

Faraday reached back into his drawer and pulled out another file, this one secured with a thick rubber band. "I have to turn this over to your uncle today," he said. "It's all the evidence we've collected against Arnold. One of the biggest pieces of evidence we found at both Tevon Tibbolt's crime scene and Payton Wyly's is a set of size twelve boot prints. It's pretty muddy on the banks of the Waliki River, and we found those boot prints all over the place, leading up to the road.

"It's always bothered me that Schroder wears a size nine shoe, and we searched his closet. He owns four pairs of sneakers and one pair of leather loafers. No boots. I thought we had him when we found his dad's boots in his mom's closet, but they're the wrong size, too, and the wrong tread."

I nodded; Donny had told me the same thing. Plus, Stubby would never wear any shoe he couldn't skateboard in. I said that to Agent Faraday and he grunted, tapping the folder on the edge of his desk like he was thinking deeply. Then he set it flat on his desk again and pointed to it. "This also includes a copy of that file your uncle gave us—the one of the kid in Willow Mill who was murdered. Guess what was found there?"

"Boot prints?" I guessed.

Faraday nodded. "Yep. Size twelve. Hell, even my guy in D.C. admitted to me on the phone today that he thinks it's the same killer for all three kids. Cigarettes found at the scene of Carter's murder match the type found at the other two scenes, but the DNA on all the cigarettes rules out both you and Schroder."

I blinked. "I thought it would take a long time to get the DNA back?"

Faraday lifted his eyes from the folder. "Carter's case was submitted back in August. The results came in last week, so we had the cigarettes from the other two murders expedited through the federal lab, which isn't nearly as backed up as the city labs. The results came in while I was grading your stack. Turns out none of the DNA matches you kids, or the blood on the knife, which turns out to be Schroder's. And yet, all the cigarettes were used by one lone individual who apparently has never had a criminal record, because his DNA isn't in our system."

I closed my eyes. I felt a mixture of relief and also anger. "Why?" I whispered.

"Why, what?" Faraday replied.

I opened my eyes. "If you knew all of this, why are you still keeping Stubby in jail?"

Faraday sighed, but at least he had the courage to hold my gaze. "We had to be sure, Maddie. And like I said, a lot of this just came in, and so much of the early circumstantial evidence pointed to you two."

"Are you sure now?" I asked, crossing my fingers.

He shut the file, but I could tell immediately that he wasn't going to give in quite that easy. Pointing to the file again he said, "Like I said, Maddie, I'm going to give that to your uncle. He'll file a motion to have the case against Schroder kicked out for lack of evidence, and while he's doing that, we'll have a talk with the DA and tell him not to fight it."

It was a long time before I could say anything. At last I stood up and whispered, "Thank you, Agent Faraday. Thank you very much."

"Don't thank me, Maddie. Until we catch this guy, we'll continue to keep an eye on both you and Schroder."

I pressed my lips together and looked at the floor. "Okay. I guess that's fair."

There was a knock on Faraday's door, and I lifted my chin to see Agent Wallace standing there with his coat on and a somber expression. "We got another missing kid, Mack."

Faraday paled. "When?"

Wallace glanced warily at me but kept talking. "Call just came in. A thirteen-year-old from Poplar Hollow was supposed to meet his mother at their house at three fifteen for a doctor's appointment. Kid never showed and was last seen leaving school about ten minutes before three."

Faraday glanced at his watch. "It's only twenty after four," he said. "Is she sure he didn't just forget?"

"The kid asked his teacher if he could leave class five minutes early so he could make it home in time. The mom started calling his phone over and over, and then she went out to look for him. She said she heard his ringtone and found his cell on the sidewalk—but no sign of him."

"Name?" Faraday asked.

"Nathan Murphy."

I sucked in a breath.

"You know him?" Faraday and Wallace both asked me.

"Sort of," I said. "I used to babysit for his little brother."

Faraday stood and eyed me keenly. "You remember his deathdate, Maddie?"

I shook my head. "I don't. But I don't think I ever met him. I mean, I only babysat for the family when Nathan couldn't watch his little brother."

Faraday got up and grabbed his coat from the hook in the corner of the room. "Call your uncle. Tell him that we'll want to talk to the two of you in a few hours."

I started to shake my head. "It wasn't me! I've been here the whole time, Agent Faraday!"

He shrugged into his coat and put a hand on my shoulder. "I know. Go home for now and tell your uncle that we'll need to see you in a couple of hours, and he should be present. I'll call him with the time."

And with that, Faraday and Wallace swept out of the room.

Donny was so furious with me that he hung up in the middle of the conversation. He arrived at the house red-faced and still so angry that I didn't know if I should let him inside. "Open the door!" he yelled from the back step.

I took a deep breath and undid the lock. He barreled in and gripped me by the shoulders. *"Do you know what you've done?"* he roared. *"How* could you have gone down there without me?"

I waited while Donny paced back and forth in the kitchen, yelling about how anything I said to Faraday could be used against me, and how I'd now be lucky if he could keep me out of jail, and how I'd likely jeopardized Stubby's freedom, too . . . and then his cell rang. "What?" he snapped, not even bothering to look at the caller ID.

His expression changed within half a minute as he listened to the caller. "Thanks for calling, Barb. That's great news." He hung up and tapped his chin with the phone, his eyes faraway until he turned his gaze back to me, but now he didn't appear at all angry—merely stunned. *"What* did you say to them?"

"Nothing, Donny, I swear. I just had Faraday test me."

Donny scratched his head. "Yeah, well that must've been a hell of a test, Maddie, because that was the assistant DA. She's dropping the case against Arnold. He'll be free to go after they process the paperwork, which should be sometime tomorrow."

I felt a smile burst onto my face, and I was about to rush forward to hug Donny when his phone rang again. This time he squinted at the caller ID before answering. "Donny Fynn," he said crisply.

I waited through the short call to learn that it was Faraday. He was ready to meet and wanted us to come down to the bureau offices as soon as possible. Donny told him he'd be there as soon as he could.

"What do you think they want?" I asked.

"Faraday didn't give me any specifics except to say that he thought we could help."

"Do you think it's a trap?" I asked, more because Donny looked very worried than because I didn't trust Faraday. The truth was, after sitting with him in his office and seeing that he'd been true to his word about telling the DA to drop the case against Stubby, I thought I could finally trust the agent.

"A trap?" Donny repeated. "I'm not sure, kiddo, but if you don't want to go, we won't. It's up to you."

I thought about it for a minute before I made up my mind. "Let's go. But if you think they want to try and trap me, don't let me talk."

Donny eyed me through half-lidded eyes. "Like that's worked so well before."

"Sorry," I said. "I had to, though, Donny. Stubby really needed my help, and I was the one who got him into this mess in the first place."

Donny sighed and came over to give me a brief hug. "For the record, Maddie, you didn't get anyone into this mess. Stubby decided all on his own to go see Payton. And if I recall, you told me you even tried to warn him about contacting her."

"It's still not his fault," I replied stubbornly.

Donny eyed me soberly. "It's not yours, either."

We made it to the bureau offices before six. Donny had called Mrs. Schroder on the way over, and I'd heard her happy sobs through the phone. Donny promised her to have his office call the jail and hound them until Stubby was released the next day. "I'll try and get it expedited as quickly as I can, Mary Anne."

When Donny hung up I realized he was a little emotional, too. For such a tough guy, my uncle had a really sweet soft spot.

We met Faraday and Wallace in Faraday's office. They motioned for us to sit, and then Faraday took out a photograph and slid it toward me. It was a picture of a kid a couple of years younger than me with light blond hair and hazel eyes. I didn't recognize his face, but I knew I must be staring at Nathan Murphy.

"This is weird," I said, looking up at the agents.

"What?" Faraday said.

"You want me to tell you if he's dead, right?"

Faraday nodded, and after a quick glance at Donny—who nodded, too—I said, "His deathdate isn't until July twelfth, twenty seventy-seven."

They both seemed surprised. "Then where is he?" Wallace asked.

Donny sat forward, probably sensing a trap, but I shrugged. "I have no idea."

Wallace frowned. "I thought you were psychic?"

I sighed because I'd been through this with him before. The whole thing had such a weird déjà vu quality about it, except for the fact that Nathan was going to live another sixty or so years. "I can only see his deathdate. Nothing else."

Wallace's frown deepened. "Do you get anything off the photograph?" he pressed.

"What else would she get off it?" Donny snapped. "She's already told you the only thing she can see is his deathdate."

Wallace got defensive. "Hey, man, she's the one that wants us to believe she's got these abilities, not me, and how the hell am I supposed to know how all this freaky-deaky stuff works?"

"You're the ones calling us to the table!" Donny shot back. "She's been honest with you from the start, and all you did was throw her best friend in jail and put her under the microscope for the past couple of weeks. The least you could do is to have a little respect for her abilities, Agent Wallace."

Faraday held up his hands in a time-out gesture. "Hey!" he said sternly. "Can we agree to play nice for the remainder of the interview?"

Donny and Wallace both shut up, settling for glaring hard at each other.

Faraday looked from one to the other as if to make sure there'd be no more outbursts, then he focused on me. "See, the thing of it is, Maddie, we're pretty sure Nathan was abducted. A woman walking her dog said she thought she heard a kid yelling, and turned to see a man hurrying to get into a pickup truck and drive away at a high rate of speed. She didn't put it together until a neighbor told her that a kid two blocks over was missing."

I sat forward. "A pickup truck?" A cold prickle began to snake its way up my spine.

"Yeah," Faraday said. "Why? Does that mean something to you?"

My mind flashed to all those incidents when I'd seen a dark pickup truck follow me or drive down my street.

"What is it?" Donny asked, and I realized I hadn't spoken in a few seconds.

"A couple of weeks ago when I was out looking for Ma, a pickup truck chased me into the park, then the driver tried to cut me off at the other end, but I got away."

Donny nearly came all the way out of his chair. "*When* was this?" he demanded. I could see the fear on his face, and I wished I'd told him sooner.

"About three weeks ago."

"Did you see the driver?" Wallace asked, but my mind drifted to another incident with what I was sure was the same vehicle.

"No, but then I think I saw the truck again about a week later."

Faraday pulled a yellow pad out of the drawer of his desk and took up a pen. "Where?"

"It drove down my street."

"Did you get a plate number?"

I shook my head. "I was never close enough to read it."

Faraday continued to scribble as he asked me, "What color was the truck?"

I shook my head. "I don't really know. Every time I saw it, it was night. I think it might've been dark gray? But what I remember most was that it had this loud engine."

"That fits with what the witness told us," Wallace said.

Faraday looked up at me from his notes. "Are those the only two times you've seen this truck, Maddie?"

I shrugged. "Yes?"

"You don't sound sure," Faraday said.

I sighed. "The truth is that I don't know, sir. I mean, this past weekend I thought I saw the same truck on my street."

"What day and what time?"

"Saturday, around four A.M."

"Jesus!" Donny hissed, running a hand through his hair and shaking his head. I had a feeling I was going to get another lecture later.

Faraday tapped the pen against the pad of paper. "You know what I don't like?" he said to me.

I squirmed. Did he think I was lying?

"I don't like that three of these victims seem to have a sort of loose connection to you, Maddie, and now we learn there's been a mysterious truck cruising by your house and stalking you at the park."

Donny opened his mouth to protest, but Faraday held up his hand. "I'm not accusing her, counselor. I'm trying to tell you someone seems to have a fascination with your niece."

I felt a chill run through me. "Maddie," Faraday continued, "do you think you might know this guy?"

I shook my head, thinking he believed I knew who was abducting and killing these kids. "No, sir!"

"When did you say you babysat for Nathan's younger brother?" Faraday asked next, and I could tell he hadn't given up chasing the lead.

"Last summer. But it was only a couple of times, and then I went to Florida with Uncle Donny, and school started after that so I didn't have time to sit for them anymore."

"Did you know Rob Carter? Or anyone related to him?"

Again I shook my head. "No. I swear."

Wallace scooted his chair forward. "Have you met anyone recently who's given you the creeps?" he asked. "Or anybody who might be upset with you? Like a client who didn't get the news they were hoping for?"

I opened my mouth to say no, but then I really thought about it. "Actually, there're a couple of people."

Faraday's brow rose. "A couple?"

"Yeah. It's been a rough few weeks with this investigation and stuff."

Faraday hovered his pen over his pad of paper. "Can you give me their names, Maddie?"

A sideways glance at Donny told me it was okay. "Well, for one, there's this really creepy teacher at school. He drives a pickup truck, too."

"Who?" Faraday pressed.

"Mr. Chavez. He's my math teacher and he walks me to fifth period every day, but he's always right on my heels when we walk down the halls, like he wants to make me feel uncomfortable. And sometimes I hear him mutter mean things about me under his breath."

"Hold on," Wallace said, leaning forward himself. "He walks you to fifth period? Why would a teacher escort you to class?"

Donny cleared his throat. "Maddie had some trouble at school from both the students and the administration ever since word got out that you guys searched her home in connection with the murders of Payton and Tevon."

"Ah," said Faraday, and I could tell that made him feel a little bit bad. "You say his name is Chavez?"

I nodded. "Last week I heard him mutter something

about being ticked off at me for getting Principal Harris fired."

"You got the principal fired?" Wallace repeated again.

Donny held up his hand. "For the record, she didn't get the principal fired. The superintendent looked into the matter of Maddie being bullied, and found Principal Harris culpable. He may have even encouraged the abuse."

Faraday's eyes darkened and he turned to me. "He did?"

I squirmed. "I think Harris really thought I was guilty. You know, 'cause you guys came to the school to interrogate me in his office, and then you arrested my best friend, and the news said that Stubby might've had a female accomplice."

Faraday sighed and made a note. "Do you know what kind of car Harris drives?"

"A black SUV," I said. "I also saw him drive by my house last week."

Donny's face turned crimson. "Please be kidding," he said.

I shook my head. I was certain I'd seen him that same night I went out on the front porch to think and get the mail.

"Are Chavez and Harris friends?" Faraday asked.

"I don't know," I said honestly.

"Do either of them smoke?" Wallace asked.

I recalled the smell of nicotine on Mr. Chavez's breath as he walked me to class. "I think Mr. Chavez does."

Faraday made a few more notes before flipping the page. "Anyone else giving you trouble, Maddie? Or just these two?"

"There's Mario Rossi and Eric Anderson," Donny suggested before I had a chance to answer.

"Who're they?" Faraday asked as he scribbled fast.

"Two kids at Maddie's school who roughed her up in a stairwell. They've been suspended."

Faraday's hand paused when Donny said the words *roughed up*. He then pressed his lips together and without looking up he asked, "Any idea what kind of car they drive?"

I thought back. "Mario sometimes drives his mom's Jeep to school. I don't think I've ever seen Eric driving a car."

"Anyone else?" Faraday said, his hand once again skipping across the page.

I thought about Cathy and Mike. They were always giving me a hard time, but I seriously doubted either of them was capable of murder. And then someone else came to mind. "Well, there was Mr. Kelly's son," I said, recalling an angry phone call Ma had taken after I'd met with Mr. Kelly, the man with pancreatic cancer. "Ma got a call from him and he said that he was super mad at me for convincing his dad that there was no hope."

"Why the hell didn't you tell me this, Maddie?" Donny barked. I could tell he was getting really upset that he knew only half of what'd been going on with me.

"He called before any of this started," I said, feeling my cheeks redden. "And mostly he yelled at Ma and hung up. He thought I'd talked his dad out of getting treatment to help fight the cancer."

"Did you?" Wallace asked.

That took me by surprise and put me on the defensive. "No!"

Wallace shrugged, like he didn't care if he'd offended me or not. "Okay, if you say so."

I glared at him and turned away. "Is there anybody else?" Faraday asked, when the room fell into uncomfortable silence.

I briefly entertained the idea of mentioning the creepy furniture delivery guy, Wes, but discarded it. He might've rattled me with his leers, but I didn't think he was especially interested in me. He probably looked at most women like that. Plus, Wallace had really put me off with his comment and his attitude, so I shook my head.

Faraday made a final note and said, "Thanks, Maddie. We'll check all this out and be in touch."

# 12-04-2014

NATHAN MURPHY WAS FOUND AT TWO A.M. I couldn't sleep and heard Donny's phone go off. Tiptoeing to the doorway of my bedroom, I listened to Donny on the phone with someone, and then I heard the floorboards creak when he got out of bed. "Did I wake you?" he asked, seeing me in the doorway.

"I heard your phone."

Donny still had it in his hand. "Sorry," he said. "They found Nathan in the woods."

I stiffened. How had I been wrong? His deathdate had been right on his forehead like everyone else's. How had I misread it?

Donny yawned and rubbed his face. "He's alive, but he was hit hard enough over the head to fracture his skull. He was disoriented and fighting off hypothermia when somebody in one of the nearby houses heard him crying for help. They've got him at the hospital, but his brain is starting to swell and they had to put him into a medically induced coma. That was Faraday on the phone. He thought we should know."

I realized I'd been holding my breath, and I let the air out of my lungs in a rush. "He'll make it," I assured Donny, who grinned sideways at me.

"Yeah, that's what Faraday's been telling Nathan's parents. He says he thinks his confidence is helping to calm them down."

I leaned against the door frame. "I want this to be over, Donny."

"We all do, kiddo. I'm heading downstairs for some of Mrs. Duncan's pumpkin cheesecake. You want to join me or go back to bed?"

I followed Donny down the stairs, and we sat up most of the rest of the night eating cheesecake and talking about my dad. Donny told me all the best stories of him that I'd already heard before, but it was still nice to listen to them anyway.

At six thirty Donny eyed the clock over the mantel and said, "I've kept you up all night, and now you've got to get to school and I've got lots to wrap up today starting with getting Stubby out of jail."

I frowned. "Can't you call me off school again?"

Donny cocked his head at me. "What's going on with you? Are they still giving you trouble down there?"

I shrugged. "Not outright, but Principal Harris getting fired didn't exactly win me any votes for prom queen."

Donny chuckled. "Maddie, this'll all be over soon. Faraday and Wallace will catch this sick bastard, and then you and Stubs will be exonerated and it'll all go back to normal."

"What am I supposed to do until then?"

Donny put a hand on the side of my head. "Until then, you hold your head high, 'cause you're a Fynn, and that's what your dad would've told you to do." I looked doubtfully at him, and he added, "And I'll make a call to the superintendent and tell her that you're still having a hard time. Maybe she can talk to your teachers again."

I nodded, but I didn't hold out much hope. Then I thought of something else. "What about Ma?"

Donny's gaze dropped away from me. "Yeah. That. I got a call yesterday that she's well enough to leave the hospital today, so after I deal with Stubs, I'll go see your mom and talk to her about taking the plea deal. Then I gotta get back to the city to focus on my paying clients."

Something about how my uncle wouldn't meet my eyes when he talked about Ma bothered me. "What?" I asked him. "What's bugging you about Ma taking the plea deal?"

He picked up our dishes and carried them to the sink. "I want your ma to choose you, Maddie. I want her to finally find the strength to enter rehab and choose you over her addiction."

I felt something fragile inside me crumble a little. "You don't think she will."

Donny stared out the small window over the sink. "She may not, kiddo. And if she doesn't, then you and I are gonna have to have a serious talk about where you're going to live. I haven't pushed the subject as much as I could've in the past because I saw Cheryl's deathdate on the drawing you made when you were little, and I've always known the both of you realize she doesn't have a lot of time left, but, Maddie, enough is enough, and I'm not leaving you up here alone to fend for yourself."

What Donny didn't realize was that I'd pretty much been fending for myself ever since Dad died.

After school Donny called to say that he'd be home late, but he had two pieces of good news for me: Ma had agreed to enter rehab, and that day at noon Stubby had been released from jail.

I'd barely hung up with Donny before I was out the door and racing over to the Schroder's. Panting hard, I rang the doorbell and bounced from foot to foot, so anxious to see Stubs that I could hardly stand it. "Maddie!" Mrs. Schroder exclaimed when she saw me. "Oh my, please come in!"

I entered and looked around the corner, expecting to see Stubby sitting on the couch, playing a video game on his Xbox. But the living room was empty.

"He's upstairs," his mom whispered. "He's resting."

"Resting?" Stubby never rested. He wore everybody else out.

Mrs. Schroder was smiling, but it was forced and her eyes were pinched with worry. "He's been through a very difficult time, honey."

"Can I see him?"

She looked up the stairs, as if she were wavering. "All right," she finally said. "But, Maddie, you should know that Arnold isn't quite himself. As I said, he had a terrible time in that prison."

I promised I wouldn't upset him, and hurried up the stairs. Stubby's door was closed, so I knocked. There was no answer. I knocked again, and still nothing. "Stubs?" I said, knocking a third time and trying the handle. I opened the door a crack. "You in here?"

The room was silent, and I wondered if he had his earbuds in and couldn't hear me, but as I took a peek into the room I found him lying on the bed facing away from me, and no sign of his iPod. "Stubs?"

"What, Maddie?"

His tone was flat and lifeless. If I'd heard him talk that way on the phone, I'd have no idea who it was. "I came over to say hi," I said, unsure about going into his room.

"Okay. You said it."

I stood there stunned and not sure what to say or do. For several seconds I simply looked at him, lying there but shutting me out. "I . . . I missed you."

Stubby didn't reply, but after a moment he rolled over to face me, and my breath caught. He had two black eyes, and his nose was so swollen it didn't even look real. Also, the fingers poking out of his cast were purple with bruises.

"Oh, God!" I gasped. "Stubs . . ."

"I'm tired," he said, his tone still lifeless.

I felt tears sting my eyes, and I blinked furiously to keep them at bay. "Yeah. Okay. I heard you got out, and I—"

"I'll talk to you later," he said, rolling over again—away from me.

I nodded even though I knew he couldn't see me. Still, I wanted to try to break through to him . . . to show him that we were still best friends. "I'll pick you up for school tomorrow," I said, then hesitated to see if he'd reply. When he didn't, I backed out of the room and shut the door quietly.

Mrs. Schroder met me at the bottom of the stairs. Wring-ing her hands she said, "Did he talk to you?"

I was too choked up to speak, so I simply shook my head and prayed she'd let me go before I lost it.

Her own eyes misted. "Oh. All right, Maddie. Maybe he'll be better tomorrow."

I swallowed hard, nodded, and hurried to the door.

The next morning I set out early to pick Stubs up for school. When I arrived at his house, however, his mother answered the door and said, "I'm sorry, Maddie, but Arnold isn't up for going back to school quite yet."

"Oh," I said, taken aback and wishing I could talk to him again, but Mrs. Schroder was standing protectively in the doorway like she was guarding Stubby from the whole world—even me. "Maybe Monday?"

"Of course, honey, but call first, okay?" And then she shut the door in my face. I was pretty stunned to be staring so abruptly at the closed door, and it took me a second to let it go as nothing more than Mrs. Schroder being overly protective. As I got on my bike and wheeled it out to the street, I happened to pass the Schroder's trash can, set out for garbage pickup. Sticking out of the top was Stubby's prized skateboard.

I paused to stare at it, and then I turned and looked up toward Stubby's window. I couldn't be sure, but I thought I saw a flicker of movement behind the curtain. With a heavy heart, I headed off to school.

I tried calling Stubs after school, but his phone went

straight to voice mail, and then I remembered that Faraday and Wallace had confiscated my old phone and hadn't given it back yet—maybe they still had Stubby's phone, too.

So I called the Schroders' residence, and his little sister, Grace, picked up. "Hi, Grace, can I talk to Stubs?"

"Hold on," she said, and I could hear her heels clapping down the hallway. I heard her tell her brother that I was on the phone, and he muttered something I didn't quite catch. "He doesn't feel like talking," his little sister said.

I swallowed hard. He was still shutting me out. "Yeah, okay, Grace. Thanks. Please let him know that if he wants to call me later, he should try this number. It's my new cell."

"Okay," she said. Then she hung up like a typical seven-year-old, assuming the conversation was over.

I sat on the edge of my bed for a long time and stared at my phone. Stubby was my only friend. I missed him so much it hurt. And I couldn't imagine what I'd do if he shut me out permanently.

Donny arrived from the city in the late afternoon, and he took me and Mrs. Duncan out to eat.

At dinner he let me know that Ma was going to be transported to the rehab center the next day. "If she does well, we'll be able to see her around Christmas."

I was so relieved she was getting help, but still, Christmas felt so far away.

On the way home, Donny said, "I've gotta go back to the city in the morning and grab some files from the office. I think I'm gonna work out of your house as much as I can for the next few months."

I squinted at him. "You trying to keep an eye on me?"

He rubbed the top of my head playfully. "Someone's got to."

I knew what he meant even though he didn't come right out and say it. The whole county was worried about this killer on the loose, and Donny wanted to stick close to me until he was caught.

And even though there was a patrol car parked out in front of our house when we got home, I felt really glad to have him in the house.

# 12-06-2014

THE NEXT MORNING WAS SATURDAY, AND I SLEPT IN. When I finally got up, I found a note from Donny on the kitchen table saying that he'd headed to the city and he'd be back by late afternoon. He also added that he wanted me to stay in the house until he got back. I rolled my eyes at that part.

The home phone rang around ten A.M. and, puzzled by the caller ID, I picked it up with a wary "Hello?"

"Maddie?"

"Yeah?"

"It's Agent Faraday."

"Oh, hey. What's up?"

"Can you and your uncle come down to the office this morning?"

"Uh . . ." I said. "Donny's in the city." Faraday didn't reply right away so I added, "Is something wrong?"

"No, no ... I only wanted to fill you two in on what we've turned up so far."

"I can come down," I volunteered.

There was a chuckle on his end of the line. "What do you think your uncle would say to that?"

I grinned. "He'd be royally ticked off, so let's not tell him."

Faraday chuckled again. "Yeah, okay. Can you be here by twelve? We'll talk and then I'll treat you to lunch."

"Sure."

"Good. Oh, and, Maddie, do you have any cash on you to take a cab?"

"A cab?"

"Yeah. I don't want you riding your bike over here. I want you to call a cab. I'll reimburse you and make sure you get home safe after lunch, okay?"

That was weird. Still, I agreed and called for a cab to meet me at my house at eleven thirty. It was interesting how, just a little while ago, Agent Faraday had thought that I was this terrible person, and now he wanted to treat me to a cab ride and lunch.

I showered and changed into a sweater and jeans, then met the cab and arrived at the bureau offices at about quarter to noon. I waited in the reception area and took in the busy office, teaming with agents and men and women in uniform. I guessed that it was all hands on deck as the whole city searched for the killer.

I heard Faraday's voice from the corridor ask loudly if anyone had heard from Agent Wallace, but I didn't hear anyone say they had. And then he came around a corner and spotted me. "Hey," he said, crooking his finger. "Come on back."

I followed him to his office and he pointed me to a seat. His desk was again piled high with clutter. There were the usual stacks of paper, but also other items like a pair of torn and bloody jeans encased in an evidence bag, and a pair of familiar-looking boots that looked brand-new. There was a yellow tag dangling off the shoelace on one of the boots.

Faraday must have seen me staring at them, because he lifted the boots and said, "Remember those size twelve boot prints we found at the crime scenes?"

"Yeah?"

"From a pair of Timberlands exactly like these. I recognized the tread 'cause I recently bought a couple of pairs myself."

My brow rose, and then something really weird happened. I remembered seeing a pair like those recently, but where? And then an unbidden suspicion came to my mind, which I immediately and firmly rejected. Faraday took his seat and said, "How've you been?"

His question threw me. "Uh... fine, sir. Thanks."

"Good," he said, leaning forward to rest his elbows on the desk. "We think we found another clue, Maddie. And it has to do with you." Faraday lifted a few articles of the clutter from his desk, searching for something, and he finally came up with a familiar-looking notebook. My pulse quickened. "First, I have a question for you."

"Okay..." I tensed, afraid again that I'd been lured into a trap.

Faraday opened my deathdate notebook to the middle

and swiveled it around so I could see. Tapping at one of the names he said, "A lot of these have the letter *C* in front of them. Can you tell me what that means?"

"It stands for client," I told him, feeling a blush touch my cheeks. I'd never talked about my notebook openly with anyone but Donny and Stubby, and it felt weird to discuss it now.

Faraday turned it back around and grunted. "That's what I thought." After flipping a few pages he stopped on a page near the end and said, "Do you remember talking with a Silvia DeFlorez?"

I cocked my head. "Who?"

"Silvia DeFlorez. She came to see you in July. She was about to undergo a biopsy, and as breast cancer runs in her family, she wanted to know what she was up against. You predicted her deathdate to be June twenty-third, twenty forty-eight."

I didn't remember. Maybe it was because I was starting to really worry if I'd made the right move coming here without Donny. Faraday was thumbing through the pages of my notebook, and then he lifted his eyes to me and his expression became puzzled. "You okay, Maddie? You look pale."

"Why are you asking me about her?" I demanded, feeling defensive because I didn't know what he was getting at.

Faraday cocked his head. "Maddie, I'm not accusing you of anything. If that were the case, no way could I bring you in here without your uncle."

I let out a breath. "Sorry," I said. "I guess I'm a little flinchy."

"It's okay," Faraday said, getting back to the notebook.

"Well, it turns out that DeFlorez used to be Silvia Carter. Rob Carter was her son."

I was stunned. "Wait, what?"

"Silvia DeFlorez Carter was your client. Her son was murdered. Patricia Tibbolt was your client. Her son was murdered. You and Schroder tried to warn Payton Wyly about her deathdate. She was murdered. You babysat for the Murphys. Their son was abducted and nearly murdered."

My mouth went dry, and that familiar chill began to creep up my spine. I believed him when he said he wasn't accusing me, but I also wondered what his point was. "What're you trying to say?" I asked hoarsely.

Faraday stared at me. "I'm trying to tell you, Maddie, that whoever this killer is, I believe he's obsessed with you. And I'm now convinced that he's also been stalking you and your clients. You're connected to each of these kids—loosely in one case, but still connected, and it worries me."

"Why would someone do that?" I asked. I shivered as that chill spread out from my spine to the back of my neck and along my scalp.

"I don't know. But this is one sick bastard we're dealing with, and right now you're our only link to him."

"Did you check out Mr. Chavez?" I asked. I was suddenly desperate for Faraday to find out who was responsible.

He nodded. "Yep. We checked out Chavez, Harris, and Kelly. Chavez admitted to being a jerk to you—something I doubt very much you'll ever have to worry about from him again as he got a pretty good lecture from us—but he swears he had nothing to do with driving by your house or stalking you. Of course we checked out his alibis, and it turns out Chavez works the four to eleven shift at a bar not far from here. The bar has a security camera, which shows him working on all the days when the kids were abducted. Plus, he's got a size eleven shoe.

"Harris also has a pretty good alibi. His mother's in the hospital with pneumonia, and he's been there practically every day since he got suspended from his job. Before that, he had several witnesses placing him in a variety of administrative meetings or at the school at the time the abductions occurred. He was helping to paint the gym on the day Rob Carter went missing—so he's been eliminated as a suspect."

"And Mr. Kelly's son?"

"Jack Kelly works for his dad at their law offices in Parkwick. It's a pretty big firm, and we've got more eyewitnesses than we know what to do with vouching for him on the days the kids were abducted. Plus, he and his dad left for New Zealand right before Thanksgiving, which means he couldn't have abducted Nathan Murphy. So Kelly's out."

"Mario Rossi and Eric Anderson?" I was grasping at straws now.

Faraday shook his head. "They also alibi out, Maddie."

I was feeling worse and worse as Faraday talked. "Then who could it be?"

He sighed. "We have another lead that we're still trying to check out."

"Who?"

"Do you know a Mr. Pierce at your school?"

I blinked. "He's my chemistry teacher."

"He drives a dark gray pickup truck," Faraday said. "We noticed it in the faculty parking lot when we went to check out Chavez."

I looked at Faraday like he had to be kidding. "Mr. Pierce is one of the only teachers who've been nice to me during all of this," I said defensively.

Faraday nodded. "Wallace and I have an appointment to interview him later today, but I doubt it's one of your teachers."

"Then who?" I repeated.

Faraday dangled the notebook from his fingertips. "I think it's someone in here."

I stared at the notebook. There had to be at least a thousand names and dates in there. I'd kept it for years and years, and I'd talked to dozens of clients and had written down the names and dates of everyone I'd ever met.

"So what I need from you, Maddie," Faraday continued, "is for you to think hard. Have any of your other clients ever gotten upset by what you've told them? Have they ever threatened you? Threatened to hurt you or get even with you?"

I sat there trying to think, sifting through the vaguest of memories I had about any of my clients who could've overreacted, but no one was coming to mind other than Mrs. Tibbolt and Mr. Kelly's son.

"It's likely this would have been a client you saw last summer, in the weeks before you went on vacation with your uncle."

I sighed. I could barely remember the clients I'd read in October, much less the previous summer. I tried not to hold them in my memory, actually. That was the whole purpose of the notebook, to write their names and deathdates down so that I could move on and forget them.

"I can't think of anyone," I said at last. And that was the truth.

Faraday nodded. "Okay. But keep thinking on it over the next couple of days for me, will you? Someone may come to mind."

Faraday was still dangling the notebook, swinging it back and forth between his two fingers when he said, "You ready to go to lunch? Wallace was supposed to join us, but I think he's out running an errand or something...."

At that moment, the notebook slipped out of Faraday's fingers, and it knocked over a stack of files, which slid into the picture frames he had arranged at the edge of his desk. We both reached out to grab them before they hit the floor, and I managed to catch one that tipped toward me.

As I caught it, my eye happened to fall on the image. It was a photo of Faraday and Wallace, their arms slung across each other's shoulders as they shared a beer together at what looked like a barbeque.

The photo caught me completely off guard, and for a long moment all I could do was stare at it, openmouthed. "Maddie?" Faraday said. "What is it?"

I showed him the picture and pointed to Wallace. "He... his... his numbers are all wrong!" Across Wallace's forehead were the numbers 12-6-2014.

Faraday's brow furrowed. "What numbers?"

But I was so shocked I could barely talk. I reached out and grabbed the deathdate notebook. Turning to one of the last pages, I scrolled down to the line marked *Agent Wallace 8-7-2051,* the date I remembered seeing from the first time we met. Pivoting the page around I showed him the line, and then I pointed to the photo. Again, I couldn't contain a gasp. Before my eyes, Wallace's deathdate went from 12-6-2014 back to 8-7-2051 . . . and then back again. "It keeps flipping!"

Faraday leaned forward and looked back and forth between the photo and the name in the notebook. "Maddie," he said firmly, "I don't understand. Please take a breath and try to tell me what you're seeing."

I stared hard at Wallace's image. The two deathdates kept flicking back and forth between 2014 and 2051, and I couldn't make sense of it. It had never happened before. "I . . . I don't know how to explain it!"

"Please try," Faraday said. I could hear the worry start to creep into his voice.

I stood up and went around his desk, still holding onto the photo. "Agent Wallace's deathdate should be August seventh, twenty fifty-one. But right now it's changed. It's showing something different!"

"What's it showing?" Faraday asked, peering at the photo in my hands like he was trying to see what only I could.

"It's flipping back and forth between that date and today, Agent Faraday. *Today!*"

Faraday's face drained of color. "Son of a bitch!" Seizing his phone he dialed quickly. He waited several seconds before he said, "Kevin, it's me. Call me the second you get this message."

He then hung up and dialed again, waiting before hanging up and trying a third and a forth time. "Damn it! He might not answer my first call if he was in the middle of something, but he'd never let a second or a third call go by."

I continued to monitor the picture. Wallace's deathdates kept switching back and forth, and I had a terrible feeling that, at that very moment, Agent Wallace was either hovering near death, or he was in terrible danger.

Faraday jumped to his feet and scooted around me. Hurrying out into the hallway, he motioned for me to follow him. I brought the picture along, and we went into the open area where all the cubicles were. Faraday silenced the room with one loud piercing whistle. "I need to hear if *any* of you knows where Agent Wallace is right now!"

Every person in the room simply stared at him with wide eyes. No one volunteered anything. But then one woman, sitting at the far end of the room, raised her hand. "I passed him on the way in," she said. "I asked him if he was headed home for the day, and he said that he was going to check on a lead."

"What lead?" Faraday demanded.

She shook her head. "I'm sorry, sir. He didn't tell me."

Faraday turned and pointed to a man wearing glasses in the opposite corner. "Steve! I need you!"

He put a hand on my upper arm to bring me with him. I walked along beside him, continuing to look at the photo. "What's it say?" Faraday asked, as we headed back toward his office.

"It's the same! It keeps flickering back and forth."

Faraday took us past his office down the hall to another door, which was locked. He stopped and pulled me to the side and said to the man following us, "Open it, Steve. Now."

Steve fidgeted nervously, but Faraday stared him down until he produced a key card and slid it through a slot right above the handle. There was a green light, and then Faraday was turning the handle and moving into the office. After switching on the lights he looked around Wallace's desk—which was as cluttered as his. He moved behind the desk and jiggled the mouse and it asked for a password. "I need in," Faraday said to Steve.

Steve's face flushed. "Sir, I don't have proper authorization for—"

"Screw proper authorization!" Faraday roared. "I need to see what lead Kevin was working on before he left!"

But Steve wasn't budging. "S-s-s-sir," he stammered. "I need the director to authorize that."

*"Then go call the director!"*

At that moment, another agent poked his head into the office. "I heard you're looking for Wallace?"

We all snapped our heads toward him. "You know where he is?" Faraday asked.

"Maybe. He said he was talking to a couple of people in Poplar Hollow who said they'd noticed a delivery truck parked down the street from the Murphy house the day before the kid was abducted. Wallace said it matched a similar statement taken by someone in the Wyly kid's neighborhood, so he was gonna look into what deliveries were made to anyone in the area on those days."

"Did he mention the name of the delivery company? Was it UPS or FedEx?" Faraday asked, his voice straining to remain calm.

The man scratched his head. "Neither. I think it was a furniture store."

I put a hand to my mouth. "Oh, my God..."

"What? *What?*" Faraday demanded.

I looked again at Wallace's photo. The flickering back and forth was slowing down, and, alarmingly, the 12-6-2014 date was starting to settle in for longer and longer periods between flashes. "Mrs. Duncan... my neighbor," I said as I began to tremble. "She gets new furniture, like, all the time. And it's always the same guys who bring it. This one guy, Wes, he's seriously creepy, and the last time he was at her house, he sort of leered at me."

"What's his last name?" Faraday asked me. I shook my head; I didn't know. "What's the name of the furniture store?"

I shook my head again. I'd seen that truck a half dozen times, and I'd never registered the name. And then I had an idea. "Call Mrs. Duncan! She'll know!"

Faraday asked me for the number as he picked up the receiver on Wallace's desk. I leaned over and dialed it for him. After a few seconds, I knew she'd answered, because Faraday said, "Mrs. Duncan, it's Agent Faraday with the FBI. I've got Maddie Fynn with me, and we have a very important question for you. Can you please give us the name of the store where you buy your furniture?"

Faraday grabbed a pen and scribbled onto a sticky pad. "Culligan's Furniture," he said. "Got it, thanks." He hung up with Mrs. Duncan and dialed 411, requesting the warehouse of the furniture company. He put the phone on speaker so that we could all hear as it began to ring.

"Culligan's warehouse," said an older man's voice.

"I need to talk to one of your delivery guys, first name Wes," Faraday said, without even introducing himself.

"He ain't here," the man said, clearly annoyed.

"Is he out on delivery?" Faraday pressed.

"No."

Faraday sighed impatiently. "Then where is he?"

"Dunno," the man replied. "But I ain't his answering service."

"Listen," Faraday said, his tone sharp as a razor. "This is special agent Mack Faraday. I'm investigating a series of murders, and I need to know—"

"Yeah, sure you're a special agent," the man interrupted with a snort. I could tell he didn't believe Faraday. "What are you, double-oh-doofus?" And then he snorted again and hung up.

Faraday's face turned crimson, and he squeezed his free hand into a fist and pounded the desktop. Steve, who'd been standing next to me jumped and muttered, "I'll go call the director and get your authorization, sir." And with that he ran out the door.

Faraday looked at me. I pointed to Wallace's photo. "It's starting to settle more and more on today!" I whispered.

Faraday grabbed up the phone again, redialing 411 but this time he asked for the address of the warehouse for the furniture store. After hanging up, he turned to the other agent who was still hovering in the doorway and said, "I need to put a trace on Wallace's phone."

"It'll take me at least an hour," the man said.

"Do it!" Faraday snapped, then grabbed me by the elbow

and backtracked to his office to grab his coat. Tossing me mine, he paused and said, "Will you come with me and keep watching the photo?"

I nodded, and we were out the door in a rush.

Faraday drove like a madman, weaving in and out of traffic so much that he started to make me nauseous. "Is he still alive?" Faraday asked, taking a turn so fast that the tires squealed.

I looked down. The numbers continued to flicker back and forth, but more slowly. It was almost like a pulse getting slower and slower. "Yes, he's alive," I told him. "But I'm not sure for how much longer."

Only a few moments later, we arrived at Culligan's warehouse. Faraday pulled up to the large bay door and ordered me to stay in the car. He then ran to a man bent with age, who was standing in the entry. I rolled down my window so I could hear, and watched Faraday flash his badge and then get right up into the old man's face, pointing at him and yelling that he was going to arrest him for obstruction unless he told him where he could find Wes.

The old man waved his arms a lot, clearly unafraid of Faraday. "I told you on the phone, pal, that I don't know where the hell that lowlife is! He never showed up for work today, okay? And the other half of his crew called off sick! Says he's got chest pains...My aunt Fanny, he's got chest pains!" My mind flashed to the memory of Rick sitting next to me on Mrs. Duncan's couch, his deathdate prominently hovering above his forehead, and I was shocked to realize that today was his deathday. With a pang, I knew that Rick had been right; it'd be his heart that would give out on him.

"Always something with them two!" the old man continued angrily. "Most unreliable crew I got!"

Faraday balled his hands into fists and looked like he was ready to pick the man up and shake him for information. I felt I had to do something so I jumped out of the car and rushed over. "Does he know where Wes lives?" I asked, trying to distract Faraday from violence.

The old man turned to me. "He lives on Thirteenth Street," he said, waving his hand in the general direction of the street behind us.

"What house number on Thirteenth Street?" Faraday barked.

"How the hell should I know? You want me to pull his file, that's gonna take me a while. They're at headquarters with HR."

"What's Wes's last name?" Faraday growled.

"Miller," the old man spat.

And before Faraday could turn away I asked, "Do you know what kind of car Wes drives?"

The old man turned large impatient eyes at me. "They're hiring kinda young down at the FBI," he said, but then he added, "He drives a pickup. A Ford F-150."

"Is it a dark color like gray or charcoal?" I pressed, the adrenaline coursing through my veins making my heart pound.

"Yeah," he said. "It's black. Why, you seen him?"

I didn't answer; Faraday and I simply turned and ran back to the car. He threw it into gear, and we peeled out of there. "Buckle up!" Faraday yelled, as I was pulled hard to the right by the force of his hairpin turn.

While I struggled to get myself strapped in, Faraday pushed a button on his dash. A woman's voice came on the line. "Grand Haven FBI, Agent Butler speaking."

"Christine!" Faraday yelled. "I need an address for Wes Miller on Thirteenth Street in Grand Haven!"

We heard nails clicking over a keyboard then, "Six-eight-six Thirteenth Street, and, sir?"

"Yeah?"

"Wes Miller has a record. Convicted of three counts of sexual assault and two counts of rape in twenty ten. Sentenced to six years in Sing Sing. It looks like he only served three and a half."

"When *exactly* did he get out?" Faraday growled, baring his teeth as he wound through traffic.

"July tenth, twenty fourteen, sir."

Faraday snuck me a glance, and then he gripped the steering wheel even tighter. "Christine, I need you to send every available agent to that address. Code ten-seventy-eight and a possible ten-fifty-two. Tell everybody we've got an ANA!"

There was an audible gasp, and then she said, "On it, sir!" The line went dead and Faraday clicked the dash again to end the call.

"What's ANA?" I asked, feeling helpless and anxious.

"Agent Needs Assistance," he said distractedly. "We only use it when one of our guys is in serious trouble."

I looked again at the photo. It was taking longer and longer for the 2051 date to come back onto Wallace's forehead. I was so worried that we weren't going to be in time.

Faraday screeched to a stop in a run-down neighborhood in a bad section of Grand Haven. He jumped out of the car almost before it'd come to a complete stop and raced to his trunk. There he got out a bulletproof vest and threw it over his head, latching the Velcro sashes. He then moved back to the open door and leaned into the car, across my legs, to pop open the glove box. He pulled out a carton of bullets and a gun clip, then slammed the glove box closed again and began to load his gun. "You're to stay put, Maddie," he said, his voice level and firm. "Under *no* circumstances are you to get out of this car. Do you understand?"

"I understand," I said, so scared I was trembling.

In the distance I could hear sirens. Lots of them. They seemed to be coming from all directions. Faraday finished with his gun, pulled back on the barrel to load the chamber, and with one last firm look at me, he shut the door.

I had the urge to call out to him to stop—I felt a terrible foreboding, but he was already across the street, running over to a white house with peeling paint and a rickety-looking porch. I watched him creep up the steps and ease his way over to the window while gripping his gun with both hands. Faraday peeked into the window, then pulled his head back. He crouched and ducked low under the pane to stand up on the other side and peek in again.

The sirens drew nearer and I whispered, "Please, please, *please* . . . wait for them!" But he didn't. Faraday moved more agilely than I would've expected, and slipped over the railing to the brown grass. He then darted around the side of the house, and I lost sight of him.

For several seconds nothing happened, and I waited and watched with bated breath. Then, almost as if a curtain had been pulled back, all sorts of cars with flashing lights appeared on the street. The tires screeched, and the sirens cut out almost instantly, but the strobe lights continued to flash. Cops emerged from their vehicles with guns drawn and vests on. They descended like a dark blue swarm on the house, and I found myself crouching low in my seat. A few agents went up to the door, others stayed on the lawn, and still others went to the right and left of the house.

For a moment, nobody moved except to make eye contact with one another and signal back and forth with their hands. In that small window of silence, I heard a slight buzzing sound coming from the dashboard, and when I could pull my eyes away from the scene outside I looked down and saw a police radio set under the dash. Quickly I reached over to turn up the volume, and as my thumb and forefinger made contact with the knob, everyone on Wes's lawn flew into action. The door to his house was kicked in and several people darted inside. My fingers turned the knob and the interior of the car erupted with sound. It was like everyone was screaming at once. "Ten–fifty-two!" someone shouted. It was so gravelly that I couldn't tell if it was Faraday or not. *"Ten-fifty-two, ten- fifty-two, ten- fifty-two!"*

And then at the door of the house, all of those agents and officers who'd gone inside came rushing back out as if the house was on fire. Suddenly, amid all the shouting I heard, *". . . gas! GAS! GET OUT! GET OUT!"*

I put a hand up to cover my mouth as the most unnatural sound reverberated from inside the house right before a giant ball of flame came shooting out, and windows and sections of the roof literally blew up in a huge, deafening explosion that cracked the glass on the driver's side doors of Faraday's car. Officers and agents threw themselves to the ground, and I dove down onto the seat, too. Bits of debris pummeled the roof of the car. and I shrieked at every thump. Shouts from the radio were drowned out for only a second or two before picking up again, this time at double the intensity. I found the courage to lift my head and peek over the rim of the door out the window, and the scene was chaotic. The house was fully engulfed in flames, and one of the patrol cars was on fire. All around, agents and officers were scrambling to help one another get away from the house. People in neighboring houses began running out of their homes to see what was going on, and those agents and officers on scene tried in vain to wave them to get back inside.

I waited and watched, unable to believe my own eyes and fearing the worst for Agent Faraday. Had he been at the back of the house when it exploded? If he had, he was probably dead. Without taking my eyes off the scene, I felt around for the photo of Faraday and Wallace. That'd let me know if both men were still alive, but it wasn't next to me or under me. It must've gotten tossed on the floor when I dove for cover.

And then, as if a prayer had been answered, Faraday appeared with singed shirt, carrying Wallace with two other agents. I saw a lot of red on Wallace's chest, and I grabbed the photo, which had, in fact, fallen to the floor. Pulling it up, I realized that his numbers were still flickering back and forth—but 2051 was now getting more play. He was still alive, and I thought he'd make it if they could only get him to the hospital in time.

As if on cue, an ambulance pulled up and Faraday shouted to the two men helping him—who were also a little singed—to move toward it. Two paramedics jumped out, and within seconds they had Wallace on a gurney and were putting him into the ambulance bay.

More sirens sounded in the distance and I knew that the fire trucks were on their way.

The moment the ambulance took off, Faraday limped his way over to me and pulled open the door. "What's the picture say?" he demanded, his face, clothing, and hair smudged with soot.

"I think you got to him in time. His numbers are still flickering, but the twenty fifty-one date is a little stronger now."

Faraday jumped in the car, and without another word he put it into gear and headed off in the direction of the ambulance.

I peered behind me. "Should we really be leaving?"

"They can handle that mess for now," Faraday said, pressing his foot to the accelerator.

When we reached the hospital, Faraday's phone was going off repeatedly. He ignored it. After parking in an illegal zone, he flashed his badge to a hospital worker, who looked like she might protest, and pulled me over to the ambulance, which was parked with the back doors flung open. Faraday went right over to the gurney where Wallace was being unloaded, and ran alongside it when he was wheeled inside. "Kevin!" he yelled. "Buddy, you gotta fight! You hear me? You gotta fight and stay with us!"

I hurried along behind the gurney but was soon crowded out by emergency room staff. Faraday was finally tugged away by a woman in scrubs who grabbed him by the elbow and tried to get a look at a bad cut on his arm. "It's fine," he said moodily, trying to shake her off.

She lifted up his elbow. "You need to let them work on your friend without you in the way. *And*, in case you hadn't noticed, you also need stitches." She tugged him back down the hall toward me. "Don't make me sedate you!" she snapped when he resisted.

I had to work to suppress a smile. Faraday caught my eye and motioned to me with his chin. I followed him and the nurse to a curtained area. The minute he was seated on the gurney he said, "He'll need blood. I'm O negative; I can donate to anybody. Hook me up and let me help him."

The nurse scowled. "Oh, you FBI boys sure know how to give orders, don't you?"

Faraday was looking around wildly. I knew he was worried about Wallace. I lifted the photo, which I'd brought with me, and peered at it. "What's it say?" I heard him ask me.

Wallace's numbers were flashing less and less frequently and settling for longer and longer periods on 8-7-2051. "He's doing better," I said. Lifting my gaze, I saw the nurse eye me curiously—but she continued scrubbing Faraday's arm and prepping it for the stitches.

I waited with him while he was stitched up, and when the nurse finally left him to answer a page, I moved over to his side. I'd been keeping an eye on Wallace's photo, and I hadn't seen it change in almost two minutes. "Anything?" he asked me.

I turned the photo so he could see it. "I think you can put this back on your desk, sir. He's gonna make it."

Faraday let out a huge sigh and grabbed the photo to hug it to his chest while turning his face away from me. "He's my best friend," he said after a few minutes, lifting his gaze back to look at me. "And you saved his life, Maddie."

"Me? You're the one who found him."

"I never would've gone looking if you hadn't seen his photo. He's got a gunshot wound to the chest. That son of a bitch shot him."

I'd guessed as much from all the blood. "Do you think Wes Miller was inside the house when it blew up?"

Faraday ran a hand through his hair. It came away covered in singed black hairs. He looked at his palm with some measure of surprise before answering me. "I have no idea. They'll need to put out that fire first and then go looking for a body, but I doubt he was inside. His truck wasn't in the drive or on the street, so he's probably running for the Canadian border by now. If I was him, that's where I'd be headed."

"Can you catch him?"

Faraday lifted his phone and tapped at the screen, wincing as his injured arm moved. "Oh, we'll catch him," he said. "Or die trying."

# 12-06-2014 (cont'd)

I LEFT FARADAY TO HEAD TO THE WAITING ROOM. He came out and sat with me while Wallace was in surgery. Faraday spent much of that time on the phone getting yelled at by his boss, who was angry at him for leaving the scene. Around four thirty my own phone rang. The caller ID said it was from Stubby's house. "Dude!" I sang happily the moment I picked up. "I've missed you!"

"Maddie?" I heard a woman say.

It took me a minute to recognize her voice. "Mrs. Schroder?"

"Yes, sweetie, it's me. I'm calling to see if you've heard from Arnold."

"Uh . . . no. Isn't he home?"

I could almost feel the anxiety from Mrs. Schroder radiate through the phone. "No. No, he's not here, and I don't know where he's gone. I came home from the grocery store with Sam and Grace, and Arnold wasn't in his room and he didn't leave me a note."

"Maybe he's out boarding," I said, and then I remembered that Stubby had thrown away his skateboard. "Oh, wait," I added.

"He threw his skateboard away," Mrs. Schroder said, and then she sniffled. "He's been so depressed lately, Maddie. I'm very worried about him."

"Maybe he went for a walk or something."

"That's why I'm worried. With that killer still on the loose . . ."

I wanted to reassure Mrs. Schroder that the FBI knew who the killer was and that he was probably on his way to Canada, but I didn't know that for sure. The truth was I had no idea where Wes Miller was. He could be roaming the streets looking for unsuspecting teens to abduct, torture, and kill.

"Maybe you should go look for him," I said.

"Will you come with me?"

I glanced over at Faraday. I didn't think he'd mind if I left to go search for Stubs, but I'd need Mrs. Schroder to come pick me up, and I didn't want to worry her about why I was there. "Sure. I'm at the hospital right now, uh . . . visiting a sick neighbor, so could you come pick me up?"

Faraday was still talking on his phone, so I wrote him a note that said I'd gotten a ride home, and he nodded and waved good-bye.

While I was waiting for Mrs. Schroder, Donny called me. "Hey, kiddo," he said with a weary sigh. "Man, have I had a day!"

I smirked. I could bet him I'd had more of one but decided to tell him about it later. "What's up?" I asked.

"My car broke down. I had to get it towed and the guy can't work on it till Monday."

"Are you staying in the city?"

"Yeah. But I don't want you in that house alone. You go over to Mrs. Duncan's house and spend the night, okay?"

I rolled my eyes. "Sure, Donny," I told him because I didn't want to argue and possibly make him mad enough to rent a car and drive up to babysit me when he really needed to deal with his car.

"Good. I'll call you in the morning."

Stubby's mom pulled up then, and I waved to her as I clicked off with Donny.

Mrs. Schroder had Stubby's two siblings with her, and they were making a racket in the back. Her face was creased with worry. "We'll find him," I promised.

We started our search in Poplar Hollow, going street by street from the Schroder residence out toward my house and beyond. We tried the park, and the school, and then it started to get dark.

I didn't get seriously worried until about seven o'clock, when we still saw no sign of Stubby. We got Grace and Sam something to eat and continued our search, but he was nowhere.

At last we headed back to the Schroders' and I helped put the kids to bed, then I waited with Stubby's mom in the kitchen, willing him to come home, but the hours ticked by and there was still no sign of Stubs.

When I couldn't take it anymore I got up from the

kitchen table and said, "Mrs. Schroder, does Stubby still have that scooter in the garage?"

She nodded and wiped her eyes. She'd been crying steadily now for over an hour. "I checked. He didn't take it."

"Can I borrow it?"

She gave me a puzzled look and I explained. "There's one place we haven't looked where I think he might be. It's over in Jupiter."

"Take the scooter, Maddie," Mrs. Schroder said. "But please be careful. There's a helmet on a hook in the garage. You have to wear that. And please call me if you find him?"

"I will," I promised, and she fished around in a drawer for the keys to the scooter. Taking them from her, I hurried out.

It took me only about ten minutes to make it over to Jupiter, and then I had to crisscross through a neighborhood to the skate park, which was always well lit until eleven at night. I'd had a thought that, even if Stubs hadn't gone there to skateboard, maybe he'd gone to watch the other boarders.

As I pulled up into the lot, I saw one lone kid zipping up and down the ramps. I knew immediately who it was.

I reached into my pocket and called Mrs. Schroder. "I found him," I said.

"Oh!" she cried. "Oh, Maddie! Where is he?"

"He's at the skate park in Jupiter. I'll bring him home in a little while."

After hanging up with Stubby's mom, I sat on the scooter for a long time and watched my best friend whiz up and down on what appeared to be a brand-new board, doing twists, turns, and other tricks.

Something had changed in Stubby—he was far less

clumsy and stiff on the board. It was as if he'd lost the fear of screwing up and was committing himself to every stunt, as if he didn't care what happened. That courage proved to be exactly what he needed to land the trick.

When I was so cold I was starting to shiver, I walked over to the ramp. Stubby flew up the opposite side, flipped his board around with his feet, landed perfectly, and whizzed back down out of sight only to reappear at the top of the ramp closest to me and land his board on the rim. I looked at him in amazement as he grinned down at me—his eyes still black and blue and his nose swollen, but grinning all the same. "Mads!" he exclaimed, clearly happy to see me—and I knew that my friend was back.

"Nice board," I called, pointing to his new ride.

He stepped off of it and onto the rim of the ramp, then did a little kick with his foot, and the board flipped up to land neatly in his left hand. "I got it today!" he gushed, already moving toward the stairs.

I waited for him at the bottom. "Your mom's been worried sick about you," I said when he landed next to me in the grass.

His face fell and he eyed the skyline. "Aw, man! How late is it?"

"It's after ten."

Stubby's jaw dropped. "It is not!"

I showed him the display on my phone and he palmed himself on the forehead. "I lost track of time," he said. "Is she really mad?"

I handed him my phone. "Better ask her yourself."

Stubs talked to his mom for a bit, and mostly he just said

he was sorry over and over, and then he asked her if it was okay if he and I went to McDonald's 'cause he was starving. She told him to be home by midnight, and once he hung up he grinned at me again. "Crisis averted."

Stubs drove us to McDonald's, and we sat in a booth and joked and laughed like old times. I told him about what'd happened earlier at Wes Miller's place, and Stubby was so amazed by it all that he made me tell him a second time. It was after eleven by the time we left the restaurant to get home before Stubby's curfew.

Stubs dropped me at my driveway, and I handed him his skateboard and he strapped it to the scooter with a bungee cord he kept in his seat. Then he saluted and was off again.

I watched him go with a wistful sigh. It felt so good to have my friend back. I turned toward my house and thought about what Donny had said. Looking at Mrs. Duncan's darkened windows, however, convinced me not to wake the old woman. Plus, the patrol car was parked between my house and our neighbor's on the other side. I could faintly make out the dark outline of the police officer inside, and I waved to him and headed up the drive.

As I rounded the corner of the house I sniffed the air. Something smelled familiar—then I realized: it was cigarette smoke wafting toward me. When I got to the back door, I saw that the kitchen light above the stove was on and the back door was open. Only the storm door was shut.

I opened the back door tentatively, the smell of cigarette smoke growing stronger. My first thought was that Ma had somehow escaped rehab and had come home. My heart lifted. I missed her so much. "Ma?" I called excitedly, stepping into the kitchen and shutting the back door before locking it. I heard the noise of a throat clearing from the vicinity of the living room.

"Ma?" I called again, hurrying to the doorway between the kitchen and the living room.

The orange glow of a cigarette butt caught my attention immediately. A figure was sitting in Dad's chair, lifting the cigarette to their lips and making it glow bright.

"Ma?" I asked one more time, as a whisper of alarm snaked up my spine.

I started to back up, but then the light next to the chair was flicked on. "Hey, Maddie," Rick Kane said.

My breath caught in my throat as my mind filled with questions. What was Rick Kane doing in my house? How had he gotten in? Had he heard about his cousin? Did he know that Wes had nearly murdered an FBI agent? Did he know that Wes had also murdered all those kids? And hadn't he called off work because he'd been having chest pains? How had he survived?

While all my questions tumbled over each other in my mind, Rick stood up, and a smile spread slowly across his face. But it wasn't a nice smile. It wasn't the smile he'd offered me each time we'd met. This was a sick smile— similar to the one his cousin had worn. Sinister and dark, but perhaps even more evil. This was the smile of a serial killer.

"No," I stammered, backing up as my mind started to put it all together with a thousand synapses firing all at once, like the finale of a fireworks display. It'd been Rick. All along, it'd been Rick. And now, here he was. In my house. Stepping forward to kill me, too.

I took another step back and began to turn, intending to run, but Rick came at me so fast I barely had time to react. In an instant, he had me twisted around with my right arm pulled up behind me and his free hand pressing hard across my throat, cutting off most of the oxygen.

I struggled, but he pulled up harder on my arm, and I would've screamed in pain if I'd had any air. "Ah, ah, ah, Maddie," he said softly . . . tauntingly. "If you struggle, I'll hurt you so much worse than if you don't."

I shut my eyes; tears were leaking out of them and streaming down my cheeks. Rick eased up a bit on the pressure of my arm and at my throat, and I sucked in a lungful of air. I was about to scream when I felt a sharp prick at my neck. "Scream, and I'll cut your throat," he said.

I held back a sob and more tears flowed down my cheeks. "Why?" I gasped. He'd been so nice. He told me I'd helped him by giving him a year to prepare and take care of his family in the event of his death.

"Why?" he repeated. "Well, Maddie, that's an interesting question, isn't it? But I think you deserve an answer, so I'm going to tell you." Rick pivoted me toward the mantel, and my gaze landed on the photo of my dad.

"See, when I first came to see you," Rick began, "and I heard what you had to say—that I'd die on December sixth, twenty fourteen—well, I believed you meant it. Like I told you before, I've got a few health issues, and I figured it was perfectly logical that I'd bite the dust at fifty-three. My dad died at fifty-five, and I've got an uncle who kicked the bucket at forty-nine, so it runs in my family.

"And like I also told you, I decided to get all my affairs

in order and make sure my family was well provided for, and I did all that, Maddie. I did it all. But then those dark cravings that I'd fought against my whole life started to crop up again, and I had an amazing thought. I was going to die soon anyway, right? Why not act on some of those thoughts? I've wanted to my whole life, you know. And I wondered what it'd be like to stop trying to be someone else and instead let me be me. So I did. And I can tell you it's been *awesome*."

I was so scared that I felt light-headed.

"I considered choosing you, you know, as my first. I mean, you gave me such a gift, I wondered if maybe you had more to give?"

I squeezed my eyes shut and shuddered, and Rick squeezed me tighter. "But we both know I didn't pick you first, Maddie. I wanted to, but I thought it might be too easy to trace your death back to me. So I watched your house and waited, and one day I followed a woman home. And wouldn't you know it? In her house was the perfect little lamb.

"Oh," Rick continued, sighing pleasurably at the memory. "He was so sweet. He took such a long time to die, Maddie. It was the greatest bliss I've ever known. I thought he'd be enough. And for a while he was, but then I started to have those cravings again. So I watched your house some more and followed the lady with the fur coat to the next little lamb. And, Maddie, he was even sweeter than the first."

I was crying now in earnest, and it was hard to breathe. I desperately wanted to pass out, to shut my ears to the horrors Rick was whispering to me. How had I not seen it? How had I not guessed?

"I thought little Tevon would satisfy the cravings, but the opposite happened. They got worse. I kept thinking that you were the key, Maddie. You'd led me to this new freedom, and you kept connecting me to all the right lambs. I thought it must be kismet. Maybe if I got very close to you, I could find one that would satisfy me enough until I died."

Rick was whispering into my ear, and he ran his cheek along mine seductively. I stiffened, and my stomach lurched. I squeezed my eyes shut even tighter and tried not to be sick, but I could taste the bile at the back of my throat.

He continued as if he hadn't noticed. "That kid you hang out with, he looked interesting. So I followed him for a day, and he led me to the girl...Payton. She was so ripe for the picking that I couldn't resist. I set up a roadblock and snatched her right off the street. But she died too fast— hardly worth the effort. The cravings started right back up. I thought again about taking you, but then I missed you that night at the park. So I decided to go back to the summer when I trailed you to your babysitting job."

I stiffened again, and Rick laughed. "Ah, you didn't know I was watching you back then, did you? It paid off when I grabbed Nathan. I wanted to take my time with him, stretch it out over a few days, you know? I wanted to get the most pleasure out of it, and I thought it'd be so easy to hide him in my hunting shack. Nathan was so scared... I didn't think he was very smart, but he was. He got away from me before I could do much damage, but I doubt he'll remember me."

I shuddered. I was so petrified it was hard to think.

"Yeah," Rick whispered, stroking my cheek again with

his. "That's it, honey. Be scared. Be terrified. I saw you downtown with the feds, and I knew you were working with them. Eventually you were going to lead them to me, but I only had a few days left to worry about. I thought I could control the cravings and wait for that heart attack, but every day the cravings got worse, even though physically I felt fine.

"I told my wife that I wasn't feeling good. I called off work a few times and watched you and the feds as much as I could. That's how I found the key to your house, Maddie. It was hidden in that fake rock by the back door. You were going to be my ultimate prize, but I didn't think I'd be able to grab you with the feds watching your house while they closed in on me. And then, I remembered you said that my cousin was going to die on the same day as me. I know what you were thinking, that we'd be in some sort of accident. But I had a better idea.

"See, Wes wasn't a very smart guy. In fact, he was pretty stupid. But he'd seen the blood in the back of the truck from that day I nabbed Payton. Wes had called off to go buy some weed, and I'd had to make the deliveries myself. He knew we were delivering in Jupiter that day, and when he saw the blood I could tell he'd put two and two together.

"So, this morning I went over to his house, and I shot him."

I made an involuntary squeak, and Rick laughed. "Yeah, I shot him in the head and then I shot that FBI agent. I saw him through the window about a second after I shot Wesley. He was too slow with his gun. Then I rigged the house to explode, and took Wes's body up to my hunting shack. I made sure to leave Wes's suicide note and his confession to the murders next to his body. They probably won't find him for months.

"Anyway, after dealing with Wes, I went to my favorite fishing spot. I figured I'd be dead in a matter of hours, so I waited. And waited. And waited."

Rick stopped talking for a long moment, and I was so afraid I didn't think I could stand it. "Do you know what happened all day today and tonight as I was waiting, Maddie?" he finally asked. I didn't answer, and he squeezed me tighter, hurting me. "I said, *do* you?"

I shook my head a fraction.

"*Nothing* happened," he spat. "Nothing at all."

With a jolt I realized what he meant. Rick hadn't died.

"All those plans," he snarled, squeezing my wrist. "All that extra life insurance, and making sure my family would be taken care of... all of it wasted. By eleven o'clock tonight I knew you'd lied to me. I knew you were wrong."

I felt cold all over.

Rick tilted my chin with his arm, and I saw that he wanted me to read the clock above the mantel. "It's two minutes to midnight, Maddie, and I'm not dead. My family isn't getting their money, and now that I've had a taste of those sweet little lambs, I know I can't stop. It's only a matter of time before your FBI buddies catch up with me, isn't it, *Maddie?*"

He snarled out my name and pulled up on my arm with a jerk. There was a loud pop, and I screamed as a pain like lightning radiated up and down from my shoulder to my fingertips.

Rick pressed his arm over my mouth to muffle the

scream. "*Shhhhhhhhh.* Quiet down, Maddie, or I'll rip your arm right off."

I squeezed my eyes shut and ground my teeth together to keep from crying out again, but it was the hardest thing I'd ever had to do. The pain was excruciating. In the back of my mind I wondered where the patrolman was. How had Rick come into the house without being seen? Why was there no one to save me?

"I know what you're thinking," he told me. "You're thinking, why doesn't Rick kill himself? That would solve all his problems, wouldn't it? But that would nullify the life insurance. My family would get zip. And here it is, Maddie, one minute to midnight, and I'm still alive."

I was sobbing so much that it was hard to breathe. I thought I was going to pass out, and I prayed for it. I wanted to black out and not hear or feel one more thing.

"I'll make you a deal, Maddie. Want to hear it?"

I didn't reply, because I couldn't. Rick started talking again anyway. "The deal is that we'll watch the time together, and if the clock strikes midnight, and I'm still alive, then I get to finish what I started with you. You get to be my next little lamb, but I'm going to drag it out for as long as I can, because people who lie about such important things, well, they deserve to feel some pain, don't you think?"

I shook my head; the terror and physical agony I felt was overwhelming. And then I heard a soft click as the big hand on my dad's clock slid over the little hand and it began to chime softly. One chime . . . two chimes . . . three chimes . . .

I realized Rick was waiting out the chimes. He'd wait until exactly midnight to begin the real torture, and I was beyond desperate. I acted without thinking. A rush of adrenaline coursed through me and I remembered a move from a self-defense class I'd taken freshman year. Wedging my hand between the blade and my neck, I let my legs go limp, sinking down in Rick's arms. He bent forward, and as he did I swiveled in a tight circle, relieving the pressure on my arm but taking a deep slice to my hand.

Ignoring the pain I focused on aiming my knee up into his groin and kicked him as hard as I could. With a loud grunt he let go of me and bent double. I took a step back, moving my weight to the other foot, and I kicked out at him again just as he swung his fist in an arc to punch me in the side of the head. We both reeled away from each other. I saw stars from the force of Rick's blow and staggering back, I lost my footing and fell, slamming my head against the window. There was a second explosion of bright sparks behind my eyes, and shards of glass clinked to the ground. Searing heat erupted at the back of my scalp. I sank to the floor, knocking over the lamp next to Dad's chair as I went.

Once on the floor, I didn't think I could move or even breathe. I lay there, trying desperately to stay conscious. Dully, I was aware that the clock had finished chiming and across the room Rick was cursing and spitting with rage. He'd tripped over the ottoman and had fallen against the opposite wall. He held his left hand up, and I saw the handle of the knife sticking out of his palm.

I struggled to take a deep breath, and as I did, some of the stars crowding my vision dimmed. I took another shuddering breath and willed myself to move, but none of my limbs would cooperate. My good arm flailed next to me, and my legs only bent at the knees. I had no strength left to fight, and then the stars started to spark again and a wave of dizziness washed over me.

*"You little bitch!"* Rick screamed, gripping his wrist and rocking in pain.

I took a third deep breath and tried in vain again to get up, kicking my legs feebly. The world was fading in and out of darkness, and I fought as hard as I could to focus my eyes. In a haze I saw Rick lurch himself to a crouched position, baring his teeth at me, and then he pulled down hard on the handle of the knife. With a loud growl he freed it from his hand and then he started for me again. "You're going to pay for that!"

I opened my mouth to scream, but only a hoarse whisper came out, and then there was a loud *BOOM* from the kitchen, like the door being kicked open, and from the light in there I saw a figure emerge. I blinked again as Rick turned toward the figure, raising the knife. I squinted through the fog and haze of my clouded vision, and suddenly, I saw my dad standing in the doorway, his black hair sleek and his blue eyes bright. He grinned at me, looking proud. Then he raised his arm to wave.

"Dad?" I croaked, drinking in the sight of him. *"Daddy!"* And then the most incredible thing happened. His waving hand made a loud popping sound. Then another. Then two more times. In front of me, Rick Kane dropped like a stone, and a red stain began to spread across the carpet like a burgundy stream.

I shut my eyes and fought another wave of dizziness, and when I opened them again I saw that Dad was gone, and in his place was Agent Faraday, holding a smoking gun. He holstered the weapon, pulled out his phone, and began to speak into it so rapidly that I couldn't catch any of the words. As he talked he moved over to Rick, kicking the knife out of his hand before bending to check for a pulse. He stood up again, clicked off the phone, and rushed over to me, stooping low to try and pick me up, but I cried out when he touched my arm.

He backed away and looked me over. "Your arm's out of the socket, Maddie," he said gently. The pain in my shoulder began to flood back, and I whimpered.

"I can put it back in," he said. "It'll hurt like hell for a second, but you'll feel a whole lot better after it's done." I nodded. If it would stop the terrible throbbing, I'd do anything.

Faraday gingerly sat me forward, lifted my arm above my head, and stood up. I was trying with all my might not to give in to a sob that would only cause more pain, and as I was concentrating on that, Faraday pulled up hard on my arm and there was a loud snap and I screamed.

Once that initial agonizing pain had faded, my shoulder felt sore, but the pain was bearable.

I realized then that Faraday was talking to me. "Maddie?" he said as he wiped the hair away from my face. "Look at me, sweetheart. Can you hear me?"

"Yes," I croaked.

"You okay?"

I nodded dully, but then a wave of emotion came over me and that sob I'd fought so hard to hold inside gushed out, and it was followed by so many more.

Faraday lifted me into his arms and carried me over to

the couch, where he held me protectively against his chest. "You poor kid," he said. "The ambulance should be here in a minute, honey." In the distance I heard the sounds of sirens closing in.

I leaned against his chest and shut my eyes, grateful to be alive.

"Hey," Faraday said after a few seconds. "Did you know your clock's still ten minutes fast?"

# 12-07-2014

FARADAY STUCK TO MY SIDE LIKE GLUE. HE RODE
with me in the ambulance even though I overheard someone tell him to stay at the house and give a statement. He'd
told that guy to stuff it... or something to that effect. He'd
said they could find him at the hospital and take his statement there.

I was so glad he came with me. I felt beaten to a pulp,
both emotionally and physically. When the ER doc ordered
Faraday to go wait in the lobby, he glared hard but muttered
something about needing to give his statement anyway. He
promised me he'd be back soon and left.

I had a long slice in the palm of my hand and a bad cut
on the back of my head that both needed stitches, and my
shoulder was X-rayed. Then they put my arm in a sling, but
the doctor didn't think there would be any lasting damage.
He said I'd be free to go home as soon as they could find
someone to drive me.

I pressed my lips together. I no more wanted to go home than I wanted my arm out of the socket again. But a few minutes later the curtain around my bed was pulled back, and Mrs. Duncan was there, wearing a coat over her night-gown and looking more concerned than I'd ever seen her.

"Oh, Maddie!" she gasped when she saw me. She shuf-fled over to my bed and wrapped her thin arms around me, hugging me very gently before stepping back. "I can hardly believe what Agent Faraday was telling me!"

My gaze dropped to my lap. I didn't know what to say, because the nightmare was still too fresh.

"And that poor patrolman," Mrs. Duncan added. My chin lifted, and I saw that her eyes were shiny.

"He's . . . dead?" I guessed. And then I knew how Rick had gotten into my house. He'd killed the patrolman and walked right up the drive to the back door.

Mrs. Duncan wiped her eyes. "I'm so sad for his family, but at the same time, I'm so relieved and grateful that you're still with us, Maddie." She reached out and smoothed my hair. "Agent Faraday says I can bring you home to my house right after he gets your statement. But if you're not up to it, then I'll tell him to wait until you've had some rest."

I swallowed hard and had to wipe my own eyes. "Thanks, Mrs. Duncan. I think I can talk to him now."

She looked like she wanted to convince me otherwise, but then Faraday was pulling back the curtain and stepping over to stand next to Mrs. Duncan. "How's she doing?" he asked her.

Mrs. Duncan smiled proudly at me and winked. "She's her father's daughter, Agent Faraday. And he had the heart of a hero." Then she patted him on the chest and said, "I should let you two talk. Come find me in the lobby when Maddie is ready to leave, would you?"

"We won't be long, Mrs. Duncan," Faraday promised. After she'd gone he grinned at me, too. "She's one tough cookie."

I found the corners of my own mouth lifting. "She's pretty great."

Faraday looked around and grabbed a stool from right outside the curtain. Pulling it over to sit down, he took out a small notebook and said, "Tell me what happened tonight, Maddie."

I did. It didn't take very long. I'd been alone with Rick in my house for ten minutes. It'd just felt like an eternity. When I was finished, I had my own questions for Faraday.

"How did you know?" I asked him. "How did you know to come to the house?"

Faraday shrugged. I saw that he'd cleaned up a little from that afternoon. The soot from the fire had been washed away, but there was a good section of hair on the side of his head that was patchy and black. "I waited here until Kevin was out of surgery, and I was about to leave when one of the nurses found me and said that he was asking for me. He was pretty groggy, but when I got to him, all he kept saying was 'Wrong guy.' He said it over and over, like he was really worried about it, so I told him I'd look into it.

"Anyway," Faraday continued, "at the time, that didn't make much sense to me, so I headed back to Culligan's to look through Wes's locker, and you know what I found?"

I shook my head.

"I found a pair of Timberlands. Size nine and a half."

"Wrong size," I said, with a knowing nod.

"Exactly. So I started digging a little more. Miller's boss had said there were two guys on the crew. I asked the old man about the other guy. I finally got it out of him that Wes's partner was his cousin, Rick Kane—a guy in his early fifties—right in the age range of the profile from my buddy in D.C. I checked out Kane's work locker next, but it was empty. That seemed kind of odd to me, you know? Not even a jacket or an extra shirt in there. So I went to Kane's house. His wife said she was worried about him because he hadn't been feeling well lately. She had begged him to go to the doctor, but he'd refused. He'd also told her something that stuck with her—he'd said it wouldn't do any good. I remember standing on her porch and thinking about that. . . . That's something a dying man says.

"Before I left her house, I asked if Rick owned a set of Timberlands. He did. Size twelve."

"The size from the imprints at the crime scenes," I said.

"Yep. Oh, and his wife said that after quitting for twenty years, her husband was back to smoking again. He'd started up again this past summer, and his brand of choice was Marlboro Lights. By the time I finished interviewing Mrs. Kane, it was going on seven o'clock. I tried calling your house, but I got no answer, so I sent a patrol car out there to watch over you until we could find Kane or his cousin."

Faraday stopped talking again, and he dropped his gaze to the floor. I had the sense that he was feeling guilty over the patrolman. "Anyway," he said, after clearing his throat, "to be sure I was on the right track, I headed back to the office and checked your notebook. I found Kane's name in there, and his deathdate was for yesterday. I didn't quite know what to make of that, but after I called his wife again, she told me he liked to go hunting and fishing up near the Waliki River. It took us almost two hours, but we found the hunting shack, and Wes Miller's body, but no sign of Kane. I didn't believe for a second that the suicide note and the confession Kane left for us to find was real. So I had dispatch look up Kane's vehicle to put out the BOLO, and wouldn't you know it, he also drove a pickup—but his was charcoal gray."

"It all fits."

Faraday nodded. "Yep. I tried calling you again to ask you if you remembered reading for Kane, but I couldn't get an answer on your line and I didn't have your new cell. Your uncle wasn't picking up my calls, either," Faraday said with a frown.

"Donny probably went out with one of his girlfriends, and he doesn't always hear his phone when he's out," I told him. I didn't want him to think badly of Donny. None of this was his fault.

Faraday shrugged and got back to his story. "I tried to get patched through to the patrol officer assigned to watch your house, but I couldn't get him to pick up his cell, either. I was worried he'd fallen asleep on the job, so I drove over to straighten him out, but when I pulled up I found him slumped over the wheel. It was a minute or two before I realized he'd had his throat slit. And, right as I was about to call it in, I heard a crash from inside your house. . . ."

Faraday seemed to end his story there, and I dropped my gaze to my lap again. When I felt I could talk I said, "Thank you, Agent Faraday."

I felt his hand on mine. "Hey, Maddie?" he said, and there was a little humor in his voice. "I shot a bad guy for you tonight. The least you could do is call me Mack."

Donny arrived at the hospital around three A.M. as I was being wheeled out to Mrs. Duncan's car. He pulled up driving one of those Smart cars, and to see him squeal to a halt and jump out wearing only his boxers, a T-shirt, and a panicked look on his face sent all of us into hysterics.

I knew I shouldn't be laughing, but it was just so freaking funny that I couldn't help it. Belatedly I also realized he had a sleepy-looking woman in the car, and I knew he'd been on a date and hadn't had a choice as to how he got up to Grand Haven. It was her car or bust.

Once we'd all had a good laugh, Mrs. Duncan invited Donny and his girlfriend to stay at her house, but the girlfriend didn't seem to want to go for that idea, so Donny checked her into a hotel and then came back to be with me and Mrs. Duncan.

She settled me into her daughter Janet's room, and I lay back on the soft pillow and nestled into the flannel sheets and thought there was no way I was going to sleep that night. A moment later, I was out cold.

# The rest of December 2014

AFTER THE ATTACK I DIDN'T GO BACK TO SCHOOL for a few days. All I wanted to do was sleep and let Mrs. Duncan take care of me. Also, I was having a hard time keeping my emotions in check. I'd start crying for no reason at all, and a lot of my dreams were more like nightmares. Donny made an appointment for me with a therapist named Susan Royce (12-30-2055), and after hearing what was going on with me, she told me that everything I was feeling was perfectly normal, but I had a few issues that she thought we could work on. I was a little surprised to hear that one of the issues she wanted to work on with me was Ma.

Still, after talking with Susan a couple of times, I started to feel better. I had fewer nightmares, and I felt okay about going back to school.

Stubs helped me a lot, too. My first day back to school, he picked me up on his scooter, and as a joke he wore his red cape. I laughed until my sides hurt.

At school there was a big shift in attitude toward both of us. Stubby and I were pretty banged up, but word started to spread that the serial killer, Rick Kane, had attacked both of us, and we'd fought him off until he was shot by the feds. Stubby did nothing to try to correct the rumor, and neither did I. We walked the halls with our heads held high, and I thought my dad might be proud.

And then, one afternoon right before Christmas break, there was a surprise assembly and the whole school was herded to the gym. Stubby and I sat next to each other on the bleachers, and we were shocked to see the person standing at the podium up on the stage was none other than Agent Faraday.

He didn't look at either of us, but after everyone was seated he started his speech, and Stubby and I were blown away. It was all about us. Faraday told the whole school that Stubby and I had played a critical role in stopping Rick Kane, and if not for the two of us, more lives might've been lost.

I felt the whole school turn their eyes to Stubs and me, and for once it felt amazing. Stubby puffed his chest out and winked at me. And then Faraday said, "Maddie Fynn and Arnold Schroder, would you please come up here?"

Shaking a little, I got up, walking past Cathy Hutchinson, who was maybe even more stunned than I was, and headed with Stubby to the stage to stand next to Faraday.

From the podium, Mack lifted two plaques, one for me and one for Stubs. "I would like to commemorate Madelyn Fynn and Arnold Schroder's bravery with these honorary badges from the FBI, and also, to give them each a check for fifty thousand dollars, or half each of the reward money posted by the families of Tevon Tibbolt and Payton Wyly for information leading to the arrest or capture of the man who murdered their son and daughter."

Stubby looked at me incredulously. Fifty thousand dollars would give both of us a huge chunk of money to go to college with. It would change our lives.

But more than that, the standing ovation the whole school gave us as we accepted the plaques and the checks was enough to heal so many old wounds.

Later, after the assembly, when I was getting my books out of my locker, I noticed someone standing next to me. Turning I saw Mario Rossi there, smiling shyly at me.

At first I was a little alarmed. I mean, I knew Mario was back from his suspension, but I was really wary of him since getting beat up in the stairwell. "Hey, Fynn," he said.

I didn't say anything. I simply waited for whatever was about to come next.

Mario seemed to read my wary expression, and he dropped the smile and shuffled his feet. "Listen, I want to say...I'm sorry. I..." his voice trailed off, and my brow furrowed. He sighed and added, "I really am. I think what you guys did to catch Kane was pretty awesome, and I only wanted you to know that I won't bother you or Stubs ever again. In fact, anybody ever gives you trouble, you can ask me to step in, okay?"

He lifted his eyes back to me and there was nothing about his expression that seemed false. In fact, he looked hopeful.

For a long moment I stood staring at him, just completely shocked. I think he misread it for dismissal, because he dropped his gaze again and said, "Yeah. Okay. See ya."

On impulse, as he began to turn away, I reached out and touched his shoulder. He stopped and looked back at me. I hesitated at first because Donny and I had had a long talk about the deathdates, and we'd both decided it was a good idea not to tell anyone about them unless I was absolutely positive there'd be no negative fallout. But I thought the risk might be worth it with Mario. "There's something you should know," I said as he eyed me quizzically.

"What?" he asked.

I bit my lip, hesitating again, hoping I was doing the right thing. "You know what I can see, right?" For emphasis I tapped my forehead.

Mario's own brow furrowed. "Yeah?"

"Your date," I whispered, pointing now to his forehead. "It's the same as Eric Anderson's. It's on July twenty-fifth, twenty seventeen."

Mario blinked a few times as he thought through what I'd just said, and then he sucked in a breath and his eyes opened wide. I held his gaze, though, refusing to look away. We stood there, staring at each other for a few seconds, and then, the most amazing and wondrous thing happened. Mario reached up and rubbed his forehead, and in an instant his date changed. It went from 7-25-2017 to 4-14-2076. My mouth fell open, and I pointed to his forehead. "Ohmigod! Mario!"

"What? *What?*" he exclaimed, rubbing his forehead even more.

I put a hand up to stop him. "It just changed! Your death-date just changed to way out in the future!"

Mario eyed me cautiously. "You're sure?"

I smiled. "Positive. And you know I'm never wrong about this stuff, so don't worry. Now you're going to live to be an old man."

Down the hall, a voice yelled to Mario. "Yo, Rossi! Come on, dude!"

We both looked to see Eric Anderson glaring at us impatiently. Mario turned back to me, and I offered him an encouraging smile. He turned back to Eric and yelled, "You go ahead! I gotta be somewhere!" And then he hurried away in the opposite direction from Eric.

I couldn't help it. I laughed at the incredulous expression on Eric's face. I had no doubt that once Mario got over his shock, he'd let Eric know what I'd said, and hopefully, his date would change, too.

Donny drove me to see Ma six days later. She looked thin, but her eyes were clear, and her speech wasn't slurred. I could tell she was a little uncomfortable with us there, but she seemed to really be trying. We exchanged presents—Ma had made me a picture frame with wire and beads. In the frame was a photo of Dad holding me when I was an infant. It was the best Christmas present ever.

# February 2015

I STAYED AT MRS. DUNCAN'S HOUSE DURING THE week for the next few months, enjoying her bright spirit and the way she fussed over me. As February began to wind down, I found myself growing sadder. The date on Mrs. Duncan's forehead drew nearer, and I didn't know how I was going to get through the days leading up to her deathdate without telling her.

The odd thing was, I swear, somehow she knew it was coming. On the weekends, Donny and I spent our days fixing up our house, and one weekend Mrs. Duncan insisted both her daughters come for dinner, and we heard the sounds of little kids playing in her backyard and adults laughing with one another. I watched through the window as Mrs. Duncan said good night to both her daughters, and I thought she squeezed them extra tight.

I also saw a lot of visits to her home from the Salvation Army truck that February. Mrs. Duncan said she simply felt like de-cluttering her home, which had always been full of stuff, from furniture to knickknacks, and slowly over the course of that month she whittled her belongings down to the bare minimum.

On Friday the twenty-seventh, I raced home from school to her house and found her busy in the kitchen. She'd been cooking all day. "I felt like making all of Mr. Duncan's favorites!" she exclaimed. Afterward, I did the dishes while she sat in the living room sipping her tea. It wasn't lost on me that after all that cooking, Mrs. Duncan had barely touched her own dinner.

I finished the dishes and came out to find her barely able to keep her lids open. "Oh, my," she said with a chuckle when she saw me staring worriedly at her. "I must be more tired than I thought."

I helped her up the stairs to bed and then went back down to take her teacup to the sink. There I sank to the floor and wept as softly as I could for a long, long time.

The next morning I was laying curled up into a ball on the couch when there was a soft knock on the door. I opened it to find Agent Faraday there. He looked very sad. In his hand was my notebook. "Is she gone?" he asked after taking one look at my tear-stained face.

I nodded, unable to speak. I'd found her twenty minutes earlier, after I'd woken up and gone to her room. She was lying so peacefully, with her hands folded under her head and the sweetest smile on her blue lips.

Faraday folded me into his arms while I mourned my sweet neighbor's passing. Later, he called Uncle Donny and escorted me back over to my house to wait with me while they took Mrs. Duncan away. And then, about an hour after Donny arrived and was rocking me back and forth to comfort me, Faraday came back to the house and held out an envelope to me. "We found it on her dresser," he said.

I took the envelope and realized it was addressed to me. Opening it up I saw that it was a copy of a letter that Mrs. Duncan had sent to the Cornell admissions office.

In the letter she told them that she and her husband had always been proud alumni supporters of the school, and that she would like them to consider very closely my application for enrollment as she found me to be an exemplary individual, and exactly the kind of student that would fit right in at Cornell. She also told them that she was enclosing a check for one hundred thousand dollars payable to the alumni fund. She hoped that the institution could find good use for it— perhaps to help support an incoming freshman—like me.

# 6-20-2015 . . . and beyond

"THE MOVING VAN'S HERE, MADDIE," MA CALLED.

I was upstairs going through old notebooks from school, trying to figure out which ones to keep and which ones to toss. School had let out a few days earlier, and I was sick of looking at the stack. I'd almost forgotten that a new family was due to move into Mrs. Duncan's house.

"Maddie?" Ma called again. I smiled. She no longer called up the stairs impatiently, and we no longer had clients going into that back room. Ma had turned it into an office for herself. She'd started to take some courses to get her nursing certificate back, and she spent a lot of time in there studying.

"I see it, Ma!" I called down to her after standing up and taking a peek through the curtains.

"Why don't you go over and introduce yourself?" Ma asked.

I realized she'd come up the stairs and was talking to me from the doorway of my room.

"Why don't you?" I asked her playfully. These days I loved looking at her. Her skin glowed now that she was off the booze and the cigarettes. She'd even taken up yoga and had turned vegetarian. The rehab center had completely transformed her. In fact, according to the new date on her forehead, 8-16-2065, it'd actually saved her life.

She grinned. "Me?" she said, looking down at herself. 'Oh, honey, I've been in the yard and I look awful!" Ma had been trying to do something with the garden in the backyard for days, but mostly all that was happening was that a lot of weeds were making their way into the garbage can. "You go over there first and tell me if they're nice," she urged.

I had a feeling she wasn't going to let up until I said yes. Rolling my eyes, I gave in. "Okay, but text me in ten minutes in case I can't get away."

Ma laughed, and I smiled reflexively—hearing her happy never got old.

Once outside, I kept close to the house as I made my way down the drive. I was hoping to sort of scope out the neighbors before actually walking up to them. I heard the sound of a basketball bouncing off the pavement, but I couldn't see who was playing with it through the pine trees that separated our properties.

Taking a deep breath I moved past the trees and looked up the drive. What I saw froze me to the spot. There was a boy taking aim at the basket above Mrs. Duncan's garage. He was shirtless, and his shoulders were broad and his arms well-muscled, and he wore a halo of soft black curls.

I stood, unable to move for several seconds as he tossed the ball and it fell right through the hoop without touching the rim. "Nice shot," I heard someone else say. A voice I recognized.

I turned my head and saw Agent Faraday coming down the back steps of Mrs. Duncan's house. He spotted me, and his smile broadened. "Maddie!" he said happily. "I was about to come over and introduce you to my son."

My mouth opened but no words came out. I swallowed and then said, "You *live* here now?"

Mack laughed and waved for the boy with the basketball to come over. "I bought it the second it went up for sale. I needed a place big enough for Aiden and me." Turning to his son, Faraday said, "And this is my son, Aiden."

My head swiveled again and I saw that Aiden was grinning at me, too. "I know you!" he said. "We met at the park last fall."

Heat seared my cheeks as a thousand little pieces slid into place. Faraday at the Jupiter game, sitting in the stands—not running surveillance on me but in the bleachers to watch his son. The boots on his desk, and that memory of seeing them before—he'd bought a pair for Aiden. The conversations with his ex-wife . . . all of it came together in a moment of synchronicity that made me want to shiver with excitement. But then, I realized that both Aiden and his dad were staring at me curiously. "Uh . . . hi," I said, trying to regain my composure.

"You two have met?" Faraday asked curiously.

Aiden nodded, never taking his eyes off me. And then he said, "Hey, Dad, is that your phone?"

In the distance I heard ringing, and Faraday patted his pockets and said, "Must've left it inside. Excuse me."

He took off and then Aiden and I were alone. "So *you're* the famous Maddie Fynn?" he said.

I felt a giggle burble up from inside me, and I was helpless to keep it down. "I don't think I'm famous," I told him.

Aiden's brow shot up. "No? Well, my dad says you're amazing, and he's usually right about stuff like that."

The heat to my cheeks got hotter.

Aiden dribbled the basketball, and then he seemed to think of something. "Is it really true that you can tell when people are gonna die?"

That threw me, but Aiden had a smile and a kindness in his eyes that I thought I could trust. "Yeah," I said. "It's true."

He cocked his head. "Even mine?"

I swallowed hard. "Yes."

Aiden pursed his lips, looking at me with playful fascination. "Would you tell me?"

I started to shake my head, but he tucked the ball under his arm and put his hands together. "Please? I can take it. I promise."

I started to laugh and then I almost couldn't stop. "What?" he asked, but he still had that playful smile.

I took a deep breath and let it out. I felt in my heart that I could tell him. "Your deathdate is July sixth, twenty eighty-four." And then I grinned so big I had to look away.

"What?" he asked again, knowing there was more.

I lifted my chin to look at him again. There was a secret I'd kept to myself about Aiden's deathdate and why it'd felt like magic when I'd first seen the beautiful boy with 7-6-2084 on his forehead. "What?" he repeated with a chuckle, trying to coax it out of me.

"It's the day after mine," I confessed.

Aiden's expression changed from playful to something a little more awestruck. "Think we'll still know each other in twenty eighty-four?" he asked, his smile growing as big as mine.

I felt light as air. Somewhere deep inside I also felt a knowing so strong that I couldn't quite describe it. Still, I only shrugged and said, "Maybe."

Just then a soft breeze came sweetly up the drive, lifting that halo of soft curls around Aiden's forehead, and in a magical instant, I saw a series of other numbers dance across his skin. They appeared in the space between us as if they were as much for me as they were for him. Behind each new date was a glimmer of insight. There were dates for movies and dances and graduations and marriage and children and anniversaries and so much more.

And in that enchanted moment, as I watched the dates skipping lightly across Aiden's forehead, instead of death, all I saw was . . .

Life.

# Acknowledgments

THE BEGINNING OF EACH NEW BOOK ALWAYS FEELS like a new mountain to climb, but in many ways this novel was my Everest. And yet, I wouldn't trade any moment of the climb, because it has truly provided some spectacular views.

These days, however, I will freely admit to preferring to hang out at base camp and enjoy the hot cocoa, and it's while I'm slurping away some chocolatey goodness, all cozy in my writer's tent, that I can now reflect on the many people who've provided no small measure of support, effort, and encouragement on the way to the summit.

First, I want to thank Jim McCarthy, whose short title is: "Victoria's agent," but who *really* is: "Victoria's muse/confidant/supporter/counselor/conscience/financial advisor/life coach/ally/conspirator/humorous sidekick/treasured friend." This book would never have been written if it weren't for Jim's unflinching belief in me, and his unwavering support. And also *maaaaaaaaybe* a *weeeeeeeee* bit of his patience, which, thank God, he is in no short supply of. Thank you, Jim. Always and all ways.

Next I'd like to thank my fantabulous editor, Lisa Yoskowitz, who wrote the most beautiful love letter to Jim and I when she was looking to acquire the book, listing all the ways Maddie's story moved her and why she'd be the perfect fit to edit *When*. She had me completely sold three lines in, and she's since proven herself to be one of the most dedicated, hard-working, insightful editors I've ever had the sincere pleasure to work with. *Definitely* the perfect editor for the job! I'm so thrilled and pleased to have you in my corner, Lisa. Thank you for all that effort and dedication and especially for your diehard enthusiasm! You've been my Sherpa and I'm so oodley grateful for all that you do, and of course, to be a part of the amazing Hyperion team!

I'd also like to thank the cover artist Tyler Nevins for his incredible vision. I couldn't have imagined a more perfect cover, Tyler. You took my breath away when I saw the direction you were headed in, and without a doubt this is one of my all-time favorite covers of any book I've ever written. I'm smitten, I tell you! SMITTEN!

To my copy editor Lindsay Walter; regarding your skills as a copy editor I would like to express a sentiment that can only be summed up thusly: WOWSA! You absolutely blew me away with your attention to detail and eagle eyes. I've never had such a fabulous or more thorough copyedit, and I am incredibly grateful for how careful and detailed you were with my work. Thank you, thank you, thank you! And an additional Hyperian-Team shout-out to Julie Moody, whose patience and attention to detail proved to be a godsend in the final stages of editing *When*.

Last, but certainly not least, I'd like to thank all those friends and family members who've inspired, encouraged, supported, and believed in me. Specifically, they are: Brian Gorzynski, Sandy Upham, Steve McGrory, Matt & Mike Morrill, Katie Coppedge, Leanne Tierney, Karen Ditmars, Sandra Harding-Hull, Hilary Laurie, Nicole Gray, Shannon Anderson, Nora, Bob, and Mike Brosseau, Catherine Ong Kane, Jennifer Melkonian, Anne Kimbol, Sally Woods, John Kwiatkowski, Matt McDougal, Dean James, McKenna Jordan, Drue Ehrhardt Rowean, Juliet Blackwell, Sophie Littlefiled, Nicole Peeler, Thomas Robinson, Meg Guzman, I.J. Schecter, Laurie Proulx, Terry Gilman, Maryelizabeth Hart, Suzanne Parsons, and Betty & Pippa Stocking.

There are days when the only thing holding me up is your love and friendship, and for that I'm eternally grateful.